WHIRLWIND

ALISON RHYMES

To request permission, contact: alison@alisonrhymes.com

Editor: Zainab M. at the blue couch edits
Proofreading: Nicole Bailey at Proof Before You Publish
Cover Design: Ben | Pilcrow
Cover Photo by: Katie Cadwallader Photography
Formatting: Sunshine Tucker
Sensitivity Reader: Laura Trujillo

A NOTE FROM ALISON RHYMES

Any trigger or content warnings for Whirlwind, or any of my other titles, can be found on my website: alisonrhymes.com

Please see the Afterword when you have completed your read for important information.

Once, I was alone.
Then, a Nightmare took my hand.
And I found safety.

Whirlwind is dedicated to every survivor. To every victim of sexual assault, abuse, violence, or harassment. Your story matters. No matter how small, it matters. You matter and I hear you.

1
KIT

U *gh.*

The last thing I want to do after today is go to a party. I spent the day—my first day at my new job—cleaning up the mess left by the person who previously held the position. Data analysis isn't for everyone, as is painfully obvious by the disaster this Mark made of every report I looked at today.

Every number on the defensemen was off. By a lot. He was either superbly unqualified, or showed up every day drunk off his ass, because I don't know how any analyst could have messed it up that badly, otherwise.

I'm a statistician before I'm an analyst; that might be what has me so aggravated. I look deeper than I need to, in most cases. It's a character trait, not one I see as a flaw. The Seattle Blades must not see it as one, either, since they hired me to clean this shit up and compile accurate information that will be helpful to the team.

The job was offered to me months ago. Initially, I declined.

The only family I have is a chosen one, not a blood relation. Meeting my best friend in college, Willa Cole, was life-changing for me.

Willa is fun, determined, smart, and passionate. We clicked instantly and never had anything that even resembled an argument. Truthfully, I don't think either of us knows how to be angry at someone we care about. That isn't something I learned from examples while growing up. If anything, I learned it despite my upbringing.

We became thick as thieves and the Coles embraced me like I was always one of their own.

They have deep ties to the Seattle Blades. Willa's dad is the coach, her sister Isla works in fan development, Isla's husband is the star player. And now, one of Willa's partners plays for the team, too.

Working for the team felt like putting too many eggs in one basket, and that weight to carry would be too much. I don't want to fracture the only good thing I have.

There isn't a lot of data on the failure of business dealings when it's with friends, specifically. But up to eighty percent of partnerships fail; and I can't lose mine with the Coles. It's not something I'd survive.

The Blades courted me heavily. Eventually, the sweetheart deal they offered was simply too much to pass up. Seattle is an expensive city to live in. When I came here to attend the University of Washington, I fell in love with the city. It's different from Maine, where I'm from. But also, it's the same, in some ways. There's an appreciation here for nature, the ocean, and a hard day's work. Despite its techy reputation.

Sometimes, I miss the small-town lifestyle. Then, I remember that small-town life never did me many favors. Seattle is where I belong. With the Coles, even if that means we tangle in a little business. I won't fail them or this team.

There are only two things I love in life. My work, and the Cole family. Okay, that's not entirely true. I love video games, my independence, and learning new stuff. My life is great, all things considered. But I know it wouldn't be this great without the support my best friend and her family have given me here.

They even let me live with Willa in the condo her dad had purchased for his daughters to live in while they went to college. I offered to pay rent, but Coach would never allow that. It let me scurry away a small nest egg, which I have used alongside my newfound big girl salary to purchase my very own house. Now that Willa has moved in with her boyfriends, it feels weird living in the condo by myself. They've told me to stay as long as I want, but I quickly found a new place.

Because I love Willa so much, I will suck up my horrifically bad mood and accompany her and her two boyfriends to this party tonight without complaint. It's a birthday party for the Blades' goalie, Blom. I've met him a handful of times, on various occasions. He's a fun guy, a little weird, but being so adjacent to hockey players these past couple of years, I've learned all goalies are a touch off.

I've searched for weird stats on them to appease my curiosity, but nothing exists outside of the normal numbers and injury studies. They're the least likely to get injured, though their numbers jumped dramatically higher after the pandemic, whereas other positions didn't.

I'd love to see further study on that because I find it a fascinating anomaly. One of the things I'm looking forward to most about this new position is that I'll be able to put my eyes on these sorts of studies before they are pushed out to the public, since it all plays a part in player analysis. And, well, I'm a geek for that kind of thing.

The party is at a bar set up like a legitimate old-school speakeasy, and I'm dressed for the occasion in a frilly little cocktail dress. A hand-me-down from Willa. I'm not great at splurging on myself. Other than events with her, I don't need anything fancy, anyway. My life is basic and I'm content staying in, most nights. I prefer the quiet, usually. Low drama is what I'm all about.

My nights are often spent with takeout, eaten on my couch in front of *Alias* reruns in my underwear. Not glammed up in shiny makeup and shinier clothes. Especially now that Willa is more occupied with a relationship. We used to go out more, not a lot, but more than I do now. I didn't mind, as long as I got to spend time with her. I don't mind she doesn't have as much time for me now days, either. I'm thrilled she's in love and happy. Zander and Damian treat her like a queen, and in my book, she is one.

Besides, just because I have no interest in men doesn't mean she should have stayed single, too. I don't need a friend to coddle me. I need one who understands what I want out of life and doesn't push me to be something different. Willa has always been that for me.

WILLA:

We're here.

They arrive as I'm slipping into my shoes. I take a final look in the large mirror by my front door before heading out to the car. I look like a nerdy goth Barbie in my black lacy mini-dress, heeled booties, and black rimmed glasses that I can't see far without these days, unless I have my contacts in, but I hate wearing those after a long day. I've even manipulated my dark strands into braids, à la Wednesday Addams.

I may not fit in well with the blonde legion of NHL wives at this party, but this is me.

Isla isn't blonde, either. Nor is Odette, the wife of Gavin, a player who retired after last season but still works for the organization. We make jokes about all the other women being blonde or blonde-ish, but it's just in jest. All the wives and girlfriends are nice.

Hockey has some strange protocol when it comes to the wives group. Players must allow their significant other to be included in the group. In all the time I've been around the team, I've never met a woman who was only casually dating a player. Maybe it's not like that on every team, but this one keeps the family well protected.

That could be due to Coach Cole. He's a legend in the industry and highly regarded by his players. His team is more than a group of players to him. Like he does with me, he considers them family.

ME:

Heading down now.

I lock the door to the condo behind me.

Zander is driving, and Damian rides shotgun, while I slide into the backseat next to Willa.

"Hey, guys," I greet.

"Hi," they say in unison.

"You look especially spicy tonight," Damian adds.

"You know me, I rarely get a chance to dress up. Might as well take advantage." Cocktail dresses may not be my norm, but I do enjoy getting dolled up from time to time. Not that I'm a troll every day or anything. Only, I've never had a job that required more than casual attire, and this is the Pacific Northwest. Outdoor wear is practically dressing up around here.

"If I had legs like those, I'd show them off every chance I got," Zander says.

"You could fit five of my thighs in one of yours. If you had legs like mine, it would take you five minutes to get from one end of the ice to the other," I say. "That would seriously drag down your career."

"It'd kill it," he agrees with a laugh. "What's the cross street of this place?"

"First and Blanchard," Willa answers. "The door is in the alley with a red light over it."

"Sounds very clandestine," Damian says.

"Can't be that clandestine or nobody would know about it. This whole concept baffles me. Isn't the point of a business to be seen and popular?" Zander asks.

"Sure," I say. "There's something to be said about intrigue, though. It's sexy, and that sells."

"We are weirdly preoccupied with sex," Willa says.

"You mean, society in general?" I ask.

"Yeah, humans. Well, I guess animals are, too," she answers.

"Oh, definitely. Did you know the antechinus during mating season will literally have sex until it gives out and dies?" I ask.

"An ante what?" Zander asks.

"Antechinus," Damian answers. "It's an Australian marsupial."

"Sometimes, I forget how oddly smart you are," I tease him.

"Oddly?"

"You're too pretty and rich to have that kind of intellect, too."

"Brat." He laughs. Damian is smart. He's also kind and a natural provider. Willa and Zander are lucky to have him in their lives. They're all lucky and so in love with each other, I almost get a sugar high when I'm around them. "I happen to know plenty of *odd* animal facts. Like, whale dicks can be as long as ten feet."

"Jesus," Zander mutters, pulling into a parking spot around the corner from the bar.

"That's…substantial," Willa says.

"Male alligators always have a hard-on. It never goes away," I say.

"Dude porcupines pee on their women to get them in the mood," Damian counters.

"Hey, don't knock it 'til you try it," I say.

They all laugh. Zan and Damian don't know the details of my sex life; they just know it's non-existent. And, hell, I sure hope they know me well enough to know golden showers would be a hard limit.

The bar is lit with soft amber lighting, decorated in plush velvet jewel tones, and the music is bluesy. It's a much cozier vibe than I'd expected.

Minus the raucous hockey team laughing it up. That's par for the course with this bunch, though.

I say hello to a few of the people I know well enough, and grab myself an Old Fashioned before finding a place to be comfortable. The venue is booked for a private event; everyone here is related to the team in some way. I recognize a few people from my day at the office; we exchange friendly waves.

"Hey, Kit Kat," Hugo Blom says, falling into the seat next to me. "What are you doing over here by yourself?"

He's a big guy. Yet, not as big as many of the other players. That surprised me when I first met him. I had this notion that all goalies must be these giants standing between the net and a team full of guys line-driving hard-as-hell pucks at it. Truth is, they need to be more agile than large.

Hugo is also handsome, clean cut with freckles and dimples. More than all that, he's a big cinnamon roll of a man. The first to offer a hug, the one who is always looking to make sure everyone is included, well fed, and happy in their situation. I'm not surprised that he found me sitting here by myself.

"Just unwinding the day's tension," I tell him. "Happy birthday, buddy."

"Thanks," he says with a grin the size you'd see on a kid at Christmas. "I hear congratulations are in order."

"They are! I got myself a new fancy gig with a big-time NHL team."

"Yes, you did, and I know you deserved it. But I meant, I heard you bought a house."

"Oh, I did do that. Which means, this will probably be the last time you see me for a while, since all my money is going to my tiny little shoebox of a house. I move in this weekend."

My expectation when I signed the closing documents to purchase my house was that I would be anxious about committing to a thirty-year mortgage payment. Instead, I loved that it cemented me into a life here in the city I've come to call home.

"Ah, you're not supposed to break a guy's heart on his birthday, Kit Kat. We hardly see you as it is."

"What heart are we talking about here?" I tease.

"Ouch!" He laughs. "Seriously, though, congratulations. Tiny or not, it's a big deal."

"I agree. Plus, it has a peekaboo view of Lake Union, which makes the price tag slightly easier to swallow."

"It's an adorable house," Willa says, sliding into the booth with us. "So much natural light and in a great neighborhood."

"That's good," Hugo says. "Seasonal Affective Disorder is rampant around these parts, so natural light helps."

"I always forget you're just one of the girls, Blom," Cillian says, walking up behind the goalie and slapping him on the shoulder. Cillian is Willa's brother-in-law. Until Willa hooked up with Zander and Damian, Cill was the closest thing to a brother I'd ever known. Now, I have three sort of brothers.

For a girl with no real blood family, it can be overwhelming. It's also damn nice when I sit back and enjoy it.

"I've been taking advice from Letty. You know he says you get more women when you're in touch with your feminine side," he says, rubbing at the back of his neck, almost as if he's embarrassed to be admitting such a thing.

"He's not wrong," I agree. "This whole male loneliness epidemic nonsense is just assholes who can't learn to be nice to women, if you ask me."

"Then what's it going to take to get you to agree to a date with a nice guy like me? Want me to come decorate your new house with you?"

"Oh, hell no." I laugh. "I plan on being extremely particular about my décor."

"When you say particular, do you mean girly?"

"That question only proves how little you know about Kit," Willa tells him.

"What, no pink sofa and macrame plant hangers?"

"No, she's more likely to have a gaming chair than a sofa," Willa answers him. "Though, I can see you hanging a plant or two in macrame."

"Gaming chairs are a bitch to nap in, though," I say. "I'll probably have to find a way to fit both of them in."

"What games do you play?"

"Any one that lets me shoot a gun or kill a dragon."

"*Call of Duty*?"

"No. Not anymore. There are far too many jerks there who think a woman is only good for making sandwiches," I say, crinkling my nose in disgust. It's not easy being a girl gamer in online communities. Mostly, I can hold my own with them, but sometimes, it simply gets to be more work than value.

"You ever want to play it again; you join up with me and my boys."

"Ah, you gonna protect me, big guy?"

"I would if you'd ever give me the chance, Kit Kat." He rises from his chair and moves to chat with some of the other guys.

"That guy has a big crush on you," Willa says.

"He has a big crush on lots of women, I suspect."

"You're not wrong there, Kit," Cillian says. "I think he's still hung up on that movie star friend of Odette's, too."

"Can't blame him; Britton Macy is gorgeous." The starlet filmed a movie here not too long ago, and was a permanent fixture not only in the Blades' social events, but Hugo's bed, as well.

"So are you," Willa says with a smile before turning to her brother-in-law. "Where's my sister at?"

"She wasn't feeling too hot; she stayed home with Sadie," Cillian answers.

"Why didn't she call me?"

"She didn't want you to mother hen her instead of coming out with your crew and having a good time. So," he says, tapping her on the nose.

"Have a good time. She's okay. You know if it was something serious, I'd be home with her."

"Maybe she's queasy because her ex is joining the team," Letty, another of the players, says, from a couple feet away.

"Wait, what?" Willa asks.

"We made a trade for Murphy, today," Cillian says. "He'll be here as soon as his visa shit clears."

"Oh, damn," I say. "Bet you don't love that."

Tyson Murphy is the only other man Isla ever gave a shot. And it was only when she and Cillian were on the outs for a few years. Tyson wanted more with her, but her heart was never fully available. Not since she gave it to Cillian at sixteen years old.

I knew Tyson before I knew Cillian. Truth be told, I was rooting for him to win her heart. Even for a while after Cillian came back into her life. She picked the right man for her; I know that now. I've seen how much he loves her and the lengths he'll go for his family.

It's not like I knew the guy well or anything. But, from what little I saw, Tyson was a good man, too. He was great with Isla's daughter. I felt bad for him. Especially because he plays against Cillian. He can't avoid the situation altogether. The NHL is a small family; they run into each other more than probably any of them would like. Now, it's going to be so much worse.

"I don't love it for me on a personal level, no. It's a great move for the team, though."

"Sadie is going to be excited, she loved Tyson," Willa says.

"You don't need to remind me that my daughter had his hockey memorabilia before she had any of mine," he says with an exaggerated pout.

Cillian didn't know he had a daughter with Isla until Sadie was a toddler. Over the years, there have been some huge misunderstandings between the two of them. As well as mistrust and a healthy dose of postpartum depression. Well, and a crazed groupie woman who didn't understand consent.

That's all in their rearview mirror, now. Other than Willa's parents, I don't know of a more solid couple than Isla and Cillian Wylder. If I were looking to have a relationship of my own, I'd want one as honest as theirs. That's not in the cards for me, perhaps.

Maybe twenty-seven is too young to be saying that. When you've gone as long as I have with little to no interest in developing a romantic relationship, it's easy to convince yourself it isn't part of your future.

And, really, that's okay. I've seen enough awful relationships to understand that not everyone is meant to be in one. Plus, I'm happy. I'm fulfilled. I have a career, friends, and a good life.

A man would probably only bring drama and ruin my carefully curated vibe. Another thing I'd like to take a hard pass on. New things often trip me up; I'm not conducive to change as a perpetual overthinker who rides through life with general anxiety and is prone to occasional emotional meltdowns.

"Okay, this is veering down a road that leads to a much sadder night than I had planned," I say. "Get your ass up out of that chair, Cill. I want to dance with somebody," I sing, like I'm an eighties pop singer.

"I don't know how to dance to…who is this?"

"Etta James," I say. "Come on, I'll teach you some new tricks to take home to your pretty wife."

"How do you know *everything*?" He stands and lets me drag him to the small area that is clear of tables. It's a question he teases me with often. A favorite game of his daughter's is to ask me for facts on random items, just to see what I know.

One day, it's pineapples, the next, it might be the Hubble telescope or raccoons. She tries her hardest to stump me, and sometimes, she manages. But that's what we have smartphones for—interesting information is never far away.

"My grandma used to say I was a sponge for information. I guess I still am. Add an overactive attention span to it and you end up speeding from one subject to another. Plus, I don't sleep much, and there's the whole ADHD diagnosis."

"I don't know how you do it. I still take naps nearly every day."

"I like a good nap," I say, placing one hand on his shoulder and the other on his hip, so I can guide him to move. "But it's not like I have the rigorous schedule of a star NHL player. I sit at a desk all day."

"I suppose that could make a difference." He's stiff as a board as I lead him through some steps.

"How do you move so well on the ice and not at all on the dance floor?" Laughter erupts behind me as the guys watch. Cillian flips them off before returning his attention to me.

"You should have chosen me, darling," Letty says. "I've got moves like Jagger!"

"Oh my God, he did not just say that," I whisper.

"You can't be surprised." Cillian laughs.

"No, I'm not. I guess I just needed the reminder. It's been a hot minute since I've gotten to hang out with the team."

"You think that might change now that you're a part of the team?"

"I'm a number cruncher in the office. It's not like I'm on the bench with you guys."

"Still," he says with a grin. "You'll be around more. It'll be nice to see your face."

"Thanks, it will be nice to be part of a team, now, instead of just another faceless body in a building full of cubicles." Moving my other hand to his waist, I try to get him to sway better. "Besides, you need more lessons. You're fucking hopeless, Wylder."

2
TYSON

Being traded at the drop of a hat is never fucking enjoyable. It's even less fun when, for some unknown reason, my visa takes a week to clear. It's not the usual process, which is fairly speedy since we have so many international players in the NHL.

I should see it as a perk, not a bug. It did give me extra time to pack up what I needed from my house in Vancouver and find a place to crash in Seattle. Luckily, a friend of mine has a place down here that he usually uses for short-term rentals when he's not using it personally. He's letting me stay here for a few months, until I can find a place of my own. It's close to the arena, which is nice. Not so close to the practice facility, but it's available now, which means I won't have to stay in a hotel. I see enough of those as it is. It's a smaller two-bedroom townhome—modern, clean, and private.

I'm not selling my house back home. Since I'm only a few hours away, I'll be able to come back often. Another bonus of this trade. I couldn't ask for a better city to be traded to. They could have pawned me off to New Jersey. Or worse, Florida, where I'd be about as far from home as possible.

Being close to home, close to my family, is what matters most to me. This way, my parents and my sister aren't so far that they can't catch some of my games. I'd gotten used to having them in the stands. It's not often a pro gets to play for their hometown team; I was lucky in that regard.

It's also great that I'm familiar with Seattle already, since my ex…girlfriend? No, she wasn't that. Not exactly. My ex-hookup who I was in love with, happens to live here.

With her husband.

Who is now my teammate.

Isla also works for the team, and her father is now my coach.

Life really does have a way of kicking you in the dick. What I've done to deserve this level of karma is anyone's guess. I like to think I'm a good person. Do I sleep around too much? Yeah, probably. I don't make promises I won't keep, though. I'm a good friend, a decent human, a great son, and brother.

All I did was fall for a woman who couldn't fall for me.

Fucking Freckles.

We connected over her love for hockey. Born and raised Canadian, I've known a lot of women who love the game. It was different with Isla, though. The game was like the air in her lungs. Growing up in the industry, she understood me and my crazy schedule. She also had impeccable insight into gameplay, itself. If I was in a rut, she always had some tips to help me out of it. I scored more goals while dating her than any other time in my career.

It's not lost on me that Cillian Wylder's game has vastly improved since getting back together with her.

That man has everything I want. A successful career, a smart wife, a great kid, a supportive family. I don't hate him, but it would be easy to.

Cillian makes her happy. Happier than I ever did, regardless of how hard I tried, or what I would have given to be with her. My love for her lets me admit that. My love for her also feels like thorny rose vines surrounding my heart, serving as a constant reminder that she'll never be mine.

No matter how many other women I'm with, it's still her face I see when I fall asleep. Every fucking night. Isla is the ghost that haunts me.

I shake away the melancholy as I walk into the Iceplex. This morning is my first time on the ice with the team, and Coach Cole wants to talk before I suit up for practice. The last thing I need is to be morose when I shake Isla's dad's hand. Or her husband's.

The first person I see is Alexander Fane. Another of my new teammates, and Isla's best friend. Well, now he's Isla's sister's partner, too. One thing the Seattle franchise seems to do well is keeping it in the family.

"Hey, Tyson. Good seeing you," he greets, holding the security door that leads to the offices and locker room open for me.

"Thanks, man. Good seeing you, too. I was happy to see that they brought you up."

Fane was a solid player on Seattle's WHL team when Isla and I dated. Young and hungry is how I remember him. It didn't surprise me when the Blades picked him up and developed him on the farm team for a couple of seasons. Fane reminds me of the guys I grew up with, who all believe hockey is life. The race to the NHL was all that mattered.

"How's the move?"

"No complaints, other than how long it took. Eight days off the ice makes me feel like I've retired."

"I'm sure the guys will put you through the paces this morning," he says with a wry smile.

"I'd expect nothing less."

"See you in there, man," he says, patting me on the shoulder before heading into the locker room.

Cillian and I have a rivalry on the ice. At first, it was over Isla. That ended after a season, and now, it's feigned for the sake of the fans. They love to see it, but neither of us go out of our way to pick a fight with one another. Doesn't mean we don't check slightly harder than we should.

That will change, now, for obvious reasons. We'll need to thoroughly squash any ill feelings because our fans will be looking for it, and cracks within the team shouldn't be for public scrutiny.

I knock on the coach's door.

"Tyson Murphy, good to have you," he says as I walk in.

"Happy to be here," I lie. Well, half lie. I'd rather be home in Vancouver.

"It's not easy being traded, especially from home. You don't have to pretend with me."

"Felt like the rug was pulled out from me, but I'm ready to play. More than ready, antsy."

"Good, because we need you. Have a seat, let's chat." I sit in the chair on the other side of the desk, which is piled with neat stacks of papers. Probably stats on every player in the league. "Haven't had a conversation since you and Isla called it quits to whatever the two of you were."

I know where he's leading. As much as I don't want to talk about it, there is no avoiding the subject.

"No, sir. Not since before Wylder showed back up."

"The two of you going to have problems playing on the same team?"

"No, sir."

"You sure about that? My daughters have earned much respect from this team. Wylder won't be the only guy to have a problem if you run your mouth."

And there it is. The first time Wylder and I faced off after Isla and him reconciled, I provoked him on the ice. Said some shit about Isla purely to see how he'd react. Of course, Coach took notice. I guess now it's my turn to explain.

"I cared a lot about her, sir. I still do. There was zero chance I was getting on the ice with him and not testing his loyalty to her," I say, imagining he'd have done the same if he'd been in my position.

Coach leans back, appraising me silently, for a moment. A small grin grows before he says anything else to me.

"The truth is, I gave Cillian a right hook the first time I saw him after we drafted him. I won't hold your past animosity against you, so long as the two of you act like what this franchise needs."

"It's not a problem on my end. All I ever wanted for her and Sadie was their happiness."

"They have that," he says with emphasis.

"I know."

"Good," he says. "Then, let's talk about your scoring and what we need to do for you to pick that back up."

This season has been my worst start since I entered the NHL seven years ago. Three seasons ago, I was the top scorer in the league. My team… or, my old team, had an off year last season. We didn't play cohesively. Because of that, management executed several changes to our lineup and coaching staff.

"All I need is a team that wants to work together toward the common goal. I haven't gotten the cup. That's what I need—a team focused on that, rather than their own egos."

"That's it?" he asks, skeptically.

"I could use some new opinions on my form, too. Until this season, I've had the same coach. He was great, but maybe we got complacent with each other's style," I admit. "Like so many of us, I'm a creature of routine. That routine is no longer paying the same dividends it used to."

"You're going to be okay with us changing up your routine?" Again, he's skeptical. As he should be. Hockey players aren't just creatures of habit; it's not just superstition. It's a way of life. Some guys wake up at 8:08 every day. Not eight AM or eight-thirty. They tape their sticks the exact same way they've been doing it since peewee, absolutely no alterations. They chew their mouthguards a certain way or at certain times. Our warmup routines don't waver night to night. During the season, they eat the same food every day without variation. I'm not any different. After a while, you figure out what makes you feel your best and you stick to it.

"If you'd have asked me at the beginning of last season, I would have said hell no. After the last two months, I'm open to suggestions and seeing what may work better. I'm at least halfway through my career. I want this second half to be better than the first. I'll listen to whatever you all have to say."

"We've evaluated your tapes. Not only from your time in The Show, but also from when you were coming up. The trainers are going to work with you on a few things, they'll go over some of those today on the ice. I suspect they'll improve your personal game. As far as the team is concerned, we're a family. The guys will give you the same energy you give them," he says, then smiles. "After some initial shit is given in fun. You know how that goes."

"I expect it."

"There might be a conversation or two from the higher ups regarding your reputation, as well. As long as it doesn't affect your time on the ice, I don't give a shit what you do in your personal life. This is just a heads up that they may throw some media training at you."

This isn't unexpected, either. I had an off-season incident that tabloids ran with. Was it part of why Vancouver didn't hesitate to trade me? Maybe.

"Whatever they need from me," I say, easily. Seattle is giving me a shot; I'll give them one, too.

"If you want a place at the dinner table, all you have to do is show up. The guys here will hold a seat for you."

"Thanks, Coach. I appreciate that."

"Don't thank me, just put in the effort and I'll do my best to get you that cup."

"Will do, Coach," I tell him, standing to leave.

Before I make it to the door, he stops me.

"Tyson," he calls. "Sadie is going to be excited to see you."

"I'm going to be excited to see her, too," I admit. She's a special girl and I've missed her. "I hope that won't be weird for anyone."

"Her dad worships the ground she walks on; he'll be happy she's happy. I think you can understand, yeah?"

Coach Cole doesn't need to remind me of common ground between me and Cillian. I know it exists. I appreciate his effort, all the same. Regardless of how difficult it will be for two men in love with the same woman to play together, we'll both put Isla and Sadie first.

"Perfectly."

"Good, get suited up. I'll see you on the ice."

"Yes, sir," I say, shutting his office door behind me.

Stepping into a new locker room is a little like the first day of school. No matter how familiar it all is, you're still somewhat off-balance. When you've played elite hockey your whole life, you get used to your teammates changing up, that's nothing new. Every summer camp as a kid was with new guys. All-star game lineups are different each season, trades and drafts happen every year. If you can't get accustomed to interchangeable parts, this isn't the sport for you.

Knowing that doesn't lessen the first-day jitters. As expected, I get some razzing when I walk in to change into my gear.

"We put your cubby next to Wylder's, Murphy," Axel Wallin says. "You cool with that?"

"That was my second choice of places to be," I say.

"Where was your first?" he asks, cocking his head.

"Next to you, buddy. Heard your eyesight was going in your old age, wanted to stick close enough for you to ogle me like I know you like to do." That gets a few laughs from the other guys. Wallin is now one of the older guys, on what is mostly a younger group of guys, on the team. I've known him for years; we played in the WHL together for a few seasons. Him being the first to give me some shit is his way of welcoming me.

"Whatever, Pretty Boy," he says. "I see just fine!"

"Nice comeback, Wally." I laugh.

"Yeah, yeah. Good to see you, dickhead."

"You, too."

I move to my cubby, saying hello to the guys I pass as I go. Wallin wasn't joking; I am next to Wylder, who is already sitting there, putting his pads on.

"Tyson," he greets me with a nod.

"Cillian," I say back. Taking a seat, I start to unlace my tennis shoes. "How's it going?"

"No complaints." He doesn't look toward me for a moment or two, but I feel his gaze when he finally does. "I'm not going to let history dictate our team relationship. There are no hard feelings on my end."

"On mine, either," I say, turning to look at him. "Honestly."

"Good to hear, man. Sadie was a box of firecrackers when she heard the trade announcement. She'll be at the game tomorrow and is hoping to see you."

"Let's make that happen. I don't want to disappoint her," I say. "I've missed her."

"She's missed you, too," he says. "They both have. I'm not saying this out of misguided jealousy, more out of diplomacy. If it's too difficult for you to be around Isla, you tell me. I'll get you in front of Sadie Baby without her mom."

"I…" I start to say something, then pause to consider. "I guess I didn't expect you to be this understanding."

"We don't know much about each other. That's something I'd like to see change. As captain of the team, as the husband of a woman who respects you, and as the dad of a kid who sees you as an idol," he says. "First thing you should know about me is that I fucked my life up beyond belief and am living every day to ensure I never do anything like that again. My family is the most important thing to me, but my family extends to this team. So, it includes you now, too."

"I respect Isla, too. She never gave me any false hope, I knew where her heart was. Her making the choice to be happy isn't something I hold against her. Or you."

"Good to know. Despite the rough start, you're still one of the best in the fucking game, so I'm glad you're here. We all are."

"Damn right," Blom says from a few stalls down. "Now, if you two are done fucking hugging it out like a couple of old grandmas, can we get on the ice and see how Pretty Boy plays with the rest of us when he's wearing the same sweater?"

"I guess I got my nickname already," I mutter.

"Could be worse," Cillian says. "They've started calling Letty Fat Bottom Girl, in recent weeks."

"Do I want to know the story behind that?"

"Probably not," he answers with a laugh.

Practice goes as good as I could have hoped for. They throw me on a line with Letty and Wally, who are not only fast and capable, but fun, too. The lighthearted banter, the ribbing of other players, infuses the work with much-needed joy. Something I hadn't realized I'd missed. The three of us read each other well, better than you can expect after one practice.

For the first time in a long while, I step off the ice with a sense of optimism. After a shower, I meet with the team of trainers. We met yesterday, too, after my flight arrived. They gave me a general physical then. Today, they'll have a plan for me. And like the pro I am, I'll execute it all without complaint. At least, to them. My dad is the one who hears that side of me. He says it's his job, since he's the one that encouraged me to start playing at the age of four.

My mom carpooled me to every practice, every game, every camp. All while my little sister became my biggest cheerleader. My career became a family affair. I owe them everything.

When I spoke to my parents last night, they told me my sister, Lottie, needed to move. The occupants of the apartment above her flooded their unit, which caused Lottie's ceiling to cave in.

I came up with a solution; I've just yet to let her know. On my drive back home after practice, I call her.

"Hi, Ty," she greets.

"Hey, heard you had an interesting day yesterday."

"Mother fucking idiots," she mutters.

"Move into my house, it's empty anyway."

"I can't do that, Ty."

"Sure, you can, and you fucking will," I tell her with my stern big brother voice. She nearly always ignores it with an eye roll, but it's worth a shot. "You have the code to the door, take your pick of guest rooms. Dad will help you move anything out of the way so you can move stuff in."

"I can't afford your mortgage payment."

"Who the hell asked for you to cover my mortgage?" I ask. Truth is, it's paid off, anyway, but she doesn't know that.

"I can't live there for free," she says, and I take that as a win because she's no longer saying she can't move in.

"Pay me whatever you were paying for your apartment. You get a bigger place, in a safer neighborhood, and I get someone to keep an eye on the place. It's a win-win." What I don't say is that I'll put whatever money she sends me into a low-risk investment account for her. She'd fight me on that, too. Lottie likes to be independent. She's not very good at it yet, but she tries. At twenty-two, she's still got time to learn.

"Are you sure?"

"Absolutely. It's empty, Lottie, take advantage of it. Besides, I know you don't want to move back in with our parents."

"Not while that demon still lives with them," she says, referring to my mom's cat. The animal hates Lottie. None of us know why; it's amusing to all of us but my sister.

"It's settled then," I say, trying not to laugh.

"Fine. Now, tell me about your first day. Did you and Wylder have words?"

"Yes, but they were all good ones. He's helping me see Sadie."

"Oh, God, Ty," she says, and I register the emotion in her voice. "That's kinda fucking great."

"It is," I say, allowing some emotion of my own. My family knows how much I cared about Sadie. It's been hard having to cut that tie. "Coach and I had a good chat, too."

"I'm proud of you, Ty. Probably don't say that enough."

"I'm proud of you, too, kiddo. Now, go move into my house."

"All right, thank you."

"You're welcome. Love you," I tell her.

"I love you, too. And I'll be watching tomorrow."

"You better be."

We end the call as I pull into the driveway of my house, or Calvin's house. Whatever. As I step out of my rig, wet paws land on my calf.

"What the fuck?" Looking down, I find the smallest ball of fur I've ever seen.

"Nightmare! Damn it, I'm so sorry," a woman's voice calls out from behind me. "He got out of his harness; it's still too big."

I pick up the yappy little thing and turn around to find a familiar face.

"Hey, you're Willa's friend."

"Oh, Tyson. What are you doing here?" she asks, taking the dog from my arms.

"I live here."

"Oh," she repeats.

"I'm sorry, what was your name again? Kat?"

"Kit."

"Right, sorry. And that's Nightmare?"

"Yeah, I recently bought my house," she says, pointing to a small, black brick house across the street. "Thought it would be good to have a guard dog."

I laugh, because what the actual fuck? Nightmare weighs maybe six pounds, and considering I can't see his face under all the fur, I'm not sure he could find an attacker if he tried.

"Probably a smart move," I say.

Kit smiles at me, and I wonder why I never noticed how pretty she is. Her skin is flawless bronze, her hair is dark and falls thick past her shoulders, with a thin nose and full lips, she's truly stunning.

"What?" she asks after a moment, scrunching her nose in the most adorable way. Except, she's looking at me like she said something that I should have responded to. Did she?

"Sorry?"

"You're staring."

"You're staring," I say back like I'm a four-year-old with an undeveloped brain.

"Oh my God," she says with a laugh. "Okay, I'm going to go back home to my pizza and *Baldur's Gate*. See ya, Tyson, I'll try to keep my dog out of your hair."

"Wait," I say, stopping her. "Console or PC?"

"Xbox."

"What's your gamer tag?"

She narrows her eyes at me, but eventually answers. "HookersNBlow."

"Shut the fuck up, seriously?"

Kit smiles and shrugs before crossing the street without another word.

3
TYSON

Waking up this morning was like a rebirth, as fucking dumb as that sounds. I don't know if it was my chat with Coach, or with Cillian, or just having a great practice with all the guys. Whatever happened yesterday was the reset I needed that allowed me to get the best night's sleep I've had in months.

Like every morning, I roll out of bed and onto my yoga mat. Twenty minutes, the same routine, no variations. Like the good, weirdo hockey player that I am. The great thing about Calvin's house is that there is a small sunroom off the primary bedroom, just big enough for my mat. Which means, I get to do my morning stretches with a view of the lake. And Kit's house, apparently. Moving into the warrior pose, I watch her as she takes her Pomeranian out for his morning wee.

She's either an early riser or the dog can't wait any longer, as the sun is barely up. She laughs as Nightmare zooms around the small yard, jumping as high as he can, which isn't high at all.

Maybe I should get a dog. Nah, that's a horrible idea. I'm away from home way too much. Still, it'd be nice to come home to someone who is excited to see me. To *wake up* to someone excited to see me. Other than the random nameless woman who I then promptly kick out.

Kit bends to pick the puppy up, but he darts off before she can nab him. Her hands find her hips, as if she's annoyed, yet the smile still clearly stays. Nightmare runs back to her, bouncing until she grabs him, then he starts licking her face.

Suddenly, I feel like an epic creep staring at them as I stretch last night's tension out of my body. Thank fuck she didn't see me.

After finishing my yoga, I jerk off, shower, and eat some breakfast. Another routine. One part I'd like to switch up is my meals. I've known players that hire a personal chef; I'm considering doing the same. You get accustomed to the monotony of it all in favor of your career, but when you see top performers doing just fine while also enjoying variation, it gets harder to avoid.

There's no reason I need to be eating the same shit all the time. And I have more money than I know how to spend, with so many of my expenses covered by the team or the league. Plus, I have a damn good agent who's gotten me a couple of very lucrative endorsements.

One of which, I lost due to my tabloid scandal. I'd already made a large amount of money off it, so it sucked, but it could have been worse. Not holding up my end of any bargain makes me feel like an incredible asshole. I wish it had turned out differently. But I don't really make apologies for the things I've done, either.

Management has asked me to run into the offices this morning; I guess they forgot to have me sign some paper or another. With the stack of documents we got through, I'm not surprised something was missed. It's not like I don't have time, either, with no social life to speak of in this city.

It's game day, though, which means, I'll get some shit done early, then I'll come back to video games and a nap before running to the arena.

I get to the right building, and as I'm approaching the elevator, it starts to close.

"Hold it, please," I say, and see a hand reach out to stop the doors. When I see who it is, I smile. "Are you following me?"

"Considering I was here first, I think I should be asking you that. Besides, I already think you're a Peeping Tom, might as well add stalker to the list," Kit says.

"It's not my fault your yard is under my window," I say. Guess she saw me this morning, after all. "What are you doing here?"

"I work here."

"For the Blades?"

"Yep."

"Doing what?"

"Are you always this nosey?"

"No, but I am always curious. It also seems fate keeps sticking you in front of me. I'd like to know why."

"Fate?" She crinkles her nose again, the same way she did yesterday. "You probably have a nightstand lined with crystals. Are you into horoscopes and fortune telling, too? You know a study in 2017 came to the basic conclusion that zodiac sign stereotypes are bullshit?"

"No." I laugh. "Would you please indulge your nosey, stalker neighbor by telling him what your profession is?"

"Statistician. Or data analyst, here, I guess. It's a new position with the team; we're trying some things out."

"Are you working on our stats?"

"Yes. Sort of. I'm diving deep into how well certain plays work. How well do they work against specific teams and players. Or with certain members of our team. That sort of thing. From purely a numbers standpoint."

"Building a database that can be fed to coaches in real time," I muse.

She shrugs. "The groundwork is already there; the Edge system helps with a lot of that. This is just more personalized. More customizable for the team."

"That makes sense," I say as we step off the elevator. "Players and coaches often run on emotion or gut feeling. It's nice to have real data to go along with that."

"That's the idea, anyway," she says, giving me a little salute. "Have a good day, Mr. Murphy."

"Wait. What's your last name?"

"Ashcroft."

"Got it, thanks for the escort, Ms. Ashcroft."

After I find the right office and sign the right paperwork, I find a grocery store in my new neighborhood and stock up on a few things. There's a small pet store next door, so I make a pit stop in there, as well. When I get home, I run across the street, drop the new purchase on Kit's doorstep, then make myself lunch and settle in front of the television.

My Xbox powers up, but before I start playing a game, I search for Kit's ridiculous gamertag. It pops up and I look at the list of games she's played. It's extensive and the achievements attached to them show she doesn't play any of them casually. We have several titles in common, some I'm honestly surprised by. For some reason, I figured she'd play cozy games, like *Stardew Valley* or whatever. I sure as hell didn't expect to see a collection of the most hardcore horror and shooting games on her list.

Who is this woman?

And why is she consuming my day?

It's stupid. She's in Isla's orbit and I'm too close to that as it is. Besides, Kit doesn't seem like the one-night stand kind of woman. She owns a house and a dog, which tells me she isn't one to shy away from commitment. That isn't something I find interesting right now.

I hit the friend request button, then back out to the main menu. Shooting some aliens on *Destiny* will take my mind off everything, and that's what I need for the next two hours. Mindless entertainment before a good nap.

Then, it's time for my Seattle debut, which somehow feels a lot like my NHL debut.

We take the ice and much like this morning, there's a lightness about me. Like I'm breathing fresh air for the first time. The pregame compadre in the locker room was a vibe, all the guys get along so well. They know who to leave be and who likes to fuck around. Letty and Blom are the biggest goofballs, while Fane stays relatively quiet and focused. Wylder is a good leader, says the right things without being too wordy.

Coach was similar. He came in for the last few minutes, gave us the rundown for the game. Then said, "Set the fucking tone, boys."

That's exactly what we do. Within the first four minutes of play, we have eight shots on goal, with Wallin landing one of them in the net off my rebound.

"Fuck yeah," he yells as we collide in celebration. "Nice play, Pretty Boy!"

"Great shot, Wally," I tell him as we skate off to the bench.

Maybe fans think we take all this for granted, being that it's what we do each day. But we don't. Every damn goal is a big deal. No matter how many years we've been doing it. No matter how good a player you are. It takes so many shots before you get one in.

I wonder if Kit knows how many?

The thought comes quickly, and I smirk as I push it away. Game time isn't for thoughts about anything but the game.

During the next run on the ice, a guy on the opposing team, Brance, hip-checks me. It's unnecessary contact as I'm nowhere near the puck.

"Fuck off, fourth liner," I say, shoving him as I skate past. There's nothing wrong with being on the fourth line. They're a needed part of the team, allowing the other lines time to rest. But Brance is a veteran in the sport, probably should have retired a season or two ago. He rarely scores now and is more of a menace than anything. Some guys are goons from the start, but Brance wasn't. He was a goal maker. Turning into a pest before retirement is a hell of a way to go out and it's not the path most would choose.

"You fuck off, slut," he bites back, and I laugh while in my pursuit of the puck.

We don't score any more in the period, but neither does the other team. They do tie it up in the second, however, and we head into the final period with a clear directive.

Score.

Brance continues to dog me every time we're on the ice together. Who knows why he has such a hard-on for me tonight. There isn't always a clear reason. It's hockey, there doesn't need to be anything more than they're currently losing. I can't say how many times a little fight made the difference in boosting your team's morale enough to go on and score a goal.

I sweep check their winger and gain control of the puck, pumping my legs down the ice to their net. Brance is hot on my heels until Fane flies in and ties him up, allowing me the breakaway I need.

There are a few high anxiety moments in hockey. Breakaways are one. Even if the net is guarded by the goalie, like now. Or if he's been pulled in favor of an extra player on the ice, you're desperate to get the puck in and you know every eye in the arena is on you. And you alone.

This time, luck is on my side. The puck gets the height and speed I need for it to sail past their goalie's shoulder and fly into the net.

Nerves rattle me as I prepare to walk into the family room. It's not my family I'll be seeing. It's Wylder's. It's the family I once hoped to be mine.

I know the reality of the situation; there's no delusion on my end. That's not the problem. My issue is that it's the first time seeing Isla and Sadie since before she got back together with Cillian. If I let any of my emotions come to the surface, what happens then?

Is Cillian still going to be understanding? Does it push my position with the team to the outskirts of the inner circle? Most importantly, I don't want to confuse Sadie.

From the way the guys all chatter in our downtime, it's clear they're all close to the Wylder family. Like me, they're as enamored with Cillian's daughter as I always was. I don't want to be the lone player that can't be around as much because his personal issues get in the way.

Isla and Sadie were never meant to be mine. My head is clear on that. I'm not sure I can trust my heart to understand it yet.

Steeling myself, I push through the door. Before I can scan the room for them, Sadie is running toward me.

"Tyson!"

"Hey, shorty," I say, catching her in my arms as she vaults herself at me.

"You're here! Now, all my favorite players are on the same team," she says, her tiny hands landing on my cheeks.

"What about Ryan Nugent-Hopkins?" I ask in disbelief. She used to say she was going to marry him.

"I've outgrown him."

"It's about time," I say.

Laughter behind her catches my attention. It's Isla, I'd know her laugh anywhere, like a permanent tattoo on my skin.

"That's what my dad says, too," Sadie says.

"He's a smart man," I say, finally looking past her shoulder to nod at her mother. Isla smiles at me, and my heart clenches.

"I've missed you," Sadie says, mustering a stern tone. "You never visit anymore."

"I know, sweetheart," I say, setting her on her feet and kneeling in front of her. "I'm sorry about that. I've been real busy trying to find my way here."

The words mean more than she'll understand. Maybe more than even I understand just now. One glance at Isla and I know I'm not over her. Or, at least, not over the idea I had of her and me. The dream of starting my own hockey family dynasty.

"Well," Sadie says, biting her bottom lip and scrunching her brow in thought. "I guess it's okay, because you're here now. And part of the best team ever."

"Yes, I am. You'll see me lots more now, more than before, even."

"That's good. You're the only one who doesn't let me win pancake eating contests."

She releases a heavy sigh and rolls her eyes.

"Everyone else lets you win?" I pretend to be aghast.

"Yeah, it's so re...rid..."

"Were you going for ridiculous?"

"Yeah, that."

"All right, next time we're around pancakes, I'll make sure I win. Again."

"It's a deal!" She runs off to say hello to some others and I'm left face-to-face with her mom.

Isla, it pains me to say, is more beautiful now than she was when we dated. There's a happy glow to her that wasn't there before. Fuck me, I love that for her. Even as I hate that I wasn't the one to put it there.

"Hey, Freckles."

"Hi, Tyson," she says, taking a step closer. "Thanks for that, she's been dying to see you since the trade was announced. Well, before that, but you know…"

"She doesn't understand the dynamics, I get it. It's good seeing her. And you…you look happy."

"I am," she says.

"I'm glad. I mean that."

"I know you do." She smiles crookedly and it feels like the goodbye I never got before. "I hope you find it, too. You deserve that, Ty."

Do I? Am I a good enough man for that? It's easy to feel undeserving. Easier than feeling worthy, for sure. Is it enough to simply exist? To live each day in an unfulfilled rut waiting for a cosmic event or divine intervention to put the love of my life in front of me? No, that doesn't make me deserving. Surely there's more for me to do. Maybe I should ask Cillian, since he seems to have figured it all out.

"Thanks, Isla."

"You're welcome. Good game, tonight."

I nod my thanks and find my way out of the arena, where I can be alone with all these damn feelings.

4

KIT

O ne week, three different women.

Today, she's a brunette, the past two have been blondes. I was starting to think Tyson had a type. Well, I guess he does…it's not about looks, though. She probably only needs to be willing to have a good time and get the fuck out early in the morning.

They've all left shortly after dawn. Before he starts his morning yoga routine, where I can watch from my living room, a cup of steaming coffee in hand. It's a damn nice wake me up. The view and the caffeine.

He had never struck me as the player type, but I did only know him when he was in a weird sort of committed relationship with Isla. Then, there was that small scandal involving him, which shattered any preconceived notions I had of him.

It's much more likely that Tyson Murphy is a man-whore than he is the sweet, wholesome guy who had no problem dating a single mom with a ton of baggage. Can he be both? I guess. I'm not one to judge what a grown adult does with their free time, as long as it's not harming anyone else.

Besides his escapades with random women, I believe he's still a good guy. He bought Nightmare a gift, after all.

The other day, I arrived home to find a neon green harness and a custom nametag shaped like a heart wrapped up in a gift bag on my doorstep. It could have only been from him, since nobody else has met the furball of terror yet. The new harness fits him much better; he won't be escaping this one, thankfully. I swear, when he slipped loose and ran across the street, it damn near gave me a heart attack. This is my first time taking care of something all by myself.

I should have started with a houseplant. But like the bozo I am, I jumped straight off the high dive and into the deep end without so much as a single swimming lesson.

Nightmare has been easy, so far. Other than being particular about food, he doesn't like kibble, so we tried a handful of wet food varieties to find what he likes. Salmon was the clear winner. There hasn't been a single indoor accident, yet anyway. And he kennels easily when I'm not home and at night.

He seems too easy, honestly. Maybe he's a cyborg dog, or just broken. I mean, I'm not complaining. I'd rather have an easy dog than one that eats its way through locked doors or something. That's partly why I picked a small breed, I've seen plenty of videos of damage via pets. I pay too much for my little home to have extra cash for unnecessary repairs.

Tyson bends into a position that puts him on all fours. A strange little tickle sparks between my legs, making me blink in surprise. It's a rare occurrence, at best. What's more rare than rare? That's how often I feel any sort of attraction to a real flesh and blood human in front of me.

Willa asked me once if I was asexual and I had to think about it thoroughly. Which is my way with everything. Except pets, apparently. Typically, I'm an overthinker. An analyzer to my very bones. I let her question marinate for a time. After a while, I deduced that I'm not. I do feel attraction; it simply isn't common for me. I've seen men that I think are handsome, who define good-looking by my own standards, but it usually stops at appreciation and doesn't progress past that. Plus, I like watching pornography. I like getting myself off to images of beautiful people.

It's the reality of another person in my life that has never held much appeal.

It isn't that I don't wish for it. It's more that I'm terrified of it.

So why now? Why him?

I'll have to leave those questions to steep, as well. Likely, whatever it is will dissipate into the ether and no longer matter anyhow. In the meantime, I'll enjoy the view he gives me every morning. It's a nice show, since he performs his routine in nothing but boxer briefs each day. Obviously, you have to be in prime form to play in the NHL, but having it on display in front of me every day puts a whole new stamp of appreciation on how hard the guys work at it.

No fat, no flab, no wiggle, or jiggle. Tyson is all taut muscle, thick thighs, bulging biceps. His burnished curls falling low on his forehead as he contorts from pose to pose. He rocks his hips toward the mat at the same time I lift my coffee mug to my mouth, missing entirely in my distraction, and the hot fluid dribbles down into my cleavage.

"Damn it," I curse, causing Nightmare to bounce up from his bed and yelp alertly. "It's okay, buddy. Just your mom being a dumbass voyeur."

That'll teach me.

Or not.

Nightmare follows me to the kitchen to put away my mug, then to my bedroom to find clothes for the day. It's Saturday, and Willa is going with me to a few secondhand stores, as I'm still on the hunt for more furniture and décor.

The basics are covered—a bed, a sofa, a desk. Yet it still looks like a minimalist lives here, and that is something I most definitely am not. I probably lean toward the maximalist side of center. I like quirky, kitsch, and color. When I'm done with this place, every corner will have something interesting to look at. Something that spurs my imagination and activates my brain.

My dad called me Chaos as a kid. Not because I ran all over the place wreaking havoc, but because my mind never settled. I would jump from subject to subject, question to question. Never satisfied with whatever new information I'd learned, I always wanted more. I still do.

After a quick shower and a quicker bowl of Cinnamon Life cereal, I'm dressed and ready when Willa arrives.

"You'll never guess who my neighbor is," I tell her when I open the door to her.

"Who?"

"Tyson Murphy," I say. "Just across the street, in that fancy modern house that doesn't fit in with the rest of the neighborhood."

"No way! What a weird coincidence," she says, bending to pick up the dog running circles around her feet. "You must be Nightmare."

He licks her nose, making her laugh as she coos at him.

"It is strange for a city this size."

"Definitely, but I like that you have someone we know so close by. I'll worry less about you."

"You don't have to worry at all, I'm a big girl. Besides, I've been living on my own for months, now, since you moved in with your men."

"Yeah," she says, putting Nightmare down and tossing his toy giraffe for him. "But that was in a secure building. You don't even have an alarm system here."

"No, but I'm not exactly in the worst part of town, either."

"Just promise me you'll get one installed soon."

"I promise. Again." I've already told her I would. She offered to pay for it, but that's silly. I can install one myself.

I think, anyway. YouTube will help, surely.

"He's fucking cute," she says, rubbing Nightmare's head when he trots back with the stuffy in his mouth.

"He is," I agree. "I feel bad leaving him home alone all day, but he's done well."

"That's good. You ready to go?"

"Yep, let me just put him in his crate," I tell her. "To your room, Nightmare."

He bounds toward the kennel, his little bum bouncing side to side, making his nametag jingle on his collar.

"Oh my God, he needs to stop being so damn cute," Willa says.

"Right? I can't get over it." I grab my handbag and follow her out front. As we round Willa's car, Tyson comes out of his house.

"Willa Cole? That you?" he hollers from across the street.

"As I live and breathe," she answers in an exaggerated Southern drawl as he crosses the road to us.

"It's good to see you." He wraps her up in a hug. I'd be jealous if I could feel such a useless emotion. Jeez…am I jealous?

Am I capable of it? Am I feeling that right now?

No, no. That can't be it, I'm probably just hungry.

"Hey, Kit," he says to me after they exchange polite pleasantries with each other.

"Hey. I've been meaning to thank you for the gift," I say. "Just haven't seen you."

"Haven't you?" His brow raises as he asks.

"If you didn't want an audience, you wouldn't do it in front of floor-to-ceiling glass," I answer, rolling my eyes, though heat warms my chest from being caught spying through his window.

"What am I missing?" Willa asks, leaning against her car, her head bouncing between Tyson and me.

"He does yoga in the sunroom up there," I say, nodding my head toward his house.

"She watches," he accuses playfully.

"Which means you watch her, too, creeper," Willa volleys back at him.

"Touché." Tyson shrugs.

"I can't help it; you have better form than I do. It's like a free lesson every morning."

"Well, you'll have to find a different teacher for the week. We leave early tomorrow for a six-day road trip."

"You'll come back to find me so stiff I won't be able to bend over to scoop up Nightmare's poop, I guess," I say with a shrug.

Tyson laughs. Willa looks at me as curiously as I feel.

"I'll help clean up when I get back," he says, as he turns toward his house. "It's the least I can do."

"Assuming you have time between visitors," I blurt before I can stop myself.

"What was that?" he asks, turning around, brow raised but smiling.

"Men between the ages of twenty and twenty-nine are at the highest risk of gonorrhea," I say, to which Willa cracks up laughing.

"I have never had a sexually transmitted anything," he says, grinning wider. "And thank fuck I'm getting close to aging out of that demographic."

"Stay safe," I say, shrugging.

"I will, thank you for your concern," he says, bowing formally before walking across the street.

"Have a good trip," Willa calls after him. She waits until we're in her car before she addresses me. "You were flirting. With Tyson Murphy, no less."

"I was not," I protest.

"You were too!"

"That wasn't flirting."

"For you…that was absolutely flirting. Which you don't do often."

"It's nothing," I dismiss. "Neighborly banter, is all."

"With some voyeurism sprinkled on top?"

"You have eyes, you'd watch, too."

"Truth," she says with a grin. "It's okay if you're interested in him. You know that, right?"

"It's not, and I'm not."

"Why isn't it okay to be interested?"

"He's your sister's ex-whatever they were."

"Isla wouldn't care."

"That doesn't mean he's over her. Besides, you know me well enough to know this too shall pass."

"I also know you well enough to know this isn't a normal reaction."

"If it stays abnormal, we'll discuss it. For now, it's not worth conversation."

"Okay," she says, accepting my lack of interest. "Let's go shopping, then."

"Can we get food, first? I'm starving."

"Glo's?"

"Fuck yeah! Smothered hashbrowns sound amazing right now."

"Rough night?" Willa teases.

"As rough as it gets for me. One of my old coworkers started playing *Fallout 76* not long ago and wanted to take advantage of the double XP this weekend. We farmed the queen for hours."

"I know what very little of that means, but I'm glad you had fun."

"I did, thank you."

"What level are you now?"

"Fourteen-hundred and something."

"Damn, girl," Willa exclaims. "You were low five-hundreds before I moved out."

"Yeah, I have less best friend time, now, which means, more game time," I say. Then, I notice the frown on her face. "Don't do that, Willa."

"Maybe I shouldn't have moved in with the guys so quickly."

"Of course, you should have."

"But you're alone."

"That's my normal, you know that. It was weird living with someone else," I tell her. Though we both know it's a white lie. I loved living with

Willa, but I wasn't upset that she fell in love and moved out. "I like my me time almost as much as I like that you're happy."

"I know you do. I worry about you, though."

"I took care of myself before I knew you. I'm sure I haven't forgotten how."

"You didn't manage breakfast this morning," she reminds me.

"Okay, true," I admit. "But only because I was distracted."

Willa glances my way and laughs.

"By a certain NHL player doing yoga?"

"Shut up," I say, making her laugh more.

We grab breakfast and conversation steers clear of my neighbor. Instead, we talk about the trip she's planning during the off season. She finished her PhD program last summer. Zan and Damian promised her a celebratory trip this year. They're talking about Thailand in one of those fancy over-the-water bungalows. Willa is ridiculously excited, and who could blame her? Two weeks on a beautiful beach sound amazing.

Even I wouldn't be opposed, although I'm partial to low humidity and lower temperatures.

After breakfast, we hit the first of the secondhand stores we plan to visit. It's a smaller, carefully curated collection of items. Each one is unique, and I find a side table with a purple giraffe base. It reminds me of Nightmare's favorite toy, so I can't pass it up.

Willa snags a vintage duster that looks like something Stevie Nicks would have worn on stage.

The next few stores aren't as fruitful, but we still manage a couple of treasures.

I'm pooped by the time we get the haul home, unloaded, and I take Nightmare for a walk. When I finally settle for the night in front of my television, there's a friend request sitting on my Xbox that I hadn't noticed before.

I click on the profile, realizing it can only be from Tyson, and see a long list of sports games, as well as the shooters that are most popular with men. We do have a handful of games in common, though.

Finding it harmless, since he knows where I live anyway. I accept the request from PuckBuddie.

5

TYSON

F uck, I get it. Isla is amazing, but Cillian never shuts the hell up about her.

Not that I would, either. But it makes it damned hard to quit thinking about her when I have constant reminders. I've had a different woman in bed with me almost every night since my first game with the Blades. All in a vain effort to rid myself of the image of her that plays behind my eyes when I close them.

It's not working.

Hell, this morning, when I was pleasuring myself, it was her face trying to creep in. Every time, I'd pause my movements, try and shake her away, imagine any other hot as hell woman, but those freckles kept coming back.

I'm an asshole, but I'm not the asshole who's going to beat off to the image of his teammate's wife.

In the end, I gave the fuck up. She wouldn't give me any peace and I was frustrated all day because of it. Then, we got to the arena for today's game and Cillian was recounting his earlier conversation with her and Sadie.

I don't know how to escape this. It's not like I can just turn off my feelings.

After the game, I brought a woman…the guys would call her a puck bunny, back to my room. It's frowned upon by the league and team management, but it happens. I didn't even ask her name. Instead, I avoided conversation, fucked her, and politely kicked her out.

It was a day game, and now I'm left with the evening to myself, wallowing in self-pity. When your life consists of as many nights in a hotel as it does at home, you learn ways to cope. Every guy is different. Some hit the gym, some take baths, some watch sports. Some, like me, travel with a game console.

It's a way to relieve aggression, to relax, to spend some down time without getting into trouble. This trip, it's my spare Xbox. When I power it up and log on to the internet, I'm happy to find HookersNBlow is online, too. She accepted my friend request. I haven't known many women gamers. The ones I do are careful about who they let into their world. Men, and boys, are brutally misogynistic on mic.

I'm glad I made her cut.

Within seconds, Kit sends me a message through the console.

KIT:

We need a fourth. Do you have a mic?

ME:

Yeah. I've mainly played killer.

KIT:

I assume you can learn new tricks.

An invite to her party chat pops up. I accept it and put my headphones on.

"You know what they say about assumptions," I say.

"We have no problem showing our ass here, sir," an unfamiliar female voice says.

"Tyson, that was Ramona," Kit introduces. "Sydney is also in here."

"Hi, Tyson."

"Hi, everyone," I say as I load into *Dead by Daylight*. It's a game where you play as a killer trying to eliminate survivors who are trying to repair enough generators to power up an exit gate. Or as a survivor trying to escape the killer. It's intense, but a great time, if you don't take it too seriously.

"What killer do you main?"

"Ghostface," I answer. "But I'm more the type of killer to help survivors get their challenges done than the type to be toxic and go after a 4K."

"Ah, we love a fun killer," Ramona says. "Micheal Myers is my favorite, though."

"Only because you're weirdly diabolical," says Sydney.

"What can I say? I love a man in a mask."

"Okay, I'm in the game."

"Sending an invite," Kit says. "Can you skill check without blowing the generators?"

"With the right perks equipped."

"Do your best to keep out of sight, we'll do the heavy lifting," Sydney says.

"Protect the baby at all costs," Ramona says.

"I'm the baby?"

"You are now, sweetheart," she says. "It's okay, though, I like kids."

I laugh, going with it. Comedic relief is what I need. A good time. If I am the brunt of playful jokes, I'm okay with that.

"How does everyone know each other?"

"I stalked these two on a women-in-gaming Discord group until they relented to being my friends," says Ramona.

"No matter how many times we blew her off, she just kept coming back. She's like a stray dog," Sydney teases, as Ramona barks and whimpers.

"Syd and I met at school," Kit says as the loading screen starts up for the game.

"At U-Dub with Willa?"

"You know Willa?" asks Sydney.

"Yeah, I dated her sister for a time."

"That's how you know Kit," she says.

"Yes, but we're also neighbors." The game loads us into the map. There are different ones, some inside, some outside. This one is outside, which I prefer, as it will give me more places to hide. This is one of the bigger maps, too. "Rotten Fields, nice."

"Tons of corn for you to hide in, kid," Ramona says.

Following instructions, I crouch and start creeping around. I won't be dead weight to the ladies, but I don't want to be a burden to them, either. Cautiously, I find a generator and start repairing it. An easy enough task, but it takes several minutes, and you can't drop your alertness. The killer can easily sneak up on you.

"Oh, fuck! It's a Pig, don't ask me how I know," Kit shrieks. "I'm going to loop around the house."

"I'll work on the gen in the barn while you keep her busy," Sydney says.

"Headed your way, Syd," Ramona tells her. "You good, Baby Boy?"

"Yep, on a gen on the other side of the map, Mommy."

They all titter.

"Oh, this must be a baby killer. They're whiffing like crazy," Kit says.

"Let's make some progress, then we'll ease up. See if they're a fun killer," Sydney says.

"So, what's your story, Tyson?" asks Ramona. "Married, dating, kids? What do you do for money?"

"Single. No kids. I play hockey."

"Like, for fun?"

"No, for money. I play pro."

"No shit?"

"No shit. Just moved to Seattle to play for the Blades. Was in Vancouver before this."

"Wait a fucking minute," Sydney says. "Tyson Murphy?"

"That's me."

"We're playing with Tyson Murphy? A heads up would have been nice."

"You would have been weird about it," Kit says. "Like you're being now. He's just a guy who plays video games in his spare time."

"Fuck," Sydney curses. "I should have put it together from the cheesy gamertag."

"Ouch." I fake outrage. "You follow hockey, eh?"

"Not really. But I have brothers and I grew up in South Dakota. It's not something you can avoid. They're going to freak the fuck out."

"Shit, I lost her. Not sure what way she went," Kit says. "I'm going to jump on the gen upstairs."

"Almost done here," Ramona says.

We manage to complete all but the last generator without the killer hooking any of us. Further proof that this killer is inexperienced. We decide to go easy on them and form something of a conga line, following one another around the map until we find them. Eventually, we do, and they join in for a few minutes before we let them get some points on us.

The next couple of matches don't go quite as easy, but these ladies are fun as hell to play with, and by the time I log off for the night, my cheeks hurt from laughing so much.

I send a message through the console to Kit.

ME:

Thanks for tonight, I needed some fun.

I give her my cell phone number, telling her I'm being neighborly. A few minutes later, a text message comes through.

KIT:

> Thank you for joining. We hate playing with randoms. Glad we could help, hope your trip is going okay.

ME:

> It's going well enough. Still a little awkward.

KIT:

> Because it's a new team?

I weigh my response before sending anything. Kit isn't someone I know, but I have to assume she knows more about my situation than the average person. Does that mean I can trust her with my secrets? My feelings?

My heart tells me I can. My brain strongly protests. This is someone deep inside Isla's circle. If I were to tell Kit how hard this is for me, it could get back to people it would affect the most. It could jeopardize the team dynamic that I'm already on the outskirts of.

ME:

> Basically.

For my own self-preservation, I keep my response vague.

KIT:

> I imagine it's difficult. A new team, a new city. Especially when you've been in your hometown. You have family there, yeah?

ME:

I do. Mom, Dad, and my sister, Lottie. I don't
have anyone in Seattle, outside of the team.

KIT:

I didn't have anyone when I moved here, either.
I'm an only child though, and didn't really
have anyone back in Maine either. But I found
Willa. Found family counts. Hopefully you'll
find something like that. In the meantime,
at least you have a friend in a crazy little
barking ball of fur across the street.

ME:

Just the fur ball? Not his friendly owner?

KIT:

His owner barely plays well with
others on her best day.

ME:

I feel like that's not true.

KIT:

Didn't anyone ever tell you not
to trust your feelings?

ME:

The opposite, actually.

I'm smiling again. It comes easy with this woman; and suddenly, moving into my own place, out of Calvin's, doesn't feel like something I need to rush. Kit's right; I need to find my people here. Until then, it might be nice having her close by.

KIT:

Wow. You must have shitty parents.

KIT:

I'm kidding! Shit, we probably don't know each
other well enough for jokes like that yet.

ME:

Relax, I knew you were kidding.

KIT:

Okay, good. I'm...awkward with people
sometimes. I apologize in advance.

ME:

Consider me a safe space for awkwardness.
My sister is on the spectrum. I don't judge.

KIT:

Thank you, that means a lot to me.

Her words hurt me. Partly because I hate that people with autism, general anxiety, or who are simply prone to social awkwardness are made to feel worse because people refuse to take the time to understand. Partly because I know Lottie's lived with that her whole life. I'd be her protector forever, if I thought that's what she needs. It's not, though. She needs, and wants, to be independent. Even if that means her life is harder. I respect that.

ME:

I mean it. I need to crash, but thanks again.
Hope you let me play with your crew again.

KIT:

Anytime.

For the first time in years, it's not Isla's face that immediately illuminates behind my closed eyes as I lie down to sleep. It starts with my pretty neighbor, instead. My curiosity about her is what lulls me. Mentally, I tally a list of questions I want to ask her. I'll never remember them all. Besides, it's not like I can show up on her door and bombard her with them just to slake my wonder.

The more I know of her, the more I want to know. What was her life like in Maine? Why doesn't she have people there? What heritage does she have that makes her skin the perfect shade of sun-kissed bronze, even in the depths of the PNW's cloudy season?

She comes across as a carefree spirit. Smart, but playful and funny. I can't imagine her being awkward. What triggers her?

Is that why she's single? Fuck, is she even single? I have no idea; it hasn't come up in conversation. I just assumed.

I fall asleep imagining the answers to all my questions.

When I wake, it's from a familiar dream of the woman I once loved and the family I thought I might have. The mind is a devious cunt.

On the plane to the next city, I avoid Wylder. It's not hard, and probably even expected. Instead, I take a spot several aisles away, with our goalie, Blom.

"How you settling in, Murphy?" he asks after we take off.

"Eh, you know how it is. Mid-season trades are messy. Especially for us singles who don't have a partner to handle the logistical shit."

"I hear that. When I went from Anaheim to Toronto, it was a nightmare. You don't have a home. Which, I guess we should be used to since we're in hotels so much, but you need that base to reset at."

"Yeah, I'm crashing at a friend's house while he's not using it. But it's not the same. Nice place, though, and I have a friendly neighbor," I say.

"Hot and friendly? Or, like, a nice grandma who will bake you cookies kind of friendly?"

"Definitely hot. Fucking gorgeous, really. And funny. But it's not like that."

"Why the fuck not? I've seen you leaving the arena with women. Having someone next door would be convenient as hell," Blom says.

"Or more complicated," I argue. "I don't know that much about her. I mean, I met her before I moved down, but I didn't know her, you know? I'm not even sure she's single. Maybe Zander knows."

"Zander? Why would he know?"

"She's a friend of Willa's. That's how I met her before, when I was…" I trail off.

"Ah, right. Wait a fucking minute," he says, turning in his seat to look at me. His eyes narrow into small slits, a frown forming on his bearded face. "Are you talking about Kit Kat?"

"Kit Ashcroft?"

"Motherfucker." He plops back in his seat with a long, drawn-out sigh.

"What am I missing? Is she not single?" I ask.

"Oh, she's single," he grumbles. "I've been trying to get her to let me take her out for months. With no damn success, and now I have you, the Pretty Boy, to contend with. What hope does the weirdo goalie have?"

"Come on, man. You're selling yourself short. I heard you had a hot and heavy affair with that actress."

"I did, but Britton Macy is hung up on one of her old co-stars. Again, how do I contend with that?" He crosses his arms over his chest, pouting like a toddler. It's almost adorable. "I'm doomed to be second choice."

"I'm probably not the right one to ask about that," I say glumly. "I'm pretty good at being the runner-up, too."

"Yeah, I guess you would be," he says. "I look at Wylder, Zan, and Gavin and think there's someone out there for everyone. Fuck, just wish it was my time."

"You lonely, big guy?" Letty asks from the seat behind Blom.

"Yes," Blom answers. "And also, fuck you."

Letty laughs and they trade a few more jabs at each other. While I ruminate on what Hugo Blom has just said.

I wish it was my time.

It hits my heart, because I wish the same. Growing up, family was as big as hockey for me. I thought I'd have what my parents do. They fell in love young, had me not too long after, followed by Lottie. My childhood was good, active, and healthy, thanks to my parents. My mom is a natural nurturer, my dad is the type of guy who wants to teach everyone everything he knows. If he doesn't know it, he'll learn it along with you.

They're who I wanted to be. I still want that. A partnership where we support each other through life. A wife that will help me grow as much as she'll let me help her. That's what I pictured my life would be.

Then, I met Isla. For a while, my dreams were on track. Before we both realized she wasn't over Cillian. After he came back into her life, I spiraled into the man-whore people expect professional athletes to be. Shamelessly, even. After my issues one night in Montreal ended up in the tabloids, I settled down some. My mother had a lot to do with that, she put me through the wringer for days. She can lecture like no other.

Now, being in Seattle, with the constant reminders of Isla, I can see myself falling into old habits. Bad habits. Habits best left behind.

I'm reminded of something Mom said to me.

"You'll never find the love of your life while you're distracted by one-night stands."

"Say that again," Blom says, and I realize I said it aloud.

"My mother told me that, once. You'll never find the love of your life while you're distracted by one-night stands."

"Well, fuck my life."

"Right?"

"Does that mean we have to be celibate until we find our person?" he asks, aghast.

"Probably. Though, I haven't cut those off yet."

"What if she's right?"

"Then all we're doing is prolonging our own misery."

"Sure feels good, though," he mumbles, balling up his hoodie to use as a pillow against the window. "Be careful with her."

"How do you mean?" I ask.

"That Kit Kat has something fragile about her," Blom says. "I don't know what it is, but I've caught a faraway look on her face a couple of times. She's special, but something haunts her. I'd bet my Stanley Cup ring on it."

It shouldn't, but that information only makes her more intriguing. Who is Kit Ashcroft?

6

KIT

Nightmare growls from his crate just outside my open bedroom door. The soft glow of light leaking in around my window blinds tells me it's morning, which is good. I'd rather deal with an intruder in daylight than in the pitch-black middle of the night.

Not that I'm keen on having an intruder at any time of day. It's likely nothing more than a passing neighbor walking their own dog.

Despite how tough I pretend to be to Willa, living alone in a house is an adjustment. Every weird sound late at night makes me a tiny bit anxious. I'm sure it will pass as I get used to it all.

Rolling out of bed, I grab a pair of sweats, pulling them on quickly. Nightmare spins in circles, wanting outside to investigate, his growls getting louder.

"I'm coming, buddy. Hang on." He's in such a rush to run for the door, I barely get ahold of him to latch the leash onto his collar. "Damn, son, chill out."

Nightmare jumps at the door as I unbolt the lock, and as soon as I have it open a crack, he's pulling on his lead and barking.

"Good morning, Nightmare," Tyson says, kneeling to pet him.

"Hasn't anyone ever told you it's weird to be creeping around a woman's yard early in the morning?"

"Sure. But I promised I'd help when I got back from the road trip. I keep my word," he says, holding up the shovel I keep leaned against the side of my house for scooping poop. "I think I got it all. Sorry, if it woke you up."

"Did you promise?"

"Didn't I?"

"I don't think you did," I say, leading Nightmare a few steps away as he sniffs out the perfect spot for his morning wee. "It's appreciated, but it wasn't necessary."

"You're welcome," he says with a teasing roll of his eyes.

"Thank you," I say, laughing.

"What are you up to today?"

"I'm installing a security system. Especially now that I know I have such nosey neighbors," I tell him. "Then, I have a date with Henry."

"Oh," he says, a small frown on his face. "Want some help with the security system?"

"Do you know much about installing a security system?"

"Nothing at all. How about you?"

"I've read the instructions, so I guess I know more than you."

"Only until I read the instructions."

"Fair point," I agree. "Come on in, you can read them while I make coffee and get dressed."

"Don't do that on my account," he says under his breath.

"What? You don't drink coffee? Are you one of the twenty-nine percent?"

"Twenty-nine percent of what?" He tilts his head, looking at me oddly.

"Twenty-nine percent of people who drink coffee have the urge to shit within thirty minutes."

"No, I'm not one of those," he says, his frown now a wide grin. "I wasn't talking about coffee."

"Good, so my toilet is safe from you, at least. Come on in," I say, opening the front door for him. "Hope you don't mind…busy."

"Busy?" he asks, then pauses, looking around my living room that opens into the kitchen at the back. "Oh."

I've been an active decorator this week. While my bedroom and bathroom are still rather bare, my main living space is done, mostly. I've painted the walls dark blue with a little hint of green. The furniture is an array of different jewel tones, and I've placed all my favorite quirky things around. Including my collection of pinned moths in shadow box frames, and my lamp that is a 1940s-style woman blowing a bubble that is the lightbulb. She sits on the newly acquired giraffe table. There's a lot to look at, and most of it is vibrant or weird.

"I like stimuli."

"It's not busy. It's eclectic. I like it."

"Really?"

"Yeah, why do you sound surprised?"

"Because I am surprised? How else should I sound?"

"No other way," he says, shrugging. "Where's this security system?"

I point to a box at the foot of the sofa. Then retreat to my bedroom to put on real clothes. Pulling off my sleep shirt, I realize I've had this entire interaction with Tyson while not wearing a bra. It's late winter and not warm outside. While the chill doesn't bother me, my body reacts to it in its own way.

Does that mean he was talking about my nipples earlier, not coffee?

God, I'm so bad at this human interaction thing. *How embarrassing.*

The first thing I grab is a damn bra. Then, a clean T-shirt. I leave the sweatpants, because I have no plans to leave the house today. After a quick brush of my teeth and hair, I go back out to find Tyson lounging on my couch, reading the installation manual.

"This looks really easy."

"I thought so, too. It's such a small house; it shouldn't take long."

"Nope. So maybe you'll go get lunch with me when we're done."

"Do you require a chaperone?" I ask, filling the coffee pot with water.

"Sometimes, sure. I don't like eating out by myself if I have another option."

"Why not?"

"I don't know," he says, sitting up. "It's always been a thing for me. Maybe because I've always had so many guys around from hockey. When I'm alone, it feels weird."

"That makes sense, I guess. I can't relate, but I understand," I say.

"You can't relate?"

"Nope, I've spent more time alone than not. For me, it's stranger to be in a crowd."

"Because you're an only child?"

"That's probably a big part of it. I did sort of raise myself," I say, then quickly change the subject. "Where did you want to go for lunch?"

"I drove by a place called Grappa, last week. Thought I'd try them."

"Sold," I say. "They have a great lasagna, and I have no patience to make that shit myself."

"That won't ruin your appetite for your date?"

"My date?" *What's he talking about?*

"Yeah, with Henry." He's looking at me strangely again.

"Oh! Henry of Skalitz, he's the main character in *Kingdome Come*."

"The video game?"

"Yeah," I say, watching the coffee drip into the pot. I wish it was quicker. I had one of those one cup machines, for a while. The speed was great, the coffee, not so much. Quality over quickness was what drew me back to a standard machine. I need it black as night and strong as fuck. Even though I only allow myself a cup a day. Otherwise, I get jittery.

Tyson laughs, shaking his head slightly, then goes back to reading.

"How do you drink your coffee?"

"What kind of creamer do you have?" he asks.

"None."

"So black is my only choice?"

"Yes."

"Then why'd you ask?"

"Curiosity," I answer honestly.

"Black is fine," he says, laughing again. Nightmare runs over to him, hopping on his lap. Tyson pets his head, and it hits me that I'm uncharacteristically comfortable with him in my house. He's not exactly a stranger, but I don't know him well, either.

I know Isla, and trust that she wouldn't have had a relationship with him, or let him anywhere near her daughter, if he wasn't a good man. Is that why I'm so comfortable?

Furthermore, why is he so comfortable? Why is he even here? With me and my dog on a rare day off.

"Why do you want to hang out with me today?" I ask, handing him one of the two mugs I poured. His has Krampus on it, mine has a giant octopus wrapping its tentacles around a pirate ship as if trying to sink it.

"Why wouldn't I want to hang out with you?"

"Have most of our conversations been in the form of volleying questions to each other?"

"Have they?"

"Haven't they?" I throw back.

"This right here is why I want to hang out with you, Kit," he says, setting the manual aside and looking at me. He has a nice smile, it looks genuine and not forced. The kind that carries to his eyes. "Because you're fun. You're playful. With such a public job, like mine, there's a lot of pressure not to let people down. When I have the chance to step away from it, I don't want to take life too seriously. You seem like you don't."

"You don't think I'm a serious person?"

"Is that what I said?"

"Repeat what you said, so I can be sure before I answer." I don't make the request to be funny or trite. It's a genuine ask because I don't always clue in to social cues properly.

"I said you're playful," he says. He reaches out to hold a couple of my fingers, gently rubbing his thumb over them. I don't pull away. It's not making me more anxious, just…more confused. "You're also intelligent and curious. If I'm making you uncomfortable, tell me. I'll stop doing whatever you don't like, or I can leave."

"I'm not uncomfortable," I say, moving to sit on the opposite side of the couch. "That's what has me confused."

"Why is that confusing?"

"Because we don't know each other. Yet here I am, being more myself than I am with most people," I say. I'm careful with strangers, by default. When I'm in a crowd of people, I focus on what I'm doing and saying, not wanting to be strange or awkward. That's not been much of a thought process this morning, though.

"I disagree. We know each other, we've known each other for years."

"You didn't remember my name," I accuse, and his cheeks redden.

"In my weak defense, I had a lot on my mind that day. Any trade is hard; this one was a gut punch. I am sorry, though, Kit Ashcroft," he says. "Is Kit short for something?"

"According to my birth certificate, no. According to my grandmother, it's short for Kitpu which is Mi'kmaq for eagle. My mother shortened it at my dad's request when I came out a girl instead of a boy."

"Your grandmother told you that?" Tyson's brow furrows.

"My mom wasn't available to ask. She was gone before I was two," I say. "She had traveled to Montana for a funeral and never came back."

"What do you mean?"

"My father said she met someone there and decided to stay."

"Damn, Kit. That's heavy."

"I was too young to remember any of it. And it wasn't much talked about by my dad. He suspected she knew before she took the trip that she wasn't coming back," I tell him, trying to convey by tone alone that I don't want an amateur therapy session about it. My mother wasn't a presence in my childhood home. My dad didn't keep pictures of her on the walls or lull me to sleep with stories of how wonderful she was.

As I grew older, I was able to ask my grandmother some questions about her, but her knowledge was limited to that of a mother-in-law who only knew my mother for a few short years. I've never known much about her, which means, I never grew much connection to her.

Sadly, she's just a name to me…Nimii. A blank memory. Everything I know of her is a fantasy I've made up in my own mind. Often, I've wanted to look for her, but I'm not sure where to start.

I'm also terrified of what I might find. If she's been living happily with a family full of healthy, well-adjusted children, how would I feel about that? I'm not sure I want to know. It's one thing to have grown content without a mother you never knew. I imagine it's something else entirely to know that she wanted a family, just not one that you were a part of.

"Your mother's family is Mi'kmaq?"

"Yeah, I don't know any of them, though. Apparently, she wasn't close to them. Dad said none of them showed up for their wedding or contacted him about me after she left."

"You're close with your dad?" he asks, and now I *am* uncomfortable. Because, no, I'm not close with my dad. And that's not something I want to discuss. My past is not high on my list of conversational topics, even with people I'm close to.

"Was this trade harder because of Isla and Cillian?"

Tyson's gaze narrows on me, registering my redirect. For a second, I think he's going to call me out on it, but he doesn't.

"Yes, and Coach Cole. History isn't always so easy to ignore. Plus, I wasn't sure if the other guys would distance themselves in favor of keeping Cillian comfortable."

"You were in love with her, weren't you?"

"It felt like I was," he says after some hesitation.

"Isn't that all the definition you need? If it feels like love, it's love."

"Because love is just a feeling?"

"Isn't it?" I ask with a smile, because we're still doing the question thing.

"Is it?"

"I wouldn't know. I've never felt it. Not like, romantically, anyway."

"Are you always this insightful?"

"No." I laugh. "You were right when you said I'm curious, though. I don't like not knowing things."

"On that note, let's get installing a security system under our belt," he says, draining his mug and standing up. I get the feeling he's deflecting now. Since he let me get away with it, I'll do the same for him.

Within two hours, we've completed the task. I set it up on the Wi-Fi and my phone, while Tyson placed the sensors and motion detectors, saying I'm too short to reach.

I snarked at him for that, but he's right. I'm far shorter than him. They never look that big on the ice when you're watching from the stands or on television. But almost every guy on the team is six foot or taller.

Conversation didn't wane while we worked. Tyson chattered a lot about his family, especially his sister, who seems very important to him. He worries about her, and I find it sweet. When I was young, I wished I had a sibling. A big brother to protect me from the shadows under the bed.

I'd bet his sister never had those thoughts. I bet she felt safe.

After we're done, he goes home to change, which gives me the chance to shower and dress in real pants before we go to lunch. When I get in his truck, he waits to start the engine until I've got my seat belt fastened. I never ride in a car without one, but I'm still amused by how adamant he is about it.

"You're a gentleman at heart, aren't you, Tyson?"

"What do you mean by at heart?"

"I mean, I don't know how gentlemanly it is to bring a different woman home every night. But it is gentlemanly to help your neighbor with her alarm system and make sure she's got her seat belt on correctly."

"How much of my business can you see from your tiny house across the street?" he asks, once again blushing some.

"I don't mean to be nosey, but your friend's house basically takes up the whole view from the front of my house. It's hard not to notice the visitations," I say. "Besides, I don't judge other people's sex lives."

"You just said it's not gentlemanly to screw a different woman every night," he accuses.

"Shit, Tyson. I'm sorry, I didn't mean for that to sound like some kind of insult," I stammer.

"Kit," he says softly, picking up my hand. "I'm teasing. It's fine."

"Both hands on the wheel, please," I say, pulling my fingers away. "Sorry, I told you I can be awkward. I'm not always good at reading people."

"You do just fine," he says, looking at my other hand gripping the door handle. "Does being in a car make you nervous?"

"Only because it's the first time. Once I know how you drive, I'll either be okay, or never ride with you again."

"Past trauma with a car accident?"

"Nope, just one of my quirks," I say, trying to sound casual about it.

"You say it like it's a bad thing," he says. "Quirks are good. They make us interesting. Imagine if we were all the same, it'd be like living in some sort of Stepford world."

"Aren't you too young to know about Stepford living?" I ask.

"Technically, sure. But I love horror. Movies, books, you name it. I read *Rosemary's Baby* on a plane to hockey camp as a teenager. It sent me down an Ira Levine rabbit hole. Besides, I'm an old twenty-nine years of age."

"That's hardly even old by hockey standards."

"You'd think so, but they're drafting younger and younger these days. Soon enough, we'll have sixteen-year-olds in the league."

"I can't argue. The average age in the NHL is twenty-eight."

"Is it?" he asks, carefully looking for traffic before taking a right turn.

"Yeah, and peak is between twenty-seven and twenty-eight. Unless you're a defenseman, then it's about a year older. But you're a forward, so you're past your prime. Statistically."

"Well, shit."

"Sorry," I say, once again feeling like I said something I shouldn't have. I scoot farther toward the door, turning to look at the window instead of at him. "It's not like it means anything, though. Not really. Gretzky was thirty-eight when he retired."

Of course, not every player is a Wayne Gretzky, but I keep that to myself. Tyson is an excellent player when he's on his game. I looked at his stats the other day—his first few seasons were far above what's expected of the average player. When he was dating Isla, he was considered one of the hottest new players in the league.

His performance has fallen over the last two seasons. I don't know if it had to do with Isla, but if he loved her, it would make sense. Personal lives take a toll on your work life. Or so I believe. I've never had much of a personal life to contend with.

"Don't apologize, you're only speaking the truth. It's a good reminder that I need to keep my head in the game and on my career if I want to keep playing. Which I do, for as long as I can, anyway," he says. "What are some of your other quirks?"

"I spew facts and data at random and often without forethought or consideration," I say, and he laughs. "Do you have quirks?"

"Of course."

"Like what?"

"My favorite thing to do when I'm stressed out is eat an entire pint of ice cream," he says, and I turn back to look at him skeptically. That's not weird at all. But then, he continues, "It has to be rocky road, and I have to eat in a bath that's so hot my skin turns red."

"Why?"

"The ice cream is nostalgic, it's my dad's favorite and he never goes a night without eating it. The hot bath…maybe so I can feel something other than my thoughts."

"Is this something you do often?"

"Nah, I don't get stressed out easily. But when I do, I get messy. That's what Lottie calls it."

"You and your sister are close?" I ask.

"We are. She's my best friend. Has been since she was born," he says.

I picture him as a little boy, peeking over her crib to watch her nap, or holding her hand while they walked in a park. He seems like the type to have been overly protective.

"What's another quirk of yours?"

"I don't like quiet. I don't mean sound as much as just in general. I need constant stimulation. It's why my house is busy. Maybe you caught on to that already," I say.

"I assumed by the fact that you had the television on, and I could hear music playing from somewhere else in the house."

"My bedroom," I say with a nod. "I almost never turn music off in there."

"Even when you sleep."

"Especially then," I say quietly. It would play softer when I lived with Willa, but then, I wasn't alone. Now, it plays a little louder. Loud enough to drown out the world. To silence the memories. At night, in bed, trying to fall asleep is when I feel most alone in the world. When I'm vulnerable.

Tyson doesn't say anything else as he pulls into a parking space at the restaurant. He doesn't move to exit the car right away, either. Instead, he reaches his hand across the center console to place it on the seat right next to mine. Not holding my fingers as he did earlier, but giving me the option, if I want it. Silently, I think he's telling me he's here if I need him, while also telling me I can keep to myself.

It means a lot that he understands. I've never been diagnosed with anything else, but surely, I'm more neurodivergent than just my ADHD. Over the years, I've found my own ways to cope with my triggers and trauma. Willa is the only one I've ever opened up with completely, and that took me a long time. She understood, too, and gave me the space to get there in my own time.

I may never get to that level of comfort and trust with Tyson. Or with anyone else. I don't know, but it's still nice to have someone else that doesn't push me to be what I can't. I appreciate it more than he could know.

7

TYSON

Hugo is right about Kit. The more time I spend with her, the more I see that something in her past weighs on her. The more time I spend with her, the more I want to know her, too.

She reminds me of Lottie in many ways. The best ways, really. Her inquisitiveness, her honesty, and bluntness. Sometimes she holds back, as if she's afraid what she wants to say will offend. But if I call her on it, she opens back up.

With most things, that is. If I get too close to what plagues her, she clams up tight. I want to know. I find myself wanting to know everything about her. Yet, I'm also afraid of her telling me. Scared that, if I'm correct in my assumptions, I'll never know peace until I find who hurt her. Because I don't think it's as simple as growing up without her mother.

Kit doesn't know peace, though. Not completely, or not always. Why should she be alone in that? The answer is, she shouldn't be. Nobody should feel alone in the world. And I don't want that for her. I wouldn't let my sister be alone in that. Maybe Kit isn't; she has the Cole family, who I know love her. But when she drifts off into her own head, she looks like the loneliest person I've ever seen.

Her sad stare breaks my fucking heart.

I hadn't realized that I had much heart left to break. Not after Isla. I thought what I had left was strictly reserved for my family and for my career.

The past couple of years I've quit letting people in. If you don't get close, you don't get hurt. There's something different about this woman, though. She's capable in so many ways, yet in my head, she's fragile and needs protection. I can't make sense of my feelings when I think of her. Which is more than I'd like to admit.

The little hints she's given about her life before coming to Seattle stay with me like a plague. I can admit I've lived a fucking privileged life. Not only financially, but with a loving and caring family, with friends, with a community. Death didn't touch me until I was old enough to understand it. Hardship wasn't something I understood. Mostly, I still don't.

The most tragic thing to happen to me is heartbreak. Not a loved one who has been missing for twenty-five years.

Kit is a fascinating mystery. One I want to solve.

Zander and I are working out with trainers today, none of the other teammates are here this morning. I use the opportunity to my benefit.

"Hey, Fane. What do you know about Kit?"

"A lot. And also, not that much," he answers, looking at me strangely. "You'll need to be more specific. Then, I'll decide if I want to answer."

"That means you get it," I say. "She's different. Special."

"Different than who? The random women you take home after a game? Most definitely."

"They're all the same," I dismiss. Does that make me an asshole? Probably. It doesn't make it less true, though. The random women I fuck only care about being able to tell their girlfriends they bagged a pro athlete. Maybe in the back of their minds they hold hope that they'll land a rich husband out of it, but most know better. "I mean, she's different than most people I've known. She's blunt, honest, and…I don't know, fun. Sassy."

"You dated Isla. None of that is new to you. She's all those things, too. But I get your meaning. What's your intention?"

"I want to be her friend."

"Is that it?" he asks.

"You think I'm not capable of that?" Fane is being cautious of me in favor of his friend. I love that about him, and I love that for Kit.

"I know you are," he says, laughing. "But you do have a reputation."

"That was a one-time fuck up," I protest at the same time my trainer, Jesse, adds more weight to the leg press I'm on. I feel the burn in my thighs. It's a good fire, a reminder that I can be stronger. And a good distraction from the tabloid debacle I ended up in when I was caught with a sex worker after a game on the road. Being caught by the press would have been bad enough; being caught by police was much worse.

My reasoning for being with the woman made it worse, still, not that I ever admitted that reasoning to anyone.

"Kind of a big one," Zander mumbles.

"Okay, yeah. But I don't see every woman as a conquest. I don't want to fuck my way through every vagina in Seattle."

"Do you want to fuck Kit?" Now, his brow furrows in concern.

"No," I say, but I can hear my own lie.

"No?" He raises an eyebrow and stops mid-squat.

"Listen, she's fucking beautiful. I'm not blind. But that's not what I'm looking for from her. Kit is the first woman I've wanted to know since…" I let the sentence drop. We both know I'm talking about his best friend.

"Since Isla," he finishes for me. "Who you did want to fuck."

"Fair point." I sigh in exasperation. "Right now, I only want to know her. She's, like, I don't know, man. She's like the fucking sun and I just want to be in her warmth."

"Dude…"

"What?"

"That's not something you say about a woman you want to be just friends with."

"Why not? Don't you feel that way about Isla?"

"Of course, I do," he says. "Is that what you want from Kit? You're looking for a best friend?"

"Maybe. I haven't had one since I was a kid."

"Is it possible you're lonely, being in a new city and away from your family?"

"I mean, yeah. But I feel like that completely discredits how fucking awesome Kit is." I can't argue how much she reminds me of my sister. Hell, I think they'd be two peas in a pod if they ever got the chance to be friends. They match nervous energy and bubbly enthusiasm.

But I'm not looking for someone to replace Lottie. Nobody ever could, even if they tried.

That knowledge doesn't change the fact that something about Kit feels a little like home.

"You really like her," he states.

"I do, man."

"She doesn't date," Zander says solemnly, after a moment. "She's never told me why that is. Not that I'd share it if she had, that's her business. I only know that it's something she doesn't seek. If she becomes more than a friend to you, you'll be climbing Mt. Everest."

"I'm not asking you for her secrets. That wasn't my intention," I say. "Blom mentioned that he thinks something haunts her. I've seen it, too."

"What *are* you asking?"

"Fuck, I'm not even sure anymore." I sigh and signal to Jesse that I'm done. "I guess, I worry about her. You know, when we're away, I find myself worrying about her."

"Sounds like more than friendship, my dude."

"He's not wrong," Jesse chimes in for the first time.

"Yeah, yeah, all right," I say to their laughter. "I think friendship is all either of us is capable of, though."

Eight days on the road never gets easier, no matter how many times I've done it. No matter that I'm not going home, even. I'm still crashing at Calvin's. It's been two months since the trade, and I haven't so much as looked for a real estate agent. Cal said not to worry about it until the off season, which is still another few months out, if we make playoffs. And it looks like we will.

All I do when I get home is change my clothes before I'm back out the door and crossing the street. Nightmare barks when I knock on Kit's front door.

"It's me, buddy," I say, and the yapping turns into an excited whimper. We've officially become pals. As I have with his pretty owner. When she opens the door, I scoop up the pup, then wrap Kit in a hug. "I missed you."

"Oh," she exclaims. We haven't been huggers before this. It was an instinct, but since she doesn't pull away, I don't, either. "How can you miss me? We've been playing *Destiny* together more nights than not."

"Party chat isn't the same." I pull my arms back but don't step away. "You look good."

She looks down at herself before looking back at me, a skeptical grin on her face. She's wearing purple shorts emblazoned with croissants and a bright yellow Pikachu tee, that I'd guess she's had since she was much younger and less developed. Her chest strains under it, and I force my gaze not to linger.

Which is a testament to how much I respect her, because, holy fuck, she has great tits.

"I know that goon with Utah got a shitty hit on you, but they said it didn't crack your bucket," she says.

"It didn't," I say. "But I like that you checked up on me."

"It's what friends do. Besides, when I asked you about it, all you did was grunt."

"Some guys like to be babied when they're bruised up, I don't." I plop Nightmare on his bed that sits on the end of the sofa. He curls up after a few spins to find the right spot, but his eyes follow me. The past couple of times I've been over here, I've sat next to him, letting Kit have her space at the other end of the couch.

That's not where I want to be tonight. I'd like to be closer. The conversation I had with Fane a while back has been heavy on my mind on this road trip. Every new interaction with Kit brings me closer to the truth, which is that I am interested in more than just friendship with her.

I physically ache to touch her. To press my lips to hers. To feel her skin against mine.

To sink into her and never fully back out.

Making any of my normal moves would send her running to hole up in the nearest cave, though, I'm sure of it. Getting women comfortable with my interest in them is as foreign to me as rocket science. It's always just happened naturally, probably thanks to my chosen profession. Not to say I'm not charming and shit…because, of course I am.

Or I think I am.

No, no, I am. I'm sure I am. Right? I'm a fucking catch. My mom says I am.

Fucking hell, I'm losing my mind.

"Tyson?"

"What?" I shake my head to clear my thoughts and find Kit standing in front of me, peering at me with an odd expression.

"Are you sure you're all right? They checked you for a concussion?"

"They checked, it's all good."

"So why are you standing in the middle of my living room, looking like you don't know how you got here?" she asks.

"I walked across the street."

"Yeah, I'm aware of that. Glad to hear you are, too," she says, cocking her head. Her dark hair falls across her forehead. Tentatively, I tuck it behind her ear with a couple of gentle fingers.

"Maybe I'm just taken by your beauty."

Her cheeks flush but she doesn't look away or tense up.

"Are you high?"

"No," I say after a burst of laughter. "Do you not know that you're gorgeous?"

"I don't know," she says, shrugging. "I don't think I'm ugly, but I'm odd."

"You are not fucking odd."

"I am, Tyson."

"No, you aren't. You're God damned perfect."

"Okay, now you're seriously worrying me. Sit down." She points to the couch, and I do what she says, sitting right in the middle.

"I'm fine, Kit. You should have higher confidence in yourself. Once in a hundred years, a woman like you is born."

"Do I get an ice pack or call 9-1-1? Do you know there's eighty concussions in the league, on average, every season? And I have no idea how to care for one."

"You watch a movie with me," I say, tugging her down next to me. "You said you didn't want to watch *Heretic* alone. I don't have a concussion, I promise, I'm fine."

She watches me skeptically for a few more moments, then relents and grabs the remote. I pull the blanket from the back of the sofa and adjust it over our laps, keeping a close eye on her for any sign that she's uncomfortable with my closeness.

At first, she's reserved, a little tense. I don't know if it's because we're sharing a blanket or if she doesn't believe that I don't have a brain injury. Eventually, she falls into the movie and relaxes into my side.

I hyperfocus on every point where our bodies touch. Her knee against my thigh, her shoulder pressing further into my arm every time the movie makes her nervous. At one point, she pauses the film to go on a diatribe about The Matilda Effect. How men have stolen advancements from women for centuries. She's passionate and animated as she spews case after case, spurred by something the villain in the movie says.

As soon as she has it off her chest, she presses play, tosses the remote aside and curls up against me.

She's a fucking whirlwind and I am endlessly entertained and equally impressed by her brain. The other night when we were on a video game together, she simultaneously planned out how our team should take out the hardest boss in the game while she rattled off information about all she'd learned over the past week. She bounced from a giant seamount that was found on the ocean floor near Guatemala to a runaway black hole in space, before she finally landed on minerals, telling us all sorts of random facts about the oldest of them. Even with the most mundane subject, her enthusiasm always makes for an interesting conversation.

By the time the movie ends, I've managed to wrap my arm around her shoulders without her bolting off the couch. Nightmare has crawled onto her lap, hindering me from getting more comfortable, *the little cock blocker.* It's probably for the best.

I turn my head toward her and catch her peering up at me.

"You're really okay?"

"You're really that worried," I state in wonder.

"You've been acting different, is all," she says. "Is everything okay with you and the team?"

"Yeah, it's better than I'd hoped for."

"Your family is good?"

"Yes, Kit. Everything and everyone is fine. I promise," I reassure her. Except it doesn't work, there are still worry lines around her narrowed eyes as they bounce around my face, looking for an explanation. I could give her that. I should give her that. Even though I'm afraid of how she'll react, it's the kind thing to do. And I don't want to be anything but kind to her. "You've been on my mind."

"What do you mean?" She tries to sit up straighter, but Nightmare protests the move with a disgruntled whimper.

"I mean," I say slowly as I drop my forehead to hers, "that I think about you more or less non-fucking-stop, Kit."

"You don't have to worry about me when you're away. I'm okay."

"I know you are, and that's not how I mean."

"How do you mean?" she asks, pulling away an inch so she can focus on my face.

"Promise you won't run away?"

"To where? I'm in my house," she says, making me smile.

"I don't just worry about you when I'm not around, Kit. I fantasize. I dream of kissing you," I say, barely loud enough for her to hear.

"Oh," she says, her mouth not closing fully after the tiny word escapes. I'd love it if that was an invitation. But I won't make a move without her expressed invitation.

"I know you don't date. So, I'm not sure what to do with my feelings."

"But you're in love with Isla," she tells me, brows furrowed.

"I'm not."

"I don't know if I believe that."

"Why not?" I ask.

She hesitates, thinking her answer through before speaking it.

"I'll admit I don't have much experience with the subject matter, but I don't see how it's possible to fall out of love easily." She nibbles on the inside of her lip, still contemplating. It's a tick of hers I've noticed several times, now. "Infatuation is more like a dopamine effect and will fade quickly, right? But true love…doesn't that have to last? Maybe it takes years and years for it to fully fade."

Fucking hell, I love her brain.

"I suspect it's different for everyone," I say, to start. "It's been a couple of years, maybe that's plenty of time for me to fall out of love. Or maybe it was never true love to begin with."

Kit's nose scrunches up as if she doesn't fully believe what I'm saying, but again, she pauses before responding.

"Have you dated anyone since her? Or have you only had hookups?"

"I haven't dated," I say truthfully, knowing this won't win me any points.

"I'd be your trial run," she says, picking Nightmare up as she stands to walk into the kitchen. She doesn't sound mad.

Hurt. She sounds hurt and I don't know how I've fucked this up so epically.

8

KIT

"**Y**ou had control of the puck two minutes and twenty-four seconds longer than Vegas in that period."

"We," Zander says.

"What?" I ask.

"We," he repeats. "You're part of the team, now. We're a we."

"Oh," I say, smiling. I like the sound of that.

"Yeah, that's a long time. We should have had more shots on goal than we did."

"You can't win them all," I say.

"We can sure as hell try, though. That's kind of the job description."

"True," I say.

"No more hockey talk," Willa says, setting down a fresh plate of cookies. Damian is the baker, these days, and every time I come over, he's baking some new recipe for dessert. "I want to know what's going on between you and your neighbor."

"I don't know," I groan. "He wants to date."

"That's great," Zander says. "Isn't it?"

"Are you comfortable with that?" Damian asks.

"No."

"Does he make you uncomfortable?" Willa asks.

"Only because I'm so comfortable with him."

"That's great, though," Zander says again. "Isn't it?" He wears a mixture of confusion and concern, one that I'm sure mirrors my own.

"I mean, yeah. I'm not normally so easy with people, and I am with him," I confess. "Except, I don't know how to trust his feelings or intentions, I guess. He hasn't had a relationship since Isla."

"Okay, let's back up a step," Willa says. "Do you *want* to date him? If there was no past history with my sister, no baggage whatsoever. Would you want to date the Tyson Murphy you've gotten to know the past couple of months?"

"Maybe."

"Kit, a maybe from you is about the same as yes from anyone else," she says, reaching to hold my hand. "That one word is a big statement."

"I like when he's around," I say, my voice a little shaky. The edges of my vision darken, that familiar sense of being somewhere outside of my body creeping in. "But I don't know how to be with him."

"You mean, physically?" Willa asks.

"Do you want us to leave?" Zander asks before I can answer her. I'm about as close to him and Damian as I am to anyone, but they don't know my history.

"I appreciate the offer, but no. I think I need everyone's opinions. You guys are who I trust most, and if I can't be honest with you, I can't be honest with anyone," I tell him. "Yes, I mean physically. But also, emotionally. Mostly physically. I haven't so much as kissed a man for a decade."

"It's kind of like riding a bike," Damian says. "You'll pick it back up quickly enough."

"I never learned to ride a bike."

"Never?" Zander asks.

"Never. Dad wouldn't have made the time, and Grandma wouldn't have been able to keep up with her bad knee."

"I didn't learn until I was in my teens," Damian says. "It wasn't a needed skill growing up in New Orleans."

"Especially when you had a private driver to shuttle you around," Zander adds.

"Precisely," Damian agrees. "I only learned when I was brave enough to go camping with some friends. One of them brought a bike and I was drunkenly determined to figure it out. I nearly fell into the river about a dozen times, but they all had a good time at my expense. As a side-note, camping in the bayou is not something I recommend any of you ever attempt."

"I'd never sleep outside in a state that has two million alligators," I say, wrinkling my nose. "That's nearly one alligator per two people, so the odds of one crawling into your sleeping bag are too high."

"Yeah, figured that out the hard way," he says, grinning. "I grabbed my shit and drove my ass home at three in the morning after we woke up to one trying to nose his way into our camp."

"Maybe serves you right," Willa says, laughing.

"Definitely. Spoiled, rich kids with no fear don't make the best decisions."

"I've never been camping, either," I say.

"Is that something that you want to do?" Zander asks. "Not everyone enjoys it."

"I don't know. It doesn't sound like something I'd like, but how do I know if I don't try?"

"You know I love how curious you are of everything," Willa says. "But you know you don't have to try things you don't want to."

"Maybe I could try glamping," I say. "I think I'd survive a camper with power and a toilet that I could be in a semi-committed relationship with."

"You're my kind of girl, Kit," Damian says. "I agree with Willa, you know. I'll support you in anything you want to try, but don't feel like you need to do things because others might think it's weird you haven't."

"Like dating?" I ask, and his grin turns sad.

"Yes, like dating. Do you want to date Tyson, or do you think you *should* date Tyson?"

"I think I want to," I say, tears pricking my eyes.

"Why does that make you sad?" Zander asks.

I don't want it to be like last time. The only guy I was ever with was not at all who I thought he was.

"What if I'm not who he thinks I am? What if he's not who I think he is?"

"There aren't guarantees like that in life, but from what I know of him, he's a good guy," Willa says.

"You know I'm not very good with no guarantees."

"I know," she says, smiling softly. "I also know that it's your nature to gather data before making decisions."

"Dating is like data analysis?" I question more to myself than my best friend. It's an idea that my mind perks up at. Love isn't something I under-stand, but data makes sense. Collect it, evaluate it, then make a determi-nation based on that evaluation. It's how I live, how I make so many of my decisions.

I'm the gal that reads every brand label before I choose which granola bars to buy, comparing ingredients, size, price. If I do that for even the mundane things, why wouldn't I do it for the big, important things, too?

"In a way, yeah."

"Nothing says you have to commit to it, either. If you don't like dating, or it makes you too anxious, you tell him that," Zander says.

"Are you comfortable enough with him to be honest about your con-cerns, or even your past experiences?"

She means Derik. He's not someone I talk about. Willa knows, of course, but she's the only person I've told my whole story to. It's not a pleasant tale, it's shameful and tragic. Triggering.

It's not something I've told Zander, Damian, or even Isla.

I probably need therapy. No, not *probably*. I'm sure I should have been in therapy for years. But that would mean I have to face my trauma with a stranger, and that freaks me out more than facing it with a friend.

I don't think anyone is born with an innate sense of self-awareness. I've always believed it's a learned trait, and one most don't ever accomplish. Mostly because it's not in our nature to evaluate our own weaknesses, downfalls, mistakes. We're always taught to focus on the positives.

I'm no different. Coping, and learning to live with flaws or quirks, allows for me to pretend that my past doesn't live like an anvil chained to my ankle. I hear what she's saying, though. If this is something I want, any kind of relationship with another person, I need to be able to share the most vulnerable things about myself. Because I'd ask the same of them.

In a way, I already have asked that of Tyson by prying into his feelings about Isla. While simultaneously sidestepping the topic every time my lack of a dating life comes up.

"No," I admit. "I want to be brave enough to try, though."

"It can be scary," Damian says. "But we're here for you in whatever way you need us to be."

"Not only does it scare me to open myself up, but statistically, it almost seems like a complete waste of time. About seventy percent of new couples break up within the first year."

"Glad we made it past that," Zander says.

"We're only a few months past it, let's not jinx it," Willa says with a playful wink.

"Maybe it's the relationships that start with a foundation of truth and trust that stand the test of time," Damian says. "Not the ones that are based on societal pressures or that look good on Instagram. But the ones that embrace the ugly moments as much as the beautiful ones. Love is more than a kiss with a pretty sunset as a backdrop. Find the person that will hold your hand through the stormy days, too."

"What he said," Zander says. "I wouldn't have made it through the whole ordeal with getting custody of my sister if not for these two."

"I don't believe that. You're stronger than you give yourself credit for," I tell him. "But I understand what you're saying. Where is Callie, anyway?"

"At a movie," he says, crossing his arms across his chest. "With her boyfriend."

His face morphs into a disgruntled frown, and I stifle a laugh.

"Max is a good kid," Willa says.

"There isn't a horny teenage guy on the planet that's a good enough kid for my sister."

"Well, the way you scared the shit out of him when he came to pick her up, I'd be surprised if he has the guts to do anything more than hold her hand," Damian says.

"He fucking better not."

"Zan opened the door wearing just his workout shorts," Willa explains. "Poor kid had to see that thick neck, bulging biceps, and the biggest hockey thighs on the team."

"How big is Max?"

"Oh, God, Kit," she says through laughter. "He's a scrawny thing. So damn sweet, but he's not the athletic type. His eyes got so big when Zan opened the door, he looked like Barrel from *Nightmare Before Christmas*."

Zander looks smug as I laugh.

"As amusing as it was, we need to be careful that we don't alienate him so much that Callie hides things from us," Damian says.

"Shit, I hadn't thought about that," Zander says. "I was just focused on making sure nobody touches my kid sister."

The three of them go back and forth on what the best gameplan is, trying to find one that allows Zander to feel like he's fulfilling his duty, while also giving Callie the freedom to grow into a young woman with agency.

It's endearing, really. I don't know how many times I wished for a protector like Zander. A big brother, an uncle, a father who gave a shit. Someone who loved me enough to care. Or at least saw me as something other than a burden, or a tool.

Instead, I had a father that reminded me I wasn't good enough, smart enough, talented enough. One who told me I was good for very little in life, and that I shouldn't have dreams because they'd never come true.

Dreams are dreams because they're fucking unattainable, he'd say. Fantasies are lies we tell ourselves, was another of his favorites. He pounded that mantra into me day after day. More days than not, I believed him. I didn't lie in bed at night imagining a life outside of small-town Maine, not until I was old enough to recognize that he was the lie.

Luckily, that was early enough to know I had to work my ass off in high school to get scholarships and acceptance letters from enough colleges to give me choices. The first choice in my life that was mine alone.

I've savored the ability ever since. Even if sometimes it seems like it would be nice to surrender that to someone else, occasionally. I don't know how to share responsibility or control. I don't know how to share life.

Which is only another reason dating Tyson Murphy feels too daunting to ever work.

9

TYSON

"It's only a few more days," I say.

"I know," Lottie replies with a long sigh. "But it's been, like, two months since I've seen you play. Or even seen you at all. It's weird and it freaks me out."

"I'm okay, I promise."

"I know you're okay. Still doesn't feel right. We haven't gone this long without seeing each other since you did that summer intensive camp when you were fourteen."

"Yeah, I was real lucky to stay close to home for so long. But we all knew the NHL is fickle."

Lottie likes routine. Upset to her carefully created schedule sometimes throws her off balance. I think it's helped that she's living in my house, it keeps her connected to me, in a way. On top of that, I make a point of video chatting with her as often as we can. With my crazy schedule, that's not always so easy.

"Three more sleeps, then you'll be here. And there's someone I want you to meet."

"Someone you want me to meet for you, or someone you want me to meet *for me*?"

I laugh at her question, because yeah, I've tried to set her up a time or two. My sister is a hopeless romantic, but hasn't had much luck in the love department. She never takes my suggestions, though. She says hockey players are too emotional.

She's not necessarily wrong.

"Both, really. It's someone I like a lot, and I think you'd be great friends with."

"Someone *you like a lot*," she repeats. "Is it a girlfriend? Or a boyfriend?"

"How many times do I have to tell you? I'm not bisexual."

"A few more, I guess. Sports are weird. There's no way you all like to spend so much time together, especially in the gym and locker room all half naked, without some feelings happening. And that's totally okay. It's not something to be ashamed of."

"You're right, it wouldn't be something shameful. As I've said, I can appreciate a man's form without finding it sexually attractive. Much in the same way women find other women beautiful. My dick just doesn't get excited by it."

"If you say so," she says. It's what she always says. Her views on sexuality are very progressive and as simple as she finds attractive people attractive. She has no other precursor. "So, who is this woman?"

"She's my neighbor. She's also Willa's best friend."

"Isla's sister?"

"Yeah."

"That's weird, too. What are the odds?"

"Maybe it's fate?"

"Since when do you believe in fate," she asks.

"Since Kit laughed and it was like the sky cleared up for the first time." Silence follows my statement. Lottie isn't quiet, ever. She's always got plenty to say and has no filter. "Say something."

"Are you on drugs?"

"No." I laugh. "She's special, Lottie. Please say you'll meet her."

"Of course, I'll meet her," she says, as if exasperated. "I'm curious as hell, wondering who this woman is that has you tied up enough to speak in prose."

"Shut the fuck up," I say through a laugh.

"You shut the fuck up, Mr. The Skies Opened at Her Laughter."

"Yeah, all right, smartass. I'll see you on Tuesday."

"See you in a few days, Shakespeare. Love you!"

"Love you, too," I say before ending the call, grabbing my duffle, and heading onto the plane.

Lottie teasing me isn't surprising. Our relationship has always been full of giving each other playful shit. I also know, she'll give Kit a fair shot but won't blow smoke up my ass if she doesn't like something about her.

I don't see how she couldn't absolutely adore her, though. And vice versa.

We've been gone for three nights but we're heading back for a long home stand. As excited as I am to see my family in a few days, I'm looking forward to seeing the woman across the street chase her yapping dog around the yard, too.

It's been a hot minute since I told her I want to date her. Kit hasn't brought it up, so neither have I. Perhaps that means her answer is no, but I'm stubborn enough to want to hear the word before I give up the idea.

Taking a window seat in the middle of the plane, over the wings, I release a long sigh.

"Why do you always sit in the same spot," Cillian asks, taking the aisle seat in the same row. Mostly, the two of us only interact when it's necessary. It's just weird. I mean, I used to fuck his wife. That's awkward as hell.

"As a kid, I read that it was the safest place to sit in a plane. Now, it's habit."

"Is that true?"

"Honestly? I have no fucking clue. I imagine if the plane is going down, there isn't a safe place to be."

"What the fuck, man," Zander says when he takes a seat in the row in front of us. "Literally any other subject would be more appropriate right now."

"Blame Wylder, he asked."

"Not intentionally," Cillian protests. "You could have lied and told me it was superstition."

"I mean, it is that, too. Now. That's just not how it started."

"It started out of fear," Cillian says.

"Don't all superstitions?"

Cillian cocks his head, thinking about that for a moment before he answers.

"I'd never thought of it, but yeah, it is fear that makes me not change my routine up."

"Same," Zan agrees. "I freak the fuck out if I tape my stick wrong because I'm scared it's going to jinx my play."

"Then you've probably never stepped on the ice with a badly taped stick, because I've never seen you play any way but solid," I say.

"Thanks," he says, shock tinging the single word.

"You know how good you are, right?"

"We all think we're good, until we have an off day and think we're shit," he says.

"When do you have an off day?" Cillian asks.

"I have them," Zander says.

"Lies," I say. Alexander Fane never shows any sign of having an off game. He's the one guy on the team you can always count on being where you need him to be. Every single time. Defensemen don't always get a lot of praise, but he sure as hell deserves it.

"All right, you can both stop blowing smoke up my ass," he says, turning around and putting his headphones on.

"The kid doesn't know how to take a compliment," Cillian says.

"I'm not sure any of us are that great at it. Except Letty, he eats up praise."

"Letty's like a poodle," Cillian says, looking Letty in the face as he moves down the aisle.

"Woof, woof," Letty says, grinning like a kid.

"Good boy," Cillian says.

"Unhinged," I say. "Every last one of us."

"There's a lot of truth in that."

After we reach altitude, Coach Cole stops by our aisle.

"The new program is live. Check it out," he says, handing a tablet to Cillian. "You can move any combination of players onto the ice, pick a play from the left-hand column, and it will show the stats. The right column lets you pick your opponents, so you know how well you do against any team's players."

Cillian moves to the middle seat, holding the tablet between us so we can both manipulate the program.

"How current?" I ask the question because it's only been hours since our last game, and it's late. I wouldn't expect tonight's statistics to be uploaded already.

"As current as it gets. Tonight's game is included."

"Damn, this is cool as hell," Cillian says.

"She's pretty fucking amazing, isn't she?" I muse, awed.

"Kit? Yes, there's a reason we wanted her. This is just the tip of it," Coach says to me. "I hear you've been spending time with her."

"We're neighbors."

"And?"

"And I like her. She's…special."

"She is," he agrees. "Take care with her."

He takes the tablet back and moves to another group to show them their numbers from the game.

"That's the second warning I've gotten about Kit. Does everyone think I'm a monster?"

"A monster? No. A playboy who has no qualms hiring a sex worker, yes."

"I'm not the first, nor will I be the last NHL player to hire someone for sex," I argue. "I was single, too."

"Is that a dig at me?" Cillian moves back to the aisle seat but keeps his eyes narrowed on me.

"Fuck, no. That's not what I was getting at. I'm just saying that night didn't harm anyone but me. It's really nobody's business."

"You're right. But Kit is family and is our business. Everyone's just looking out for her."

"And what if that's the job I want?"

"What does Kit want?"

"She doesn't know yet. Whatever she decides, I'll live with it, because I just want to be part of her life."

"A sentiment I know well," Cillian says. For the first time, I see firsthand the regret he has for the time he missed with Isla and Sadie. For the first time, I feel a little bad for him. I've spent so long being jealous of what's he had, what he lost, what he eventually won back; that I never saw him as worthy of Isla or Sadie.

It was natural for me to envy him, which made it impossible to see that he knew regret and pain intimately. Hating that he had everything I wanted made me only see Cillian Wylder as a smug, arrogant asshole. Not a human with a heart and love for his family.

Isla once told me "Lonely people do stupid shit." I can attest to that, now. My stupid shit was mostly years of destructive thought process, but that takes a toll on you. It wears you down, day after day. Eventually, I was a husk of a man trying to fill the void any way I could. Mostly with random women. That hadn't been my life before I dated Isla. Picking up whatever puck bunny looked the hottest after a long game didn't appeal much to me. I was with women, I dated, but they were typically friends of friends or old acquaintances.

After Isla reconciled with Cillian, I stopped dating, stopped sleeping with the same woman more than once. Most devastatingly, I stopped connecting.

Then, I moved across the street from Kit Ashcroft.

"I don't want to hurt her."

"I didn't want to hurt Isla, either," he says. "Sometimes life gets in the way of even our best intentions. I wish I'd had people in my life giving me reminders of what was most important. Maybe things would have turned out differently and I wouldn't have lost so much time."

But then, I'd have not had the chance to know Isla and Sadie the way I did. It's difficult to reconcile, wishing the best could have happened for the three Wylders while also not wanting to lose what I had.

Instead of saying the wrong thing to my teammate, I say nothing.

I'm not home ten minutes before incessant rapping starts up on my front door. There's an urgency to it, and since only a select few people know where I live, I assume it's Kit. My heart rate spikes as I take the stairs back down to the first floor. The rain pelting the sheet-metal roof normally soothes me—now it just amps up my pulse.

Not to be a misogynistic, overbearing asshole, but I do worry about her living alone. Nightmare's a good noise-maker, but he wouldn't be much help if she ever needed protection.

Throwing the door open, I find her soaking wet, shivering as raindrops stream down her face. She's only wearing boxing shorts and a T-shirt, flip-flops on her feet. The woman dresses like we live in Hawaii, not next door to the Cascade Mountains.

"What's wrong?" I demand, pulling her inside and out of the downpour. "Are you okay?"

"No," she says adamantly, swiping wet strands from her cheeks.

"What happened?" I gently tow her farther inside, perching her in front of the gas fireplace. Flipping the switch, I grab the throw blanket off the sofa and wrap it around her. Kit follows my every move but doesn't answer right away. "Kit?"

"Just say it, Kit," she mutters to herself. After a long exhale, her eyes pop up to mine. "I've been thinking about what to say to you for days. Writing notes, memorizing key points. I even practiced in a mirror, like a teenager preparing for an oral exam. That's why I'm not okay. You—you're why I'm not okay. You distract me. You're like an intrusive thought. I can't focus for very long before your crooked smile conjures in my mind."

"I'm an intrusive thought?" I manage not to laugh, but my smile still forms.

"Yes! As is that smile," she accuses, pointing at me.

"Should I smile less?"

"No."

"What should I do?" I ask.

Kit's nervousness doesn't present like Lottie's. My sister turns inward—quiet, withdrawn—sometimes not speaking for days while she works through something. We learned early to let her know we were there, but give her space. Kit hasn't told me how to support her, and I stupidly haven't asked. I can tell she's struggling, walking a line between frustration and agitation. The crease in her forehead is as prominent now as when I opened the door. And I don't think all the shaking is from being cold and wet.

"How do I help, Kit?"

"I don't know." Her hands ball into fists at her hips. "I had my life figured out, you know? I was content with what I had—and what I didn't. Now? I don't know how to do any of this."

"Any of what? Talk to me. Let me help."

She shakes her hands out, only for them to curl into fists again.

"You're safe here, Kit. It's just you and me. And I don't judge, remember? You can say anything to me. I'll stand here and hear every word."

She takes a few deep breaths. Eventually, her shoulders lose a little of their tension. I want nothing more than to wrap her in my arms, carry her to my bed, and be the big spoon to her little one. I want to protect her through whatever internal battle she's waging.

While her nipples pebble under the thin, wet cotton, it's not sex on my mind right now—though I dream of her every night. Not Isla. Never Isla, anymore. Now isn't the time for those thoughts. Right now, I only want to soothe her.

"I don't date, Tyson. I never have. The one relationship I had with a man…I've come to realize it wasn't what I thought it was at the time. I haven't got the first clue how to date you, or how to be any sort of partner to you—or anyone." She pauses to steady herself while I try to keep my own emotions in check. Her dark eyes glass over as she quietly pronounces her next words. "All I know is that I want to be brave enough to try."

I take a step forward, my hands reaching before I can think better of it.

"Can I touch you?" I pause mid-motion. "Your face—can I touch your face?"

"You've never asked before." It's not an accusation, just an observation. She's right—I didn't ask before. But I've never touched her with this kind of intimacy, either.

"That's not an answer, Kit. Say the words."

"Yes." She tips her face up to mine as I take another step closer.

"There are no rules to follow with me," I tell her, cupping her face in my palms. "You don't need to know how to do anything but communicate with me. Whatever concerns you have, we'll face them together. Okay?"

She leans into my right palm, and I rub my thumb across her temple.

"I'm not a virgin," she says. "But I might as well be."

That, coupled with her earlier statement, sends a sharp pain through my chest. But I don't want assumptions—I want truth. If she's willing to give it.

"What does that mean?"

A tear spills over her lower lash. It's the first time I've ever seen her cry, and my heart rages for her. I catch the droplet on my thumb and bring it to my lips before replacing my hand on her cheek.

"If I tell you, don't look at me differently." Her quiet words sting the air. Anger pools in me, demanding to know who hurt this perfect creature.

"I can't promise that," I tell her softly, wincing when her eyes shut in pain. "I can't promise you won't say something that makes me see you as even stronger than I already thought. I can't promise it won't make me feel more connected to you. But I can promise that whatever you say next, I'll be on your side. I'll always be on your side."

"Can you promise that, though? You don't know me that well."

"I know you well enough. I've practically placed myself in your back pocket for the last two months. That's long enough for me to know your character. I hope it's been long enough for you to know mine."

We haven't had long, deep discussions about life-changing events from her past. I know when I'm getting too close to a topic she's not ready for. I've told her plenty of my own story. She holds the reins here. The control. All the power. I'm not here to pry or push, but to support.

Her eyes search mine. I let her read me, let her see what I'm offering—security, safety to be herself, to tell her truth. Her hand rests on my chest, fingers curling into my shirt. It takes her a few minutes, but I see the moment she decides she can trust me.

It's the most empowering moment of my life—to be given such a fragile gift.

"I…I didn't want it to happen. Not really. But the pressure was too much. I couldn't keep fighting it," she says, her voice the most vulnerable sound I've ever heard. "I didn't say yes, but I didn't say no, either."

"If it's not an enthusiastic yes, it's a no."

"I know that, now. Or maybe I did, then, too," she says. "It was confusing."

"Who?" The single word scrapes my throat, my hands wanting to be gentle on her skin, yet violent on his.

"My father's coworker. He was around a lot, watching sports with my dad. Drinking beer, eating pizza. It was their chosen pastime. When my dad would get belligerent, Derik would step in. I felt…obligated."

She means he made her believe she owed him. She's not saying the words, but I hear them, all the same. A thousand questions and every negative emotion rush through me. I've never felt murderous in my life—until now.

"Nobody owes that. I'm sorry you were made to feel you did. I hate that for you," I tell her, pressing my forehead to hers, not breaking eye contact, forcing my voice to stay soft.

"I tried to hold it off. I was so close to leaving—moving away. It was only weeks away, but he was so persistent. Always there. It became his mission, and I thought…"

"It would be easier to give in," I finish for her.

"It wasn't, though," she says, another tear spilling over. Her fist tightens in my shirt. She's anchoring herself—to me.

I hope to be worthy of such heavy weight.

10

KIT

Tyson doesn't say anything to that. Instead, he wraps the blanket tighter around me, picks me up with an impossible ease, and settles us both on the couch. Me, cradled like a wounded animal on his lap.

Normally, that would bother me. Being seen as delicate, or a thing to wrap in cotton fluff. I am a capable woman. Yet, I'm liking his care. The touch meant to ease my frayed edges; I could get used to it.

A terrifying thought.

Comfort wasn't offered to me as a child. Being a single parent, my father didn't adopt any maternal instincts. Hell, he didn't have any fatherly ones, either. My grandmother did her best, but if she showed too much affection toward me, my father scolded her. I never knew my grandfather, but I have the sense he was a cold man who berated her. My father learned from him and took up the mantle when my grandfather passed. Even when freed from being a battered wife, she couldn't stop being a battered woman.

It always struck me as sad, but when I got away from it, I swore I'd put an end to the generational trauma of the Ashcroft family.

Although I like the way Tyson rubs his chin against the crown of my head, and the tingle of calm it sends through me, the thoughts still swirl.

Can I trust him with my vulnerability? Is this a mistake?

If it is, it shouldn't feel this nice. That would be a cruel trick of the world. But it wouldn't be the only one—after all, the best-tasting foods are the worst for you.

Is that what Tyson is? My bacon-topped maple bar? My turtle cheesecake? My rocky road ice cream?

I laugh out loud, and his arms tighten around me.

"What are you thinking?"

"That you might be what gives me cellulite," I say, burying my face in his chest. He can't hide his bemusement when he asks me to explain. "Oddly, I'm more comfortable with you than I am with most people. I like when you touch me. I want you to. I even crave it—sort of like I crave chocolate when I'm on my period."

"Oh. So I'm like a sugar rush, or comfort food."

"I guess so. Does that freak you out?"

"Not at all."

"It does me," I admit.

"I'm guessing you haven't had many people you could count on," he says after a pause. "Whatever happens between us, I will be that for you. You don't owe me anything in return—you don't have to be or do anything for me. You understand?"

"No, but I'm trying to," I answer. "You're right, I didn't have anyone I could count on to always put my best interests first. Not until I became friends with Willa. I don't trust easily. I've never had reason to think I could."

"I'll prove that you can trust me, and I'll understand while you learn to. Deal?"

"Deal. And I'll try not to evade every tough topic."

"Take your time with it," he says, pulling the blanket up from where it's slipped off my shoulder. "Are you comfortable?"

"Yes, you make a cozy chair." He's warm, too—his body heat seeping through my thin pajamas. I like it more than I can say, his strong frame pressing against me. He makes a humming sound, but I suspect there are a lot of thoughts running through his head.

"You can ask me things. I might not answer everything, but I'll try. It may be easier than spilling my story, anyway."

My toes twitch; I curl and uncurl them. It's a weird nervous habit. I clench my fists, too, but my toes are easier to hide from other people. Not that I'm trying to hide from Tyson right now—it's just that I'm not in the practice of talking about my life in Maine.

"Did it happen more than once?"

"Yes. There were two other times," I say, the words coming easier than I expected. Usually, when I think about it, I feel ashamed. Somehow, that's not what I'm feeling right now.

"I'm trying really hard to keep levelheaded, right now. You be sure to let me know if my tension gets to be too much for you," he says, and I nod for him to continue. "You hadn't been with anyone before?"

"Never even been kissed," I say with a sigh. "Boys I went to school with were either scared of me, or I feared them. I was too awkward for the jocks, too smart for the stoners, too cute for the brainiacs."

"And those three times?"

"No. I was already skittish around men—my situation with Derik only made it worse."

"Hey." He turns my face toward his with a finger under my chin. "Your situation was rape. If you didn't want it, it was forced."

"I know," I say. "I didn't for a long time. Because I didn't struggle or scream, I thought it was my fault it happened. Or that by not saying no, I was somehow asking for it. It took me a long time to understand that I was coerced into doing something I absolutely didn't want to do. But sometimes it's still hard to forgive myself."

"There's nothing for you to be forgiven for, Kit. It's not rape because a woman struggles—or because she screams. It's because she didn't want it."

"I know. I do, I promise I do. But intrusive thoughts are hard to battle, you know?"

He makes the same humming noise as before. It rumbles through his chest, against my cheek.

"You smell good. How do you smell good after being on a plane all day? I swear I smell like French onion soup after every flight."

"The planes we fly are a lot cleaner, I guess," he says with a laugh.

"Must be nice."

"It doesn't suck," he says. "Have you ever…and tell me if this is out of bounds, I don't want to make this weird, but since you've never dated… do you feel…"

"Do I desire," I interrupt. "Do I have a sex drive?"

"Yeah. It feels like important information to have. I don't want to assume or rush. Or worse."

"I like sex, Tyson," I say, my toes clenched so tightly. "I've just only ever had it with myself. Not because I haven't found men attractive over the years. But because I've never felt at ease enough with any of the ones I did."

One of my former coworkers used to ask me out on a semi-regular basis. He was good-looking but too nice. Almost *fake* nice, like he was trying to cover a personality flaw. It was probably just my overactive imagination, but I'd rather trust my instincts to a fault than be horribly wrong about someone. Again.

That's what's been starkly different with Tyson. My creep radar hasn't gone off with him—not once.

I believe you meet certain people in life and instantly connect in some way. It happened with Willa. When we both reached for the same tea at the coffee shop, I knew by her easy laugh that she was someone I could feel lighter around after a stressful day. You could call it soulmates or kindred spirits, though I don't know how much I believe in that sort of thing.

With Tyson, I think I knew the day he helped me install my security system—when he spent the entire day with me and didn't balk at my sudden subject changes or erratic habits.

"Noted," he says. "Does your father know what happened?"

"He does. And that's something I want to be able to share with you," I say. "Not tonight, though. That story needs to wait for a day when I'm not feeling so worn out."

"Okay," he says. "Where's Nightmare?"

"I put him in his crate before I came over. It was his bedtime; I'm sure he's knocked out."

"Is your house locked up?"

"Yeah, why?" I pop my head off his chest to look up at him.

"Can you stay? Not for sex," he adds quickly. "I'd like to hold you, though. Be close. I'm not sure I can sleep tonight if I can't keep eyes on you."

"Do you sleep with your eyes open?"

"No." He laughs.

"It's a valid question. You could be one of the twenty percent who do."

"I'm not."

"Thank fuck for that. How creepy would it be to roll over and have a snoring man staring at you?"

"I don't snore, either," he protests.

"Look at you ticking off green flag after green flag," I tease.

"Lack of snoring is a green flag?"

"I don't know, but it's certainly not a red one." I shift on his lap, turning to face him more fully. My breasts brush against his chest, and I notice the twitch of his dick at the same time I notice his slight grimace. He probably doesn't want to be turned on by me—not after what I've shared with him.

Tyson Murphy, a big, bad hockey player, is a gentleman, it seems. It makes me like him even more.

"So? Will you stay? Or we could stay at your house, if that's more comfortable for you," he offers, and now it's my face with a frown.

"No. My bed wasn't a safe space after Derik. I…I don't know if I could sleep with you there with me."

"Okay," he says, brushing some hair from my forehead and pressing a quick kiss there. "Can I walk you home, at least?"

"No. That's not what I want," I say, leaning closer another inch. "I want to try and stay here. No promises, though."

"I'm not asking for promises, Kit. Just communication, remember? If you can't handle it, you wake me up and I'll walk you home. No questions asked. It's a lot to ask of you. Fuck, I haven't even taken you out on a date and I'm already asking you to stay over."

"You've taken me out to eat a couple of times."

"Those weren't dates, Kit. That was just me feeding you."

"Isn't that what dates are, though?"

"No," he says with a frown. "Whoever taught women to expect bare minimums was an asshole. Why are you laughing?"

"You're a feminist. I kinda fucking love that."

"My mom is going to love you," he says, weaving an arm around my waist so he can pick me up as he stands. "Do you want a dry shirt to sleep in?"

"I thought you jock types offered your sweaters." I wrap my arms around his neck, and it feels natural. Coming over here tonight, I thought I'd be tripping up over letting him in and sharing my past with him. Instead, I've only been tripping over how easy it is to be myself.

Proof that sometimes facing your biggest fears pays off, I guess.

"You get an A-plus for calling it a sweater and not a jersey. You can have one, if you want, but it's going to hang down to your knees and the material is ridiculously stiff."

"Can I pick?"

"Sure," he says, walking us straight into his closet and setting me down on my feet. Slowly, I spin in a circle, taking it all in. There're a lot of clothes packed in here. The hangers are full—mostly of suits, which I know is what they wear before every game. There are also stacks of jeans, sweatpants, shorts, shirts. Stacks upon stacks.

"Wow, this is…"

"Impressive, I know," he says, and I grin.

I hold a jersey up against me, and we both laugh at how comically huge it is. Sorting through a stack of T-shirts, I stop when I find the perfect one. The graphic is a UFO beaming up a man, with the words *ask me about my butthole* emblazoned across it.

"This one," I exclaim.

"Fucking hell," he says, grabbing it from me.

"You said I could pick!"

"That was before I remembered this was in here. It was a gag gift from Lottie."

"I want that one, Tyson," I say, pointing at it.

"Fine," he relents, handing it to me. "You change in here; I'll go brush my teeth and leave a spare toothbrush out for you."

Before I change, I pull my cell phone from my waistband and send a quick text to Willa.

ME:

I told Tyson I want to date. I told him about Derik. Now we're having a non-sexy-time sleepover at his house.

I promised I would check in with her, and knowing her, she's waiting up until she hears from me.

WILLA:

You're good then? Like, totally good? Do you need to talk?

ME:

I'm good. I'll call you tomorrow.

WILLA:

I'm so proud of you! Don't push yourself past your limits. Call me if you need anything. I'm leaving my ringer on. I love you!

ME:

I love you too, thank you for always being here for me.

WILLA:

ALWAYS

"You good?" Tyson asks, from the other side of the closet door. Again, he's being a gentleman and not peeking in.

"Sorry, yeah. I'm good, I was texting Willa."

"Don't apologize, take your time."

He's sweet. Or he's a normal man, and I haven't known enough normal men in my life. Either way, I could get used to it.

I change quickly into his silly shirt and rush next door to the bathroom, where a new toothbrush is sitting out for me. When I head back into the bedroom, it's with a new apprehension. I pause just outside of the door. Tyson is already in bed, scrolling on his phone, bare chest on full display.

"Hey," he says. When he notices me, his eyes narrow. "Talk to me, Kit. What's wrong?"

"You have spare toothbrushes," I say, my toes curling into the soft carpet. His face falls but he recovers quickly.

"Can you come sit with me and I'll explain?"

I debate taking a minute to think about it, but decide that's stupid. He's been so patient with me; it would be unfair to not give him the same grace. So, I move to the opposite side of the bed from him, and crawl up, keeping to the edge.

"Yes, your assumptions are correct. I do have spare toothbrushes for the occasion when I have a woman over. I just left the last one out for you."

"Better add more to your grocery list," I snark quietly.

"I have a handful more in the drawer, Kit. I meant, it's the last one, because I haven't so much as looked at another woman since my neighbor turned my head."

"Oh." Heat bursts on my cheeks, embarrassed that I've reacted the way I have. "I told you I don't know how to do this."

"Seems like you might have a jealous streak; it's sexy as fuck, if I'm honest." He throws the blankets back, inviting me under. "You still want to stay?"

"You still want me to?"

"Without question." He turns away to plug his phone into the charger. I use the opportunity to climb in without his eyes as an audience. "You make my dumbass shirt look good, by the way."

"It's a great shirt," I mumble, scooting farther under the covers. I eye his tanned skin, wondering what it would feel like, but I'm too nervous to reach out. Pulling my knees up to my chest, I lock my fingers around them.

Tyson watches, his lips twitching to smile. He fights it off well enough, then rolls to his side to face me.

"You doing okay?" he asks, and I nod wordlessly. "Do you want a cuddle?"

Again, I don't answer. I just awkwardly scoot closer without fully releasing my fetal position. Tyson ends up laughing.

"I like it when you laugh," I whisper.

"I like it when you laugh, too," he mimics my soft tone. "It lets me know your comfort level."

"Your laughter helps with that," I tell him, and he inches a little closer to me as we stare at each other. "Will you do something for me?"

"Anything you want."

"Will you…" I start and then think better of it.

"Kit, this is a safe space. Any time you're with me, you are safe."

The way he continually reminds me and reassures me makes my heart swell. An expression I never liked, since it sounded like a medical emergency. Now, I understand it.

"Can I have a goodnight kiss?" I ask tentatively.

"Fuck, yes, Kit. Do you want me to control it, or do you want to?"

"I don't know how," I say.

"It mostly comes naturally." He moves even closer. So close that I feel his body heat against mine. His minty breath across my lips. A soft gasp escapes me at how such a small thing excites me so much.

"It takes one-hundred-forty-six muscles to kiss."

"Then it's a good workout, too." He speaks the words at the corner of my mouth, and I feel it in other parts of my body. I don't want to wait any more. Nor do I want to relinquish the decision to someone else.

Leaning the mere centimeter forward, I press my lips to Tyson's. Not thinking about how it may come across as fumbling, I move my mouth against his until I find a position and a rhythm I like best. He follows my lead, only deepening it when a needy sound bubbles out of me. His lips separate, his tongue darting out to taste.

My toes curl for another reason entirely.

11

KIT

I fall asleep to delicate kisses. When I wake, it's to a hard body under me. At some point in the night, I ended up atop Tyson, plastered to him, really. My pillow is his pectoral, my blanket his arms wrapped around me, a palm resting on my ass.

I blink, take a steadying inhale of air, and evaluate the data.

My body isn't tense; I'm relaxed and well rested. No racing pulse, no pain in my temples, no signs of anxiety. No fight or flight response to waking up with a man next to me, or under me, as the case may be.

His chest moves at a slow, steady pace. His pulse vibrates against my cheek. His dick hard against my hip. An itch to reach down and touch it starts at my fingertips, and I remind myself that it isn't okay to touch him like that while he sleeps.

I'm unsure of the time. It must be early because the light seeping around the curtain is still dim. Nightmare will want out soon enough, though moving from this bed anytime soon sounds like a horrible idea.

Which tells me everything I need to know.

I didn't just survive my first sleepover with a man—I enjoyed it. My soft giggle stirs him.

"Good morning, gorgeous," he says, voice rough from sleep. "You good?"

"Better than." I stretch my legs as I say it, and he sucks in air. "Sorry."

"No, I am. Biology doesn't always know the rules."

"I don't always know the rules, either," I say. "Besides, I like that I, um… have that effect on you."

"Do you now?" he teases.

"I do. I told you I like sex—I meant that. Or my version of it, anyway." I shift again, careful of his sensitive parts, propping my chin on my hands and staring up at him.

"What has your version entailed?"

"A fairly pricey vibrator and a carefully curated selection of pornography," I say, crinkling my nose. I'll be thirty in a couple of years, and every orgasm has been delivered by the equivalent of a pocket-sized robot.

"Maybe when you're comfortable with it, you can show me this curated collection." He loops his hands under my arms, dragging me up his body so he can bury his face in my neck. His light stubble tickles in an intoxicating way while he trails kisses down and across my collarbone.

"You want to watch porn with me?"

"I want to know what you like," he says. "You smell good."

"Doubtful. I need a shower," I say, but he just grunts in disagreement. His fingers play at my side where my shirt has ridden up, brushing bare skin and making me squirm with the urge to lay hands on him, too. It's all I can think about. "Tyson?"

"Mmm."

"Can I touch you?"

"You already are," he says, nodding toward where my fingers are in his hair.

"That's not what I mean." I disentangle myself and sit up, my legs straddling his chest. "I mean—will you be still and let me touch you?"

"You mean, explore? Get familiar?"

He understands me so well for someone who's known me such a short time. My heart does that stupid swelling thing again, and I nod. He nods back, an almost sinister grin flashing across his face.

"You're excited," I say, cocking my head to the side.

"I can't think of anything I want more than for you to trace your way around my body. I'll be as quiet and still as I can be."

"Well, now I'm even more nervous."

"Don't be anything but you, Kit."

The thing is…nervous *is* me.

Oh. Maybe that's what he means. He's watching me with nothing but encouragement. No judgment. Okay, then.

Fumble away, Kit.

I start with his face, dragging my fingers down his cheek, around his jaw. Tyson just watches me intently. Still self-conscious, I stick my tongue out at him, making us both laugh and breaking some of the tension.

Is it sexy? No, probably not.

But I'm like an inexperienced teenager, here; might as well own it. Besides, sexy isn't the goal. We're not about to have sex—I'm not that ready. I just want to know what a man feels like when it's not fearful and forced. I want to see what sensations it sparks inside me. Wide awake, eyes open, and most importantly…in fucking control.

By the time I'm at his chest, the dark thoughts have faded. He hasn't shaved or waxed away his body hair. It's ruddy, like the hair on his head, but not thick—a soft smattering that suits the protector side of him he's been showing me.

When I reach the ridges of his abdomen, the muscles shift under my touch, and again, his cock makes itself known.

The blood rushes to my head like a high. Me—a nerd in an alien butthole T-shirt with morning breath—can stir the desire of a godlike professional NHL player.

How is this real life?

I take my time on his abs. No, it's more than six—this man is all edges and ridges, hard lines under smooth skin. An urgency rises in me to taste him. I want to see every part of him.

I pause, looking from my fingers at the band of his boxer briefs up to his face. His gaze is steady, intense, sending fire through my veins.

"Whatever you need, Kit," he says, like he can hear my thoughts.

Keeping my eyes on his, I bend to lick a slow line over every hill and valley of his abs. My first thought is that he tastes clean, which makes no sense. Pheromones are oddly powerful. I do it again, testing my reaction, but it's Tyson whose skin flushes and warms.

"Fuck, Kit. That's the hottest thing I've ever seen."

That sounds monstrously untrue. I've seen the women who've left his house, and Isla is effortlessly, naturally sexy. How could I ever compare? But again, I can't read a lie in his expression.

I grip his waistband tighter, forcing away my insecurities. They aren't real—they don't exist in this room, only in my head.

"Kit? What do you need?"

"To believe," I say, the words escaping before I can think better of them.

"Hey, sit up. Let me show you." His hand comes to my cheek, guiding me. I obey, watching as he slowly, carefully, scoots up to rest against the headboard. At the same time, he pushes the covers down. There's space between us; I can move away if I want.

"This is you, Kit. It doesn't matter what you know how to do—or don't. It's you my body reacts to. It's you I want." He lifts his rear and slides out of his boxers.

I barely hear him past the pounding in my ears. It's hard to focus when he's lounging like a naked god in front of me, his cock—hard, veined, and divine—resting between the V of his hips.

"Will you…" I falter, sealing my lips shut, my fingernails digging into my palms, too afraid to ask for what I want.

"Give me the words, Kit. You're safe. Ask me anything."

You're safe.

Tyson is a safe space. He's done nothing to prove otherwise. Willa would tell me there's nothing to be ashamed of, that I should go after what I want.

I want to see Tyson's hand on himself.

You're safe.

"Will you touch yourself for me?"

"Fuck," he says with a sigh of relief. "I thought you'd never ask."

The relief he shows makes me grin, until his hand wraps around his length and all the blood in my body moves to my own core.

"Damn," I whisper.

"You like that?"

"It doesn't suck," I say, and his head falls back, eyes closing.

"Oh my God," he groans, his hand working up and down his cock. I couldn't pull my eyes away from him if I tried. But why the hell would I try something so stupid? He moves slightly faster, his other hand moving to cup his balls. This live action is better than any porn I've watched. I get fidgety, shifting my weight from hip to hip when the tingling sensations get to be too much. "You need to touch yourself, Kit?"

"How do you know everything?" I ask with a mixture of surprise and urgency as I push my hand into my underwear. "Oh, fuck."

It's a sweet relief when my fingers start circling my clit.

"Beautiful," Tyson mutters. His eyes move all over me, never straying from my face for too long. "Find your rhythm, Kit. I'll follow."

Tyson rises, his heels digging into the bed. The muscles in his thighs flex, and it brings me a step closer to climax. I could watch him for hours and never last mere minutes. I slip my finger down and in. A whimper escapes me, and Tyson licks his lips.

"Tyson."

"I'm here. Right here with you, Kit. Get yourself there."

I insert another finger, picking up my pace while grinding against the heel of my hand. Reaching out with my other hand, I wrap it around Tyson's. I'm not helping him get off so much as feeling the power of him doing it himself.

It's all it takes to tip me over the edge, shaking through my climax while I watch his semen escape the tip of his cock. His cum falls into the ditches I had my tongue on only moments ago. I want it there again.

"Fuck, Kit." We're both breathing heavier by the time our movements slow. Sweat glistens on his chest, and I find even that sexy as sin. Everything about him is sexy, in this moment. "You okay?"

I can't help the laugh that escapes. It isn't humor, though—it's tearful, it's joyful.

It's fucking healing, even as it turns somewhat manic.

Immediately, Tyson's arms wrap around me. He pulls me to him, cradling me against his chest, soothing a hand over my head as my laughter mixed with sobs escape me.

"It's all right," Tyson whispers repeatedly into the crown of my head. "Let it out."

He doesn't stop petting or whispering until I've regulated my breath and my tears have slowed.

"That was the best moment of my life," I'm finally able to say after a minute or two. "I'm sorry if I freaked you out. I never really thought I'd have this experience."

"I'll help you experience whatever you want to in life, Kit," he says before bringing my fingers up to his mouth and sucking them in. His tongue works around them as he hums in pleasure.

This man's understanding ways are going to be the death of me.

Or maybe he's going to help me finally live my life.

"I was going to steal your T-shirt and wear it home, but I think the neighbors might look at me funny if I cross the street in a jizz-stained alien-ass shirt," I say after a few more minutes, when I realize what the dampness between us is.

"If you look deeper in the closet, there's one that says *I'd rather have serotonin than this huge cock.* You could take that one instead."

<hr>

"Zan said they played with the new, improved stat tracker on the way back from Florida." Willa and I are having a girls' night. For us, that means pizza in front of trashy reality television. "All the guys were really impressed. He said even Hugo, who hates most technology, loved how user-friendly it is."

"That's good. That was the goal, anyway. Mostly, all I did was build in a better stat tracker and suggest they update the user interface so it wasn't as confusing for basic users."

"You shrug it off like it's the easiest thing in the world," she says, laughing.

"Well, it's not exactly hard."

"And yet, they didn't have it before you agreed to take on the task."

"Shove another piece of that pie in your mouth and quit blowing smoke up my ass."

"It's my job to boost your ego. Top five rule in the BFF handbook," she says, tossing a piece of pineapple at me. She misses, but Nightmare is there to nab it up the second it hits the floor. "Shit, can dogs eat pineapple?"

"Yeah, it's fine. No avocado, though—which I found surprising, for some reason."

"You hear that, Nightmare? No basic bitch avocado toast brunch for you."

Nightmare whimpers, spins in a circle, then buries his face in his paws.

"Too bad. He'd make a good brunch partner for us. He's so well-behaved in public."

"You've taken him out to eat?" she asks.

"Tyson and I took him earlier for chicken and waffles at The Barking Dog. He didn't bark or pull on the leash at all—even when other dogs paid him attention."

After our playtime this morning, Tyson was hesitant to let me go about my day too quickly. I was fine, but he wanted to be sure. His overbearing side didn't bother me, though. It was…cute. For now, anyway. I like being around him a lot. More than a lot. But I'm used to being independent, and I don't want to lose that—not even for orgasms.

"Your cheeks are red."

"I was wondering when you were going to ask me about my night."

"I didn't ask anything," she says with a smirk.

"You did—just not with words."

"You're killing me here! Obviously, it must have gone okay because you didn't call me. But I've been here for"—she pauses to check the time on her phone—"exactly thirty-eight minutes, and this is the first time you've brought him up."

"I wanted to make you squirm because I knew you wouldn't ask."

"Only because I want you to tell me things in your own time."

"But it kills you when I don't do it immediately," I tease.

"Yes, you asshole," she laughs.

"It was amazing," I say.

"That's it?" Willa asks with an exaggerated eye-roll.

"He understands me, Willa. He showed patience and compassion, but he didn't coddle me."

"Is he letting you set the pace?"

"Completely. Even this morning, when I wanted to touch him and we ended up masturbating together," I say quickly, because even though she's the person I'm closest to in the entire world, it's not something I'm used to discussing.

"You did that?"

"I did. And then I cried, but it wasn't a bad cry. It was…I don't know, cathartic. And he held me through it."

"Oh, Kit." Her eyes go teary.

"I'm trying not to get too wrapped up in it all—or in him—while also trying to let myself live. You know?"

"You want to find yourself, not lose yourself."

"Exactly," I say. "There's also the lingering voice telling me it's not real, I'm not the kind of woman who can make him happy, it's going to end in flames…blah, blah, blah."

"That's normal. Everyone's insecure in their relationships—until they're not. It takes time. It's new for both of you," she tells me.

I hope she's right. Until I trust that, I'll hold on to the idea that, for now, I'm enjoying my time with him. If it doesn't work out, at least I'll have that.

"You really do like him, though?"

"I really, really do."

"Then I'm ecstatic for you, and I'll make sure you don't get too lost in being an NHL wag."

"Oh no, I don't think I'm that," I protest.

"You might end up being that, though. I mean, you're already having sleepovers," she says. "Besides, you do all the fun wag stuff with me and Isla already, anyway. You might as well get the rest of the benefits."

"What are the rest of the benefits?"

"Orgasms, mostly."

"Well, that doesn't sound so bad."

"It's divine, my friend," she says, leaning her head on my shoulder. "I'm proud of you."

Those aren't words that have been common in my life. My father never said them. My grandmother showed it on a couple of occasions, most notably when I received my acceptance to the University of Washington. She may not show her support on a regular basis, but she always tried when it mattered most.

I should call her soon. It's been weeks since we last spoke, which isn't uncommon for us, by any means. But she's getting older and she's the only family I have. Well, the only family I acknowledge having, anyhow.

Every time we talk, she asks me if I've met a handsome young man yet. No matter how many times I've told her I wasn't interested in finding random lost men, she still asks. She'll be thrilled when I tell her about Tyson. She worries about me being across the country, alone, and without a man.

She can't acknowledge that it was a man who hurt her and I both. Nor does she accept that men never stepped in to save either of us.

She's old school that way, I've come to accept her for who she is. Flawed, incapable of learning, fearful. She loves me, though, in her way.

"Thank you. I'm proud of myself," I tell her. "I went over there with a belly full of determination, almost threw it all up once I was standing in front of him."

"You didn't, though," she says.

"Nope. When he's close enough, and especially when he touches me, I forget most of what makes me so afraid. Is that weird? It feels weird." I'm not good at being dependent on anyone.

"It's not weird. You're not used to it, but it's normal. Human touch and oxytocin are good for you. Consensually, of course."

"They do say you need four hugs a day for survival," I say. Though, I've never gotten that many on any day in my whole life and I'm still very alive.

"Yeah," she says. "Eight for maintenance and twelve for growth. Seems like bullshit to me, though, I do love a good bear hug."

"Between Zan and Damian, you should be the most grown person around."

"Right? But we both know I can still be as immature as hell."

"We both have our moments," I say. "But that's what makes us fun. We can't be classy and serious all the time."

"When have either of us ever been classy?"

"Yeah, okay. Good point."

There's a lot for me to think about when it comes to Tyson. We can't predict the future, of course. So, I can either fret and worry that this won't work out, or I can take each day for what it is and enjoy that I can grow and heal with Tyson. Even if we aren't meant to be together forever.

12

TYSON

Since my night with Kit, I've been living like I'm on a high—like there's more air in my lungs, more blood in my veins. Colors seem brighter. Everything feels sharper, more in focus. It makes me feel insane, but it's like I'm remembering things I'd forgotten.

I'd swear she'd slipped me drugs, if I didn't know better.

There's something powerful when someone with trauma like Kit's decides *you* are the one they trust to help them move past it. I feel like a different man, now. There are moments in life that change you irrevocably—whether it's a death, a birth, an illness. For me, it was a witnessing.

I bore witness to her surviving her monster. It was the hardest thing I've ever done. All I wanted was to rage for her—to hop on a plane, fly to Maine, hunt him down, and bury him in the fucking ground.

There are still so many questions I want answers to, but I won't make her relive any of it just to satisfy me. That's a torture I'll live with—knowing that if I ever *do* get the chance to find that asshole, I'll make good on my desires.

And then, there was the moment she had the courage to ask me to get myself off for her. It was intimacy unlike anything I've ever known. She was so beautiful.

But I can't help wondering if she's ever had a *full* orgasm.

She came— I know she did, because I tasted it on her fingers. But it wasn't explosive; it was the smallest flicker of release I've seen since Jill Swanson and I lost our virginity to each other at fifteen. I barely got Jill there, either—had no idea what I was doing back then.

One day, I hope I get the chance to truly blow Kit's mind. I'm obsessed with the thought of it. Which makes me feel like an asshole—because while she's taking baby steps into her sexuality, all I want to do is fuck her until she's limp and can't remember anything but my name.

"Hey, Shitbrick! Wake up," Lottie says, bringing me out of my thoughts.

"Lot," my mom chastises her. We're at a restaurant on the waterfront, a nicer establishment, otherwise, Mom wouldn't care. We all talk like longshoremen at home.

"I'm awake."

"Just distracted," Lottie says. "Because of that woman?"

"What woman?" Dad asks.

"His neighbor lady."

"She has a name," I say.

"Well, are you going to tell us what it is?" Mom asks.

"Her name is Kit."

"That's a cute name," Mom says.

"She's not a kid; it's not a cute name. It's a pretty name," Lottie argues. "She isn't a kid, is she?"

"No, smartass."

"Well, that's good," Dad says, as if it was an option that I'd be dating someone underage.

"Why did I invite you all here anyway?"

"Because you miss the hell out of us," Lottie says, picking another blueberry out of her pancake. If blueberry pancakes are on the menu, she'll order them. However, she hates the blueberries being in the pancake. She picks them out one by one and eats them separately.

I don't ask questions.

"I thought I did," I say, rolling my eyes at her, then winking.

"Do we get to meet her?" Mom asks.

"She'll be at the game tonight," I say, nodding.

"In the family section?" Lottie pops another blueberry in her mouth.

"Yes, with Willa. I think Isla and Sadie will be there, too," I say, and they all stare at me. When Isla broke it off for good with me, I didn't take it well. My family saw the worst of it.

"It will be nice to see them again," my mom says. "Seems weird to meet your new girlfriend with your ex in tow, though."

"Don't call her my girlfriend in front of her," I say. "She's not comfortable with that whole idea yet."

"Why?" Lottie asks before I even have the last of my words out.

"She's new to relationships." I shrug, playing it off as if it isn't a big deal. I don't want her interrogated by my sister, who isn't the best at reading social cues. Nor do I want my family to scrutinize her all night. "Hasn't really dated much."

"But she's not a kid?"

"No, Dad. She's a couple of years younger than me, is all."

"So, my age?"

"Yes, Lot. I think you two will get along great."

"Does she know I'm neurodivergent?"

"She does, you can be yourself with her."

"Okay," Lottie says, biting her bottom lip. She gets nervous about new people, but less so when she knows she doesn't have to explain her ticks. Her confidence grows all the time, but I long for the day that it doesn't weigh on her like an anchor.

"We'll be sure to chat with her at the game," my dad says.

"And try to pay her less attention than Isla and Sadie," my mom says.

"It shouldn't be weird," I say. "Kit is Willa's best friend; she's practically a Cole herself."

"That's wonderful," she says. "But you aren't exactly versed on the ways of women, so I'll evaluate the situation myself."

She smiles at me as if she's calling me a silly boy.

"Thanks for having my back."

"Always, Ty. You're my favorite son, after all."

"He's your only son," Lottie says, brows furrowed.

"Precisely," Mom says, then takes another bite of her omelet.

They got in early this morning while I was at practice. After feeding them, I'll get them settled at the hotel before heading home to prepare for tonight's game—which includes a nap and maybe some video games.

Athletes are all different. Some hyperfocus on an upcoming game. Others, like me, do better if we don't think about it until we're in the arena, suiting up. I usually arrive an hour or two before call time so I can look at the other team's updated stats. Not all players care about that kind of thing. I do. I like to know who my opponent is and what their strengths are.

The coaches will give us plenty of information beforehand, and on the fly as they relay plays. But I like having something to sink my teeth into and mull over while I'm taping my stick. It's a ritual for me, and I don't fuck with my routine.

Mom and Lottie have enough planned for the day to sufficiently drive my dad crazy. If I had to guess, he'll end up parked at a bar with a beer while the women prowl every inch of Pike Place Market.

By the time I drop them at their hotel, Lottie already has their afternoon fully mapped out—down to where they'll eat lunch. She's food-driven when she travels. Just like me, she wants to try the best or most unique things the area has to offer. I'm a little bummed I can't hang out and experience it all with her.

I've always loved watching her try new things—whether with exuberance or trepidation. She doesn't hide her feelings about anything, and I find it refreshing—her lack of pretense, her refusal to be polite just for politeness' sake. It's one of the reasons I think being a father would be fun—kids are mostly the same way. Lottie just hasn't lost that as she's aged.

There are times when I'm with Kit that I feel like I haven't lost it, either. Which should be a good thing, but there's a pit in my stomach telling me I'm going to fuck this up if I'm not careful.

"How many are you missing?"

"Five, now, thanks to last season," Letty says. "The guys all say their teeth are safe as long as I'm still on the team." He smiles so I can see the wide gaps.

"Damn, dude. I've never even heard of a player missing that many."

"I am one of a fucking kind," he says, then puts his flipper in. A lot of guys won't play while wearing their bridge, for fear of damaging it. But Letty looks like a horror show without it, so I get why he does.

"That's the fucking truth," Wallin says. "Poor shithead, don't know how you'll ever get a woman."

"I get more women than you do," Letty argues. "Not as many as Pretty Boy, here. But more than you. That's for damn sure."

"Leave me out of it," I say. "I'm not after numbers."

"How did you find a lady friend already? You've been here for, like, five minutes?" Wallin asks.

"Landed across the street from her."

"That's some fate, right fucking there," Wallin says.

"He moved across the street from Kit Kat," Hugo says with a big frown.

"No shit?" Wallin asks.

"Lucky motherfucker," Hugo mumbles.

"Ah, come on, big guy," Cillian placates the goalie. "One day, you'll be a bride."

"Not likely," he grumps. "I'm doomed to be a bridesmaid forever."

"She's here, by the way," Zander offers, while looking at his cell phone. "Just got here with Willa and Damian."

"Thanks," I say. "She's meeting my family for the first time and I'm not there to introduce her."

"Is it fraying your nerves?" Zan asks.

"A little. I don't want her nerves frayed, you know?"

"I get it. Willa's good at smoothing things over, though."

"Yeah, I'm happy they found each other," I say, lacing up my skate. It hits me that everyone I care about is under this arena roof. My parents, sister, Kit, Isla, and Sadie. All the time Isla and I were acquainted, she didn't come to watch me play. In fact, this is the first time since I went pro that a woman I am dating is going to watch me play. I don't even know if I should label us with that. I mean, I've yet to really take her out. But what do I call her instead of the woman I'm dating? What we shared is much more intimate than any date I could take her on.

It's too soon to call her a girlfriend, I think. Besides, I hate that moniker. It feels juvenile, and if I'm on that level of commitment with anyone, they'll be more than a friend. They'll be a partner.

"I am, too. They're good for each other," he says, staring at me. "You in your head about it?"

"Am I that obvious?"

"A little." He shrugs. "I also know the signs well."

"She makes me see things differently. I don't want to fuck it up."

"She's your rose-colored glasses," Hugo says.

"Such a romantic," Wallin says.

"Fuck you, Axel."

"It was a compliment, Hugo!"

We're interrupted by Coach Cole, who lets us know it's time to take the ice.

When I step out for the puck drop, I get that same sensation—that everything's sharper, clearer, like the world is moving slower than I am. Anticipating the drop, my stick gets to it before Calgary's center, and I pass it behind me with ease.

For the entirety of the first period, I play better than I have in the past couple of seasons. Instinctual more than thoughtful. None of Calgary's players are known for telegraphing their moves, yet I'm reading them like I know their next thought.

It's fucking bizarre. Scary, even—except that it's working. We're up two-nothing when we leave the ice for intermission. I'm riding the adrenaline as we hit the locker room. Usually, I'll have a cup of coffee. I skip that tonight. I'm already amped. Instead, I grab some electrolytes and try to relax.

Wylder pulls up a tablet to check the first-period stats. He takes his role as team captain seriously, which makes him the right choice. He's nothing but encouraging to the guys, even when he's helping them fix whatever's stifling their game.

Isla's the same way. She's lived and breathed hockey for so long that her eye is unmatched. I've always been able to count on her for an honest opinion—about my skating, my shooting, my chemistry with the team. She always had an answer worth hearing.

She and her husband make a good pair. Sadie's a lucky girl.

The second period is much like the first. We score again when Fane nails the five-hole beautifully. Still, Calgary hasn't put a point on the board.

When the third starts, they come out with renewed energy. In hockey, when you're down, you pick fights—either out of frustration or to get the crowd riled up. It's a common enough tactic, and fights can rally your team. So I'm not surprised they're chippy right from the puck drop.

Their defenseman, Preston, takes every chance he gets to check me. It's annoying, but we're winning, and it's not worth giving them penalty points just to hit back—a sentiment the coaches drill into us between every shift.

"Learn to skate, fucker. Then you won't need to lean on me to stay up," I tell him, shoving him off. He skates away after the puck, but as soon as he gets another chance, he's right back on me.

The back-and-forth lasts most of the period. If we're both on the ice, he's pestering me—or anyone else he can. Mostly me, though.

When Fane swats the puck away from Calgary's winger and sends it toward Letty, Preston hops over the boards for a shift. He barrels straight toward me just as Letty passes me the puck.

I shoot at the same moment Preston slams into me, my hip bouncing hard off the boards.

I score—and I couldn't care less—because I'm already driving my elbow into Preston's chest. Then, all hell breaks loose. Both benches pile in, fists flying, gloves dropping, and the shit talk that's been building all game turning into open warfare.

It's fucking glorious.

Not all players enjoy fighting. I'm not one of them. I don't seek it out, but I'm happy to take the opportunity to put someone in their place—and Preston has been begging for it all damn game. There's a sick kind of satisfaction when my fist connects with his jaw.

Hockey rules are weird. We leave it on the ice. Tomorrow, Preston and I could grab a beer and be best buddies. But not now. Now, we get it all out of our systems.

Well, not *all*, in my case. If I unloaded every ounce of frustration, Preston would be nothing more than a bloody pile. My anger over what Kit went through can't be burned off in the arena. Maybe it never will be. I'll have to live with that—because if Kit has to carry it, she shouldn't have to carry it alone.

When the scuffle finally breaks apart—thanks mostly to the brave linesmen—I hobble off to have the trainers check my hip. The sting grows as the adrenaline fades. With only a minute and a half left in the game, I'd be spending the rest of it in the sin bin anyway.

13

KIT

"Porcupines."

"Ooh, that's a good one," I tell Sadie, who is sprawled on my lap, barely awake, but not ready to stop playing our game of quiz. "They're really good swimmers and can live up to twenty years."

"They look like they'd sink."

"I know, but I guess they don't."

"Um, slugs."

"They have four noses."

"That's gross," she says with a giggle.

"What about a slug isn't gross?"

"Nothing," she says, scrunching up her nose. "I think I'm getting a puppy for my birthday. But don't tell my dad I know."

"Okay, the secret is safe with me," I say conspiratorially, as I look up to see Willa, who seems shocked her niece already knows about the apparent surprise.

"I hope it's as cute as Nightmare," she says.

She spent the entire first intermission looking through my pictures of him.

"I'm sure it will be equally as cute."

"I guess it could be ugly, too. But it has to be friends with all the mermaids in the lake, or it can't stay," she says around a yawn.

They live on a floating house and Sadie has decided the lake is inhabited by merfolk.

"I'm sure it will love all your friends, and they will love it, too."

"They better," she says, her head popping up when she spots who's just walked out of the locker room. I expect to see Cillian, but it's not him.

"Tyson!"

Sadie sits up as he approaches, arms outstretched.

"Hey, kiddo," he says, lifting her from my lap. "What are you doing still awake?"

"Waiting for you slowpokes," she says, wrapping her arms around his neck. "You played a great game."

"Thank you," he says, pride lighting his eyes.

Tyson's mom, Francine, shifts next to me. I met his family for the first time tonight. I'd been nervous walking into the arena, but they were so kind and welcoming that I relaxed quickly.

Francine made a point of getting to know me, sitting beside me through the first period and intermission. She peppered me with questions—nothing too personal or hard to answer. When the second period started, she swapped seats with Lottie.

Tyson's sister is amazing—so full of life, I could talk to her for hours. Tyson said we'd get along great. He wasn't wrong. She's sweet, smart, and sassy. All qualities I love in people.

His father, Will, is sweet, too, and was over the moon to see his son play again. He was as exuberant as a kid, and it was contagious. I don't think I've ever had as much fun at a game. Maybe I'm just more invested, now.

Until Tyson took that hit late in the game, we'd all been having the best time. Lottie grabbed my hand when he was checked against the boards. When he started throwing punches, she cheered him on with a zeal I didn't know she had. I couldn't get excited—my anxiety over his potential injury wouldn't let me. Francine's reaction was much the same.

Sadie starts snoring softly on Tyson's shoulder, finally giving in to exhaustion. Isla notices from where she's chatting with a few of the other wives.

"Is she out?"

"Yeah," Tyson answers.

"I'll take her."

"It's fine, I've got her until Cillian comes out. Shouldn't be much longer."

"Are you sure? She's getting so big and heavy."

"I'm sure. I mi…it's fine."

Their conversation continues, Tyson's family joining in as they catch up with Isla. I tune out, letting the buzz of the room distract me from the unwanted thoughts creeping in. I'm not a jealous person—especially not with Isla, who I love like a sister.

Yet, an uncomfortable sensation twists in my stomach. It's new, foreign, and it makes me sad—mainly because I don't know how to process it. Harder still that my first time feeling it is in a room full of people, many of them practical strangers I've only just met.

My fingers tense at my side, the urge to ball them up strong. I tuck them under my thigh, which helps a little. Isla isn't the problem—she's just being herself, friendly and polite. Tyson isn't the problem, either…except my brain keeps trying to pin the unease on him.

When I glance up, I find him watching me. *You good?* he mouths.

At the same time, Willa slips into the empty seat next to me. Her hand rests beside the one I've hidden under my leg. She leans in, shoulder to shoulder.

"Need a break?" she asks quietly.

"I'm not sure," I say, answering her and him at once. "It's probably time to go home."

"Damian and I can take you. We don't need to wait for Zan—his car's here." I'd ridden with them, but the plan was to go home with Tyson, since we're headed to the same place.

"Hey," Tyson cuts in. "I can take you." He reaches out to brush his free hand along the side of my head. I look up at him, and his concern only makes me more uncomfortable—drawing attention to me when I already feel off-balance.

"I don't want to rush you," I say, glancing toward his family.

"It's all good," he says. "I'm spending the whole day with them tomorrow. Let me take you home?"

My instinct is to say no. But it's silly to refuse—especially when Damian and Willa would have to go out of their way. Tyson hasn't done anything wrong. I'm the one feeling weird.

"If you're sure you're ready," I say, linking my pinkie with Willa's before I stand and turn to the Murphy family. "It was so great meeting all of you."

"You, too, sweetheart," Francine says. "I hope we see you again before we head home."

"I'd like that," I tell her.

"We'll make it happen," Tyson's dad says, while Lottie throws her arms around me in a big hug.

"I'm so glad you like my brother," she says, making me grin.

"I like you, too," I say, squeezing her back. "Not just him."

"That makes me happy," she says, as Cillian finally comes out of the locker room and takes Sadie from Tyson. He doesn't show any sign of distress that Isla's ex is cradling his daughter or chatting up his wife.

Further proof that I'm the fucking weirdo here. When the rest of the group starts to say their goodbyes, Willa pulls me aside.

"You okay?"

"Yeah, it's...new. I'm struggling to keep my head on straight, is all."

"Because you met his family?"

"No, that went great. I don't even want to say the words, Willa."

"Why?"

"Because it's stupid to feel jealous. I'm not sure that's even what it is, but I think it is."

"Over his past with Isla?"

"Yes, and I hate myself for it." I drop my head to stare at my scuffed up Doc Martens.

"Oh, honey. It's a normal response," she says. "I even had some moments with Zander and Damian early on because they were already together, and I didn't know if I fit."

"My brain understands that. My stomach has a different opinion."

"It will catch up, I promise."

"I'm putting my faith in that," I say, pointing at her. "And thank you."

"Always, Kit. I love you."

"Love you, too."

Tyson clasps my hand in his and leads me out of the arena to where he's parked. We don't say anything until we're settled in his SUV and driving down the street. He reaches over again, taking my hand in his. I stare at our fingers—his larger and rougher than mine. I like the differences between them, even as they cling together as one.

He probably doesn't realize tonight is the first time a man has ever held my hand—whether to guide me, comfort me, or simply touch me. When he did it leaving the arena, I was surprised by how much I liked the quiet ownership in it. Not that I want to belong to him—or anyone—but it's nice to have someone who wants to look after me.

I should start writing down all the new things happening in my life. I don't want to forget them or take them for granted. They should be cherished. Well, except for dumb stuff, like jealousy. Maybe journaling would help me process it all. I've never been in the habit, but I know it works for some people.

"I'm sorry if that was all too much. My family can be a lot."

"No, they were very kind and welcoming. I didn't feel nervous around them, at all."

"But you were uncomfortable with something. I could see that," he says, his thumb rubbing circles on my skin. "Do you want to talk about it?"

The last thing I want is for Tyson to start seeing me as a patient instead of the woman he's dating—whatever it is we're doing. It's not his job to psychoanalyze me. If I tell him the truth—that I didn't enjoy watching how easily he and Isla communicate—will he think it's endearing or utterly ridiculous? Will I stop being worth the investment?

My naivete threatens to derail us before we even start, and it's so fucking frustrating.

"No," I say bluntly. "Sharing the things I'm least proud of doesn't hold much interest for me. But I also don't want to start this relationship by hiding who I am or what I'm thinking."

"I can appreciate that."

"I'll need you to do the same."

"Yeah, of course," he says, glancing at me briefly. "Do you think I'm hiding something?"

"No," I say, exasperated. I blow out a breath and stare out the window at the blurred lights of passing houses. "That's not what I think. I'm just feeling very unhinged right now."

Resting my forehead against the window, the cool glass feels like a wet washcloth on fevered skin—a balm for an unseen symptom. Tyson doesn't press me for the rest of the drive.

"Let's go get Nightmare," he says when he parks in his driveway.

I unlock my front door and free my fur-baby from his crate. Nightmare yips and circles us until we're outside, so he can relieve himself. Tyson still doesn't say anything—just laughs and plays with him, which hints that he's not upset over my drama. That's a relief; I avoid that kind of tension like the plague.

Still, my squirrel brain jumps from thought to thought—disappointed in myself, imagining how Tyson must hate dealing with me when he has such a high-pressure career.

"Kit," he says, stepping in front of me. "Grab his crate. Come home with me so we can talk you off whatever ledge you're on."

"Thank you," I say, relief washing over me like a hot bath. I run inside and grab a few things for both me and Nightmare, while Tyson entertains him outside, letting him burn off some puppy energy. When I return and lock up, he picks up Nightmare and reaches for my hand. I take it, falling into step a half-pace behind as he leads us safely across the quiet street.

"Do you want anything to drink?"

"No," I answer, stopping just inside his house. I set the small kennel down and drop the tote I'd shoved a change of clothes into.

"You gonna come in?" he asks, setting Nightmare on a blanket on the couch. As usual, the dog spins a few times before curling up with his nose tucked under a paw. "Or do you want to have the conversation over there? I'm good either way."

"Sorry," I sigh, moving to the sofa to sit beside my dog. "I'm not thinking very clearly tonight."

"Okay. Tell me what's going through that brilliant mind—maybe I can help." He sits cross-legged on the floor in front of me, tall enough that we're practically eye level. The longer I look into his hazel eyes, the more comfortable I get with the idea of opening up to him. Tyson is the deep end; I just need to take the plunge.

"I was jealous of one of my best friends tonight. It was one of the most awful things I've ever experienced," I blurt, quick and sharp. He blinks, processing.

"Do you mean Isla?" he asks, his brow furrowing. I nod.

"Of Isla and me?"

"You're so easy with them—Isla and Sadie."

"Am I not easy with you? Because if I'm not, it's only because you make me nervous." He plays with the laces of my boot. It's the first time I've seen him do something that reminds me of a coping mechanism I would employ myself. A focal point for anxious energy is what my grandmother would say.

"How do I make you nervous?" I ask, the thought never having crossed my mind before.

"Baby, by being you," he says, resting his chin on my knee. "You don't understand how great you are, Kit. Or how stunning. You make me feel like a teenager again, tripping over my feet to impress you, all while knowing I never could."

"How is that even possible? I've seen the types of women you've been with. Beautiful, confident. Sexual," I add. "I can't compare."

"You're right, there is no comparison," he says. "You outshine them all."

"I don't know how to believe that," I say as my cheeks feel warm. *Am I blushing?* "I'd never felt jealous before, Tyson. It scared me."

"I can understand that. It's going to take time, Kit. For you to trust me, for you to see that I'm a loyal guy," he says. "We have time."

"What if I don't want to waste any more of it? I've lost so much already."

"What does that mean?"

"What those other women have…what Isla has, or even Willa…I want that. I want their confidence. To be able to stand by your side and not be the strange girl, but the accomplished woman. I don't want to see myself as less than them."

"You aren't, Kit." He rubs his hand along my thigh. "Not even close."

"In some ways, I am. I don't want to fear that anymore." What I don't say is that I don't want to be a project for him, or something he works for. Those words stay sealed behind my lips, because I know enough of him to know he'll take that as me wanting to have sex for him.

That's not what I'm doing.

This is for me. He's the first man who's made me feel safe going there, and I don't want to waste that, either. Even if we don't work out, if this crashes and burns, at least I'll have had that.

"What are you saying?"

"Results of studies vary, depending on age and region, but most current data shows sexlessness is on the rise. I don't want to be in that statistic," I say, dropping my forehead to rest on his. "I don't want to wait anymore."

"That is not what I expected to happen tonight," he says, his eyes wide with shock.

"Welcome to my brain," I say.

"It goes from nervously jealous to confidently horny in a matter of minutes?" His lips twitch before he smiles.

"It does tonight, I guess," I say sardonically.

"Can I make a confession?"

"I'd love to not be the only one."

"You being jealous is sexy as fuck. I mean, I'm sorry it overwhelmed you, but it's a God damned turn-on."

"So, we're both horny?"

"I always am around you. I do my best not to show it," he says, scooting closer and wrapping his arms around me so his hands rest on my lower back.

"Could you maybe start showing it? I think I'd like that. It would help."

"You'll tell me if it isn't helpful, yeah?" Again, I nod. "And you'll tell me if things go too fast, or too far?"

"I will." It's my turn to press a kiss on him. I place one on the corner of his mouth, then the center. Slowly but chaste.

"Can I propose an idea?"

"Of course. This is a group project, after all," I answer, and he laughs.

"I propose that we don't set expectations for tonight. Maybe we start with getting naked and we see where that takes us."

"By us, you mean me?"

"I do."

"Start with a naked play date," I muse. "Without the expectation of fornication. But with the hope."

"Definitely with hope," he agrees, before grasping the nape of my neck and pushing his tongue between my lips.

Fuck, he tastes amazing.

14

TYSON

F uck, she tastes better than the top-shelf bourbon. I push my tongue further, and she wraps her arms around my neck, settling into my lap. Her legs wind around my waist, never separating her lips from mine.

Her eagerness makes it hard to remember our circumstances. As terrified as I am of rushing her, I'm equally determined not to deny her anything she wants. It's a tightrope, but I don't mind walking it for her.

I do hate that she got in her feels about Isla, earlier, though. I'm the asshole for not being more careful. Missing Isla and Sadie is something I still struggle with—not because I'm in love with my ex, but because we had more than just sex. We were friends. That's what I miss.

But nothing like I'd miss a life without Kit's perfect body grinding on me the way it is right now. She's taking the lead, and I have every intention of letting her—regardless of how out of the norm that is for me. My cock hardens to steel under her rhythmic movements.

Every mewl she makes tests my resolve further. I want her naked, but need it to be at her pace. Feeling her skin to skin is something I'd kill for right now.

As if she hears me, she tugs at the buttons of my shirt, and we separate just long enough to pull it the rest of the way off.

"I didn't expect to love kissing," she pants.

"You didn't?"

"No. I thought it would, I don't know…smell or something," she says casually—as if she isn't pulling off her top and undoing her bra. I laugh, right up until the straps slip off her shoulders, dropping the rest of the fabric and exposing ample breasts with pert, dark nipples.

"Hell, Kit. You're a goddamn goddess."

She stills, her eyelashes fluttering like she's trying to process the words.

"Do you need me to put you in front of a mirror so you can see for yourself?"

"No, thank you," she says, scrunching her nose.

"Then, I need you to admit you're beautiful." I press my lips to her clavicle. "That you're the sexiest woman in all of Seattle." I trail my mouth lower, brushing the skin of her breast. Her chest hitches. "Do you believe it, Kit?"

The wait for her answer is excruciating. The need to suck her into my mouth is as urgent as my next heartbeat.

"I've never believed that before," she says, meeting my eyes. "But I can see the truth on your face."

Her fingers tremble as they brush my cheek, then tangle in my hair the moment I take her nipple into my mouth. The pull is delicious—the perfect mix of pain and pleasure—as my tongue flicks her stiff peak.

Her moan encourages me, but we're still wearing too much.

"Upstairs," I mumble, shifting her in my arms so I can stand. "We need fewer clothes, more skin."

"Yes, please," she says, burying her face in the crook of my neck. She kisses and tastes, sending chills down my spine. If this were any other woman, I'd stop halfway up the stairs and fuck her until we couldn't tell where my body ended and hers began.

Instead, I make it all the way to my bed, setting her down gently before kneeling to unlace the boots she's still wearing. When I glance up, she's watching me with a soft smile—bare breasts unapologetically on display, no hint of distress or embarrassment.

"Hey, beautiful," I say, untying the second boot and tossing it aside.

"Hey."

"Can I take your pants off?"

"No. But you can take yours off," she answers with a sly smile.

Standing, I kick off my shoes and waste no time undressing. When I shed my boxers, her cheeks flush.

"I love that you like looking at me, Kit." I stroke my cock, her eyes following the motion like she's studying for the biggest exam of her life.

"Do you want to look at me, too?"

"Whenever you're ready for that," I say, even though my head is screaming *fuck yes*.

"Can I try something, first?" She nibbles her lip, her fingers doing that nervous tensing that's always her first tell.

"Sure," I say.

She immediately slides off the bed and kneels at my feet.

"You don't have to do that, Kit."

"Are you saying no? Or are you saying that for my benefit?" she asks, tilting her head.

"I'm fully consenting," I clarify. "To whatever you want to do to or with me. I'm…adventurous in bed. But I don't want you thinking anything is expected—especially something that won't bring you the same amount of pleasure it'll bring me."

"How do I know it won't bring me pleasure if I don't try it?"

"Okay," I say. "That's a fair point. But I can guarantee it won't be *as* good for you as it will for me."

"Okay," she mimics. "You probably never go down on a woman, then, right? Because that can't be as good for you as it is for her."

Well, damn.

"Your brain is even sexier than your body—and that's saying something, because you're hot as fuck," I tell her, pointing down at her.

"Thank you," she preens. "Now, let me do what I want before all this conversation kills the mood."

"By all means, proceed," I say, trying not to laugh. I've had fun sex before—plenty of it—but never like this. Never where the talking itself was so…mood-enhancing. Kit couldn't turn me off if she actively tried.

Her fingertips trail up my cock—soft, tentative. At the tip, she rubs around it, familiarizing herself.

I might die. Right here. Right now.

This will be what takes me out.

I hold still, though it takes every ounce of willpower. I can't stop the involuntary twitch of my muscles or the precum that escapes—which only seems to fascinate her. She drags her thumb through it, wetting it, then sucks her thumb into her mouth. I groan.

"It doesn't taste like I thought it would," she murmurs, almost to herself. Then, her gaze locks on mine. "I like it."

Fuck. My. Life.

Her head dips, stopping less than an inch away. A small puff of air escapes her before she licks the full length of my cock—base to tip.

"Fucking hell, Kit."

"Good or bad?"

"So damn good." She traces the motion again, and this time, when she reaches the tip, she wraps her mouth around it. The hum she makes almost robs me of all control—I nearly thrust forward.

"Jesus, Kit. I'm trying really hard, here."

She snorts softly and takes me deeper. After a few fumbles, she finds her rhythm with shallow bobs, then gradually pushes a little farther, a little deeper. My hands lock behind my head, every muscle tight as I fight to keep from spilling down her throat. My stamina tonight is non-fucking-existent.

Then, she hums again.

"Kit, I can't hold off," I warn, trying to pull back. She chases me, making a disapproving sound before sucking harder. There's no holding back, now—the first spurt escapes. Aside from a slight jerk of surprise, she doesn't flinch. She swallows the next, then pulls back just enough for the rest to paint her chest in hot ribbons.

I'm spellbound, watching her smear my release across her skin. When I'm spent, she licks my tip clean.

Pretty sure I just fell in love with Kit Ashcroft.

I shake the thought away. There are a million reasons to fall for Kit—her fascination with blowjobs ranks low on the list.

"It was more than I expected," she says, demure as she looks up through her lashes. I offer my hand and help her to her feet.

"Was it okay?"

"It was everything," I tell her. "You are everything."

Palming her cheek, I kiss her, not caring that she tastes like me. It only adds to the heat between us.

"Can we still have naked time?"

"Whatever you want, Kit. Whatever you need."

I duck into the bathroom to dampen a washcloth. When I return, she's still bare-breasted, unconcerned about the mess. Of all the things that make her squeamish, this isn't one.

"Will you undress me? I want you to do it," she says, her voice trembling ever so slightly.

I take my time—hands on her waist, then her hips, fingers playing along the waistband of her pants before I finally unfasten them. I ease them down a couple of inches at a time, murmuring her name and soft affirmations.

"Anything you want me to do, Kit, just tell me."

"Like my own personal sex slave?" she asks with a grin.

"Exactly like that." And I mean it. She could ask me for the vilest thing and I'd comply.

When her pants hit her ankles, she steps out and covers herself with her hands. Plain black cotton—practical, like her.

"I don't shave it," she says.

"Good."

"Really?"

"Really, Kit. I want a woman. *This* woman."

"But all the women in porn…"

"Are there for the pleasure of creepy-ass men who can't get women in the real world," I cut in.

She grins.

"What?"

"Nothing," she says with a shake of her head. "You're just cute."

"Cute?"

"Sweet," she amends. "Handsome, gentle, sexy, and you have the best cock I've ever seen."

"How many cocks have you seen, Kit?" I tease, brushing my nose against hers.

"Enough," she whispers. "I watch a lot of pornography."

Blood surges south at the thought of her touching herself to other people fucking.

"I'm dying to get my hands on you right now."

"Then, put your hands on me, Tyson."

She pushes her underwear past her hips and kicks them aside. I start at her chin, trailing my fingers down her throat, over the swell of her breast, across the flat of her stomach. Her skin pebbles; her muscles twitch. She doesn't pull away. She touches me, too, mirroring my movements, exploring, familiarizing herself with me.

I pause just above the apex of her thighs. We're both trembling—me from adrenaline and lust, her for reasons I can't quite name.

"Are you ready?"

"I'm eager," she says, guiding my hand through her soft curls until my fingers rest on her clit. "Oh, God."

"Keep looking at me, Kit," I tell her, cupping her temple with my free hand as my fingers begin to tease the most sensitive part of her. She pants, eyes glazing with lust.

"Stay with me."

"I'm here. I'm here. It feels…so much."

I slide lower, dipping one finger inside her—just enough for a taste.

"Tyson."

It's a plea for more. I press my thumb to her mouth until she pulls it in, then add a second finger inside her drenched heat. She rocks on my hand, her teeth biting into the meat of my thumb, and my cock throbs in response.

"Can I taste you, Kit? Can I make you come?"

"Please," she cries. "Please, Tyson."

I scoop her into my arms and lay her on the bed. Her hair fans around her like a dark halo—an angel with a sinful aura. Except there's nothing sinful about Kit. She's everything good and precious.

I adjust her legs, spreading them until my shoulders fit between. My hands cup behind her knees, lifting them.

"You move however makes you feel good, okay?" She nods. This will be the first time she doesn't have to bring herself over the edge. I'll only be satisfied if I blow her mind. "Dig your heels into my back, pull my hair, bite my hand—whatever you need to get what you want. I can take it. I want to take it."

She nods again, and I settle between her thighs. I inhale her scent before pressing my thumb to her folds and opening her up for my first taste. She's warm, sweet—and she jumps when I flick her clit.

One heel digs into my back, giving her leverage to grind against my mouth as I lick and fuck her with my tongue.

The way she's responded tonight is astonishing. I'd have given her all the time in the world. After what she's been through, I expected her to be timid, even afraid. Instead, she's been nothing but brave—bold in reclaiming her life.

That I get to be part of that? It wrecks me in the best possible way.

Stiffening my tongue, I fuck her with new zeal, circling her clit with my thumb.

"Tyson, I…I'm close."

I hum into her, pleased that she's nearly there. I pull at her breast, and her hips rock up. Over and over. Then, her palm lands on the back of my head, pressing my mouth to her pussy, and I give her everything I can until she cries out her pleasure. I don't stop licking, sucking, touching her.

"Oh my fucking God, oh my God," she chants until her orgasm subsides and the same sobbing laughter as last time kicks in.

"Hey, hey." Crawling up her body, I cradle her against my chest. "I've got you."

"I'm okay," she says between hiccupping breaths. "I'm sorry, I didn't know. I didn't know, Tyson."

"Didn't know what?"

"That it could be so good. That it could be fun," she says into my neck. "I'm so mad about that."

"You're mad it was fun?" I ask, already knowing what she means but wanting her to keep talking. Wanting to keep her present in the moment and not slipping into some lonely place inside her head.

"Mad that I've missed out on so much of it from being afraid."

"That's not your fault, Kit. It's a natural response," I say, turning my face to hers. "I'll help you make up for lost time."

Her hands snake up between us and cup my cheeks as she stares at me, her eyes bouncing between mine.

"Thank you, Tyson," she says softly. "Thank you for being everything I need and not running away from my messiness."

"Never, Kit. I'm never running away," I promise. "Besides, I like getting dirty."

15

KIT

We fell asleep gazing into one another's eyes like a couple of lovesick goobers. It was the best night of my life, after I came down from the rabid thought processes at the arena. It's easy to believe that every new step on my sexual journey is going to be the best time, beating out the last. Because I thought masturbating with him wouldn't be topped so easily.

In that, I had all the control, which is what I thought I needed for so long. Last night, though, I gave that to him and realized every orgasm I've had before was a microdose in comparison.

Analyzing that…it should mean that when we make it far enough for his penis to enter my vagina it will, once again, be the best night of my life. Or maybe morning. Because as I lie here, waking from a few hours of great, deep sleep, I'm horny again.

If his bulging dick is any indication, he's right there with me.

The blankets have been kicked off. Probably because our bodies were so wrapped up with each other, we didn't need additional warmth. Even though a chill settles on my skin, now, I don't pull them back up. The view is very good. Tyson's body is unreal.

There's a bruise on his side, fresh from last night's game. It shouldn't, but it turns me on more, the proof of his physicality and that he doesn't make a fuss about it.

Willa always comments about Zander's "hockey thighs." I get it now. Tyson's are thick, tight, and toned. As is the rest of his body. Nothing about him is small or weak. While that would have scared me before, it never has with him. Instead, it makes me feel safer.

Tyson has become a safe space. I'm not sure he understands how profound that is. Perhaps he does, since I think he's safety for his sister, as well.

It's been a long time since I've felt safe. Or bold. I feel bold right now.

I also really need to fucking pee.

Sneaking out of bed as carefully as I can, I manage it without waking Tyson. After a potty and a toothbrushing, I stare at myself in the mirror. It's not right that we don't appear differently after big, life-altering moments. Like, my smile should be brighter, my hair shinier, or my boobs bigger.

It's not only that I've climbed a rung higher on the sexual ladder. Honestly, that's the least important thing that happened last night. The substantial change is what happened inside me. My inner child stood up to one of the monsters under her bed. There is more to the war, but I won one battle.

It's something to be proud of, and I am.

Tyson has a discarded T-shirt on the floor of the bathroom. It smells like him, so I throw it on, and I ride a high as I quietly walk downstairs and let Nightmare out for his own potty break. It's early still, barely four in the morning. After he's done his business, I pilfer through the kitchen, looking for something to feed my little buddy. Leave it to a pro athlete to have copious amounts of protein cooked up and ready to grab. Picking some chicken breast, I shred it up and give it to Nightmare, who happily scarfs it down. Before I head back upstairs, I grab my cell phone from the bag I discarded by the front door.

At the end of the bed, I watch his chest rising and falling, like I'm a sparkly vampire in that one young adult book. If it was later in the morning,

I'd consider waking him and asking him to…how do you ask someone for sex? He needs more sleep, though. I don't know how professional athletes keep up with their schedules, let alone their training routines.

When I get back on the bed, I keep as much distance as I can. Not an easy task, since his large frame is sprawled in the center of the bed. Making sure my volume is silenced, I pull up a favorite porn site of mine. It's produced by a woman, so it isn't filled with videos of women who look too young to be legal or videos that should be reported to authorities.

I'm curious if my preferences have, or will, change. They should, I think. I mean, I imagine that's how kinks evolve. And while my preferences haven't changed so much since I first started watching porn, they have shifted some. The first time I watched anything, it was a man pleasuring himself. That's still something that turns me on, but eventually, I branched out to couples. Nothing extreme, or hardcore, or with multiple partners.

Vanilla, mostly.

There have been many times I've almost clicked on categories outside of that, but I wasn't confident in my own mental state to be able to handle it. Since I've only ever watched it by myself, there was never anyone there that would be able to help calm me if I got too anxious watching it.

Glancing over at Tyson, I tempt myself with the idea. Scrolling through my phone, I pick a video I normally wouldn't. It's in the "rough" category. I'm not sure I fully understand what that means, but I won't ever know if I don't look. It starts off the same as so many do, with the normal foreplay of him undressing her. Except, once he has her naked, his hand finds purchase on her neck. Not heavily, or overly forceful, but with enough directness to guide her to the bed, where he lays her down with her head hanging over the side. Quickly, the man unfastens his pants and pulls his dick out. The woman opens her mouth for him, and he begins thrusting in. It's deep and quick, but at the same time, he leans forward to place his mouth on her pussy.

I turn my phone, so the video takes up the whole screen; I want a closer view. He's heavy atop her, but he also pauses his fucking of her mouth on occasion to let her swallow and catch air. That makes it hotter, him showing his concern while also getting what he wants. One-sided sex isn't anything I ever want to experience again.

Tyson trying to talk me out of a blow job last night only made him more endearing. The truth of it is, I enjoyed it. Once I got past being self-conscious about it, anyway. I'm sure he's received amazing oral before, I know I can't compare, but I still made him come. That alone was a huge boost to my confidence.

He's still asleep when I scroll to a different video. Then, to another and another. I analyze each of them, looking less for my own pleasure and more to understand or learn techniques, something that never occurred to me before, since I never expected to have a partner.

By the sixth or seventh video, I'm finding a few things that intrigue me. One in particular. It's another unexpected realization.

"That's the best one yet," Tyson says next to me, startling me so much that I drop my phone on the bed between us. He laughs deeply. "Sorry, didn't mean to scare you."

"I thought you were still asleep."

"Been awake for the last few videos, you pervert." He rolls toward me, handing me back my phone.

"I couldn't sleep," I say, as if that's enough of an explanation for why I'm watching porn in bed next to him.

"You should have woken me up, I'd have watched with you." He snakes an arm around my waist and pulls me into him, back to front.

"You need sleep. I was only trying to stay turned on until you woke up, but I kind of fell into a rabbit hole."

"Again, you should have woken me up. I'm happy to be of service," he says, kissing the back of my neck. He pulls at my collar, baring my shoulder so he can press kisses there. "Did you see something you liked?"

"Besides the naked hockey player in bed with me? Yes, I think so."

"What was it?"

I roll around to face him, nervous to say it. Not sure why I liked what I did, or what it says about me that I did.

"I like when he fucks her," I say timidly. "As opposed to when she fucks him. Does that make sense?"

"Absolutely, it does."

"Then, why do I feel weird about it?"

"Maybe because you're looking at it the wrong way," he says after a moment of thought. "It's not about him controlling the experience, it's about him putting in the work."

"Oh, maybe you're right," I say, and ponder what he's said. Every orgasm I experienced prior to Tyson was solely by me putting in all the work. It is nice to relinquish that, to have someone who wants to bring me pleasure themselves. "Will you…" As bold as I feel, I still can't say the words.

"Fuck you like that?" he offers easily.

I nod, several times. More times than necessary—I only stop when I start pressing kisses below his chin, the stubble there tickling my lips.

"Yes. The same rules apply, okay? Say the word and I stop whatever I'm doing that makes you uncomfortable."

"Okay."

"We haven't talked about protection, which, in hindsight, seems fucking stupid."

"I have an IUD that I hate with the fiery passion of the depths of hell, but it serves its purpose," I say, leaving out the part that it's protection against predators, not accidents on my part.

"I'll still use a condom. I haven't been tested in a few weeks."

"A few weeks?" I crinkle my nose.

"It's part of our routine testing with the league," he says. "I promise, I'm not that big of a slut."

"I watch *Shoresy*, you're all sluts," I tease, also remembering how many women I saw leaving here before he started showing interest in me.

"She's brilliant, beautiful, and she watches *Shoresy*," he mutters, reaching behind him to dig through his nightstand. "I'm done for."

"Is it weird that we talk so much? I mean, during sexy times."

"I don't think so. It's different, but I don't get turned off by it. The opposite, actually. I like that you're vocal," he says, then rips the condom wrapper open with his teeth. He doesn't pull it out or put it on, yet, just readies it while he watches me watch him. "I want you wet, Kit. Soaking."

Jesus. If I wasn't already, those words would have gotten me there.

"Not a problem," I mumble, my voice raspy.

"Let me see," he says. His hand snakes under the shirt I wear, landing on my hip, first, then traveling to my center. Instinctively, I spread my legs wider for him to dip a finger in, then another as he curses. "Fucking hell, I love how responsive you are."

"I've been awake with your hard dick for the last ninety minutes, how else was I supposed to respond?"

"If I get my wish, always exactly like this," he says, coating my clit with my own wetness as he rubs a finger around it. "Kiss me, Kit."

He leans down, stopping when our noses touch, and waits for me to close the distance. As soon as I do, his tongue dips between my lips. He's warm, soft, and slick. Our tongues fight a battle, neither winning nor losing. All the while, Tyson continues to play with my pussy. When I can't take any more, I moan and hike my leg up over his hip. He rolls us so I'm atop him, propping me up to sit high on his chest, his hands busy behind me, sliding the condom down into place.

"Lean down for me, Kit. Your eyes stay with me, okay?"

As instructed, I run my hands up his sculpted chest and over his shoulders until they land on either side of his face.

"You ready?"

"More than," I say truthfully, even as my eyes fill with unwanted water. "Please, Tyson."

His hands hold the globes of my ass, positioning me where he wants me. Then, I feel his tip at my entrance. I gasp. Not in fear—in anticipation. I don't look away as he inches farther in. Slowly.

Excruciatingly slowly.

"Tyson."

"I'm with you, Kit." He presses kisses all over my face until he's in as far as he can go. "Is it okay?"

"No, it's more than that. It's so much more." My voice shakes, a tear spills out. "Move, now."

"Whatever you want," he says through a wide smile. Then, he slides out almost all the way. I clench around him, not wanting to lose the connection. Then, he slides back in, never breaking eye contact. Keeping us connected in every way. His hips thrust further each time, slowly increasing his speed. Still, he holds me steady.

Doing all the work.

It's exactly what I asked for. It's everything I wanted. The friction as he glides in and out of me is amazing, and yet, not enough. Pulling at the T-shirt, I yank it over my head and throw it…I don't know where, but away.

Skin. I need all of him pressed against all of me.

"Talk to me, Kit," he says. "What do you feel?"

"Good. It's so good, Tyson."

He rolls us again. Laying me on my back, he sits up on his heels. Hands travel over my breasts, down my belly, around my hips.

"The way you take me," he says quietly, almost as if he's talking to himself. "Goddamned beautiful, Kit." He looks from where he's fucking me, to my face—it's overwhelming. I want to look away, to hide from the connection that feels too intense. But I don't. I've been doing that for too long.

I'm stronger, now. Braver.

"I need to move, too."

"Do it, Kit. Get what you need."

Moving my hips, I match his flow, and we move together.

A dance, delicate and beastly. Graceful but instinctual. I let my mind go and just…be. Just movement. Sex. Sensuality. Touch. Fucking.

When I reach above my head to grab on to his headboard, he clasps one hand on my breast and the other to my clit. That spot he's getting so familiar with.

"Gorgeous cunt, gorgeous body. I'm fucking a goddess. You gonna come for me, Kit? Explode all over my cock?"

"Oh my God," I cry.

His dirty mouth does me in, and the next time he applies pressure on my clit; it sends me over the cliff. There is no breathing, no air, no words.

Just a pulsing blood rush staccato. Every muscle tenses; time stands still as I become tiny bits of energy floating in the ether.

Tyson grunts as he starts to follow, and pulls me back into my body, back to the moment and reality. I pant through it, catching my breath and losing it again when he comes into focus. Bliss veils him, like he's experiencing the same ecstasy I am. That doesn't seem possible. He's done this so much more than me.

"Is it like that every time?" I ask when I'm able to find my voice again.

Tyson falls alongside me, removing the condom and tying the end before he drops it to the floor.

"No, but it should be," he says, craning his head to look at me. "You're amazing."

"I didn't do much."

"Don't sell it short. You vanquished a demon," he tells me, his own eyes misting up.

"Thank you for being my sword," I say, then wince. "This is a really weird time for me to be imagining a *Dungeons and Dragons* scenario. Sorry."

I bury my face in his laughing chest, and he holds me until I doze off.

16

KIT

F ive days later, I still haven't told Willa. It didn't seem right texting her that I finally had sex. Over the years, she's been my biggest cheerleader in gaining confidence and control in my life. She's the only person who knew my desires and my fears. The news deserves to be delivered in person.

Besides, we've both been busy. She's been down in the capitol fighting for a new law to be passed that helps victims of domestic abuse obtain easier restraining orders, while I've been in a two-day online conference for a new data visualization program. It's more complicated and in-depth than what we currently use, but once we've learned it, I think we'll be able to do some cool things with it.

I haven't seen much of Tyson since that morning, either. He spent that day with his family, then, they were on a short road trip. Tonight, he's taking me out on what he's calling our first official date.

It seems unnecessary to me. I mean, we've had sex—we've already put the cart before the horse. He's insistent, though, saying he wants to give me the experiences I never had. Willa thinks I'm not used to the attention or being pampered, so the idea of an extravagant date makes me uncomfortable.

She's right, though I hate admitting that. Mostly because it's a reminder of the years I spent alone, fending for myself, trying to stay quiet and unseen. My father is an angry man, and I was a reminder of the woman who left him. I paid the price for what he perceived as her betrayal. For a long time, I felt betrayed by her, too. As I grew older, I understood why she would want to leave him, and I could no longer blame her. I only wished she had taken me with her.

That isn't a subject I want weighing heavy on me tonight, though. Roughly twenty-five percent of children are raised by single parents. I wasn't an anomaly. Tyson, by being as understanding as he has been, has earned the right to a night with a woman who isn't shrouded in her childhood trauma.

I'm meeting up with Willa today for brunch and shopping, because what the hell do I know about preparing for a date? She says I need a new outfit, but it's mostly just an excuse for us to have some much-needed bestie time.

Walking into Ludi's, my fingers twitch at my side, wanting to clutch up into fists, and I laugh at myself. Willa has never been anything but understanding of me. Yet, I worry that she'll think I've moved too quickly.

Because I worry that I have. Not when I'm with Tyson, but in his absence, my mind wanders and wonders.

I see her at a booth toward the back; she's already got a coffee and an orange juice waiting for me.

"It's like you know me or something," I tease, taking my seat.

"Lucky guess," she says with a wink. "Hi, friend."

"Hey, bestie. Long time, no see."

"It sure as hell feels like it. I love my guys, but I miss hanging out with you every day, too."

"Right? It's not the same, now that I can't walk down the hall to pester you about some silly new thing I learned."

"Nothing you learn is silly," she says as the server comes by to take our food orders. We both order the Ube pancakes. "My knowledge of weird facts is definitely lacking since I moved into Damian's house."

"But your orgasms aren't, that has to make up for it."

"It sure helps," she says, looking at me curiously. "How's *your* orgasm situation?"

"Jeez, is it written on my forehead?"

"Kit," she whisper-shouts. "How far have you gone?"

"All the way," I say, grimacing because I sound like a teenager.

"Oh. My. God. I should have ordered champagne with our orange juice! Tell me everything," she says. "Well, not everything, everything, but you know, *everything*."

"It was the morning after the game," I start, then stop, not knowing exactly how much to tell.

"Girlfriend," she says, sitting back against the booth. "That was *days* ago. You've been holding out on me."

"How do you type that out on a text? It seems too, I don't know, important or deep."

"It is, you're absolutely right. But I would have come over with shrimp fried rice or something."

"Is shrimp fried rice the meal for having sex for the first time?"

"I don't know." She shrugs. "It's always a good time for shrimp fried rice; seems appropriate."

"Nothing about that man is shrimpy."

"What the hell is happening here? You're making sex jokes before me, now?" She grins conspiratorially. "That means it was good. Which, yeah, obviously it was; otherwise, you'd have called. Right? You would have called me if it went badly?"

"I would have. But it didn't." I pause, taking a drink of my coffee. There's something about diner coffee that I always love. At home, I want the good shit. Out for breakfast, I want it black and bitter. "Tyson was great. Patient and caring, he listened to what I wanted and needed."

"And he delivered?"

"He definitely did," I say, feeling the blood rush to my cheeks.

"Don't be embarrassed or shy about it," Willa consoles. "It's hard to be assertive and ask for what we want, but you did that. And with a man that knows what he's doing, no less. Be proud of that."

"I am," I promise her. "I guess I'm just struggling to wrap my head around it all—it's been something of a whirlwind."

"Falling in love with the right person should always be a whirlwind."

"I didn't say anything about love," I say with a nervous laugh.

"No, but I don't think you'd have gone this far if there wasn't some deep affection happening already."

"We don't know each other well enough for all that."

"What do you know about him?"

I know he grew up in the suburbs around Vancouver. That he was immersed in hockey from the age of four, even though nobody in his family had ever played before. He loved peewee but hated junior hockey because the boys often had overinflated egos and what Tyson called "toxic behavior." He hated when they had to stay in hotels, and loved billeting because it felt more like home, and he often missed his family.

He loves baseball—the slow pace, being vastly different from hockey, intrigues and relaxes him. When gaming, he's aggressively competitive, especially against assholes he encounters. He plays *Stardew Valley* in co-op with Lottie, which is the most endearing thing I've learned about him to date.

When he was eight, he broke his arm riding his bicycle and thought it meant he'd never play hockey again. In school, despite his busy elite athletic career, he always received the highest grades. He's a perfectionist and loves challenges, yet doesn't hold others to the same standards he holds himself.

He's kind, most of all. He cares about others.

"I guess I know more than I thought," I say after several moments of her patiently waiting.

"And what does he know about you?"

That question is both easier and more complicated. He knows less about me than I do about him. My childhood wasn't filled with happy memories or stories of family vacations. I'd never left the state of Maine until I moved away for college.

"Not as much," I say, feeling somewhat defeated. "I don't like bringing down the mood."

"Honey, that's not what would happen." She reaches across the table to hold my hand. "Not if he cares about you, and I'm guessing he does."

"I know he does. It's the kind of guy he is," I say. "What I don't know is if it will last—if it can when I'm like an orphaned baby bird learning to fly and he's the stranger that happened by at the right time."

"That's not fair to either of you, Kit. Yes, this is all uncharted water for you. And, of course, there is fear involved. But I know Tyson well enough to believe he wouldn't be taking you out tonight if he was only fucking you as a favor. And I think you know that, too."

"Ugh, you're right. You're right," I concede. "My self-deprecation is at an all-time high. I'm overthinking all the things I've already overthought four times. It's hard to understand what he sees in geeky, inexperienced me."

"I get that. Except, I imagine most women who meet professional athletes feel the same way. Isla and I grew up in this world, and even I was weird around Zan when I learned he wasn't gay and was maybe interested in me," she says. She had nerves and uncertainty—I remember that. Not quite on my level, but most people aren't at my scale of social dysfunction. "You might need a confidence boost, is all. Well, and time to adjust. Sharing your life with a partner is a big change."

"A confidence boost? That sounds helpful. What store sells those?"

"I don't know, but we'll find it," she promises.

"Fucking hell, woman. Warn a man before you open the door looking like that," Tyson says when he picks me up for our date. This is the first time he's seeing me dressed up in anything but casual wear. Admittedly, I went for a sexier look than I'd normally choose for a night out. My new dress falls only a handful of inches below my ass. Though the green floral fabric has full-length sleeves, it's balanced with an extreme plunging neckline. I decided to use boob tape instead of a bra. Besides the dress, I splurged on a pair of delicate lacy panties—something I've never done before. But knowing that I have them on is the exact bolster to my ego that I needed, like my own little hidden secret waiting to be exposed at the right time.

He presses a kiss to my temple. "You look amazing."

"Thank you," I say. "Is it too much? You didn't give me much to go by." He was adamant about surprising me. I went for dressy, but I still have my Doc's on my feet.

"It's going to be hard keeping my hands off you, but it's perfect."

"I never said you had to keep your hands to yourself, sir."

"Yes, ma'am," he says in a deep, growly voice. Then, his mouth meets mine, his palm on my ass drawing me in and up to him. "Hi."

"Hi," I say, a little dazed from the searing kiss—something I'm still not used to. Hopefully, I never am. I'd like it to always be this exciting and fun. "I feel like a teenager every time you kiss me. Like I want to pull you to the couch and have a make-out session."

"If we weren't on a timeline, I'd happily indulge you. But we are, so your insatiable libido is going to have to wait," he says. "Do you have a coat? You'll probably want one for part of the night."

"Is insatiable bad?" I ask honestly, moving to grab my long teddy coat. It's a bit ridiculous and over the top, but it's like wearing a hug—and who doesn't need that from time to time?

"Your best friends are with hockey players. You have to know insatiable is the best thing," he says, taking my coat and helping me into it. "This is great—it's like a Snuggie. If it goes missing, don't come looking for it at my house."

"Have you ever dressed in drag?" I ask as he loads me into the passenger seat.

"I was Lady Gaga once for Halloween," he says as he settles in the driver's seat.

"You were? Do you have pictures?"

"Yeah, a few years back, I copied her little hooded red hot suit," he says, pulling his phone out of the center console and handing it to me. "Look through the pictures—it's on there somewhere."

I'm awestruck that he so easily hands me his phone to pilfer through. It's surprisingly well organized, every app in a neat folder. When I click on Photos, those are all sorted into folders, as well. I scroll past *family*, *promo*, *ice time*, almost pausing on one titled *Isla and Sadie*. But I think better of that—besides, I wasn't invited to look through everything. Not explicitly, anyway. Eventually, I get to one called *holidays*. Sure enough, there are several photos of him hamming it up in a red bodysuit with fishnet stockings stretched to an inch of their life over his huge thighs.

"You look good as a woman."

"I appreciate that," he says with a laugh. "It also made me appreciate all the shit you women do on a daily basis, because nothing I had on was comfortable. At all."

Flipping through a few more shots, I land on one that looks like he's mid-twerk.

"This one is hot as hell, Tyson. Kind of flooding my basement right now."

"Oh my fucking God," he says around a cackle. "How the hell do you simultaneously crack me up and make my dick hard?"

"Men get something like a dozen erections in a day. I don't think I'm accomplishing much," I say, pausing on a picture of Lottie dressed up as Buffy the Vampire Slayer.

"I assure you, that's not accurate data, in my case."

"More or less?"

"Less. Definitely less. Can you imagine if the whole team got that many in a day? We'd never win a game, let alone get through a practice."

"You'd have to have circle jerks every intermission," I say, and again, he laughs. "Have you ever done that? I always imagined that was a thing in sports, since you guys practically live with each other all season."

"Have I ever jacked off in front of other guys?"

"Yeah. It's a thing, right? Or are you going to say no and ruin my fantasies?"

"You have fantasies about athletes masturbating together?"

"Not regularly, but a few times, sure," I say, turning to watch him as he drives. He's got the biggest grin—the kind that crinkles at the corners and shows a lot of teeth. Genuine. I like that I amuse him, and not because he's making fun of me. "Guys think about sex a lot; it would only make sense. Not just with athletes—I bet musicians do it, too…all that time spent on tour buses."

"No, I never have, to answer your question. Though, yes, it happens. Especially in juniors. Boys are horny and generally gross," he says. "I'm much more interested in these fantasies of yours."

"Men masturbating is a favorite," I say. "You probably get told this often, but you have a great smile."

"I don't think anyone but my mom has ever said that to me. And she's got a big bias." My bias is running deep these days, too. But I keep that to myself, afraid to let him know how connected I feel—how dependent I can see myself becoming on his easy, calming charm. Willa reminded me earlier to not overthink the *what ifs*, so I try to force out the thoughts of how great a partner, a husband, a father Tyson could be to someone. The bond he has with Sadie lets me know that's something he'd want. But I don't know that *wife* or *mother* are in the cards for me. I don't know how to be either of those, never having had examples.

"I smile more around you than I do most others, though," he says, pulling into a parking lot at the marina.

"Are we going out on a boat?"

"Yeah. I checked with Willa to make sure that wasn't something you'd hate."

"I was with that traitor all day and she never said."

"I bribed her with a donation to that women's clinic she's been working with."

"That'd do it," I say. "We normally don't keep secrets."

"A surprise, not a secret. Wait there—I'll come around."

I watch in a bit of disbelief as he comes around to open my door and help me out of the vehicle. In my whole life, I never felt truly cared for. My safety and upbringing were an afterthought for my father—something he felt obligated to do under duress. Fatherhood wasn't natural or innate to him.

My fingers tremble as Tyson takes my hand. He doesn't ask if I'm okay, but his eyes bounce around my face, looking for signs. Stretching to my toes, I press a kiss to his cheek. "Thank you."

"You're welcome."

He leads me by the hand to an actual fucking yacht—not a huge one, but still an expensive vessel.

"I've never been on a boat bigger than a rowboat," I whisper as we near it.

"Really? Not even a ferry?"

"No," I say with a shake of my head. "We have the largest ferry system, and I haven't been on a single one of them."

"Hello, Mr. Murphy, Ms. Ashcroft," a man greets us when we walk up the small ramp to the boat. "I'm Severan, and I'll be making sure you have everything you need this evening."

"Thank you, Severan," Tyson tells him as we follow him to the back of the boat. A table has been draped in white linens, decorated with bursting bouquets of hydrangea, and lit by flickering festoon lighting above.

We sit, and Severan pours wine and points out a card placed between Tyson and me. It's a seven-course pre-determined menu with the chef's name on it—a name even I recognize.

"Tyson, what have you done?"

17

TYSON

"Called in a favor. Wanted it to be special," I say, as if it's no big deal to hire a Michelin-star chef for a date night on a random Thursday. It was simple enough to set up, since Luther is a friend of mine. "Why are you looking at me like that?"

Her eyes are wide, tinged with a sparkle of wetness as the boat starts to troll away from the dock.

"I'm a little overwhelmed."

"Why?" I ask, palming her cheek to keep her looking at me.

"It's really nice."

"Nobody has ever spoiled you," I say. No point in asking, since it's so obviously true.

"The Coles have taken me on a couple of vacations with them," she says. "I think those count as spoiling."

"Where to?" I ask, but Kit waits to answer until after Severan has come up with our first course and explained what it is. It's tiny, bite-sized onion cakes that look like miniature works of art.

"Costa Rica and New Orleans," she says, then takes her first bite. "Holy shit, Tyson!"

"Luther's brilliant, right?" I ask, and she hums her agreement, taking another bite. I keep her talking about the vacations with the Coles over the next course. She loved both places for different reasons. In Costa Rica, she was obsessed with the titi monkeys, while in New Orleans, she wanted to learn about the history and culture of the city.

"Did you go on many vacations as a kid?"

"Never," she answers. "My first plane ride was when I flew here for college. I'd barely been out of my small town, other than an occasional field trip to Bangor. I'm not worldly or well-traveled," she says with a grimace.

"If you could go anywhere and money wasn't an issue, where would you go?"

"The Galapagos," she says instantly. "Joshua Tree, and the Shiraito Falls in Japan."

"You've put some thought into that," I say with a laugh.

"My lack of travel isn't because I haven't always wanted to. I spent a lot of time in the local library as a kid, thumbing through travel books and imagining myself in the different places." She takes a swallow of the small cup of broth placed in front of her. "Why do I feel healthier after one sip?"

"Luther makes the best soups."

"How do you know him?"

"He was my neighbor growing up." His family lived a few doors down and he was the biggest punk on the street. I'd have never guessed he'd end up being one of the most acclaimed chefs in the Pacific Northwest.

"You could have taken me to a restaurant, you know? I'm easy to please. Though, I'm not complaining. This is the best meal I've ever had."

There's a lot I want to say to that, but I let it go, for now, focusing instead on the food, the wine, the view of the city skyline lit up in the distance. Kit keeps her enthusiasm through the remaining dishes, especially dessert.

"There's probably not extra down there, is there?"

"I can check for you, Miss Ashcroft," Severan answers her with an amused grin. When he disappears, I reach over to lift Kit from her seat to my lap.

"Thank you," she says quietly, dropping her head on my shoulder.

"My pleasure," I say. "I'm preoccupied, every day, trying to come up with the best ways to spoil you."

"It's bad for you to have preoccupations," she says, bringing her hands over her face. "I don't want to be that for you."

"I compartmentalize just fine when I'm working," I say, dipping my fingers under her coat to drag up her bare thigh. "Besides, you're the best fucking distraction I could ever ask for."

"Are you sure?" she asks, peeking through her fingers at me for a few seconds before she drops her hands. "I don't want to be a Jessica Simpson or something."

"I'm a much better man than Romo. I can play to my best ability while being utterly infatuated with a woman," I assure her.

"You know that because of Isla," Kit says—not in accusation, simply as fact.

"Do you still believe I'm in love with her?" Since my first conversation with Kit about Isla, I've thought about what she said—that if we think it's love, it must be.

"In my whole short life," she starts to answer, adjusting herself so she can snake a hand around my waist. The position gives me more access to her while keeping it hidden under her furry coat. "I've never known anyone who fell out of love with someone. My brain is preprogrammed to believe we only love once in a lifetime."

"I'm inclined to believe you," I say, and watch the light in her dark eyes dim. I'm saddened to hurt her, but it tells me that her heart is somewhere near where mine is. "The flaw in your argument is that sometimes people think they're feeling love, only because they've never truly been in love. When you do finally fall, everything you thought you knew about it before pales in comparison."

"How do you know?"

"Because," I say, pausing to press a chaste kiss to her lips, "what I feel for you already surpasses anything I've felt for another woman before."

She doesn't say anything as I watch emotion after emotion flash across her features. She's confused. I get it—this is all new for me, too. Still, I have much more of a foundation under me than she has. There are things I can look back on for reference.

Kit has no baseline for love. She's raised herself mostly with its absence.

All I want to do is shower her in it—to fill her up with it the way she fills me up with joy. I'm like those sappy videos all over social media, when the girlfriend films her boyfriend in a crowd and once he sees her, he grins sappily. That's me when I even think about her.

Kit Ashcroft alters my perspective of all things.

"This is hard for me." Her voice carries the slightest tremble, and I hold her closer to me, moving my hand higher up her leg. "All of the things I naturally reject are the things you remind me of. I don't believe in fate or kindred souls. But I can't deny how at ease I am with you. Things I can't explain or find answers for frighten me. Then, I put this pressure on myself to not be so wrapped up in it, which only makes me more manic."

"Maybe you have a spiritual side that you've never explored."

"What do you mean?"

"You're Indigenous," I say. "In peewee, I played with a kid who was Squamish. I didn't pay as much attention to what he talked about as I wish I had, now. But I remember he was always so grounded in nature. Tribes are all different, I know. Maybe your mind and something more inherent inside of you are battling each other instead of working together. I'm just spitballing ideas, here. Have you ever thought about learning more about your heritage?"

She doesn't talk about her family much, at all, outside of an occasional reference to her grandmother. Other than the first conversation we had about her mother leaving when she was a child, she's never mentioned her again—or that she's half Indigenous.

Severan comes back to deliver a plate of two more perfectly crafted small bites. "Chef had one more trick up his sleeve for you," he says.

"Ooh, thank you," Kit says, sitting up to grab them. She places the first one in my mouth, her fingers lingering long enough for me to nip at them. Shock briefly shows on her face and her head tilts. "I think I liked that."

I laugh as she pops her own dessert into her mouth and moans in appreciation. Then, she stands, taking my hand to pull me behind her as she moves to the railing. I perch behind her, an arm on either side, my chin resting on her head as I wait to see if she'll circle back to our conversation or veer into another topic, which is a habit of Kit's.

The biggest lesson I have learned being Lottie's brother, though, is that I can't force someone else's timeline—especially a neurodivergent. They'll get there when they're ready.

"Do you want to know why I chose Seattle for college? Other than it being so far away from Maine?"

"I want to know everything you want to tell me."

"Careful what you wish for," she teases, then points to a spot in the distance. "Over there, you can't really see it from here, but there's a big black building. People nicknamed it Darth Vader, though, really, it looks like the Sandcrawler that the Jawa move around in. I loved that. It felt like a city where I could be my geeky self and fit right in. You do know *Star Wars*, right?"

"Of course," I say, grinning. "I know I'm supposed to say that *Empire Strikes Back* is the best in the franchise, but I happen to think it's *Rogue One*. And I'll fight you on that."

Her chin drops, and I wait for the same argument I hear every time I say this to a fellow fan. I've heard them all; the story is superior, it's better than the first in series, which is nearly impossible for any sequel. You can't compare a Disney movie to an original Lucasfilms.

"How do you keep getting more perfect?" she asks instead. "Nobody ever says that, and I'm left arguing about how even ESB's amazing storytelling pales in comparison to the raw tragic drama of R1. Which also happens to keep the light comedy without the hyper-cheesiness. It's so fucking good."

That settles it. I'm in love with Kit.

"Glad we agree. I wasn't prepared to argue with you where you could easily push me overboard," I tease, wrapping my arms tighter around her. The night air is cooling quickly as the boat slowly makes its way back toward the marina.

"About what you said earlier," she starts, then turns in my arms to face me. "I've never explored that part of me because I don't want to face what I've lost. Or, that I've been too afraid to find what's been lost."

"I'll help you. If you decide you want to learn or if you want to find her. You don't have to face any of it alone."

"I wouldn't even know where to start," she says. Resting her cheek on my chest, she nuzzles in.

"What about with your dad?" For how little she speaks about family, her father gets the least attention, yet the biggest reaction. I'm not sure she's aware of it, but the couple of times he's come up in conversation, the tension on her is visible.

"No," she says adamantly. "Maybe my grandmother."

"Hey." I cup her face, pulling her up to me. "Whatever he did, I won't let him hurt you again. Okay?"

"He also can't hurt me if I don't ever talk to him again," she says.

"Fair enough," I say, pressing a kiss to her lips. Kit grabs the back of my neck and keeps me there, deepening the kiss. We stay like that for the remainder of the cruise to the marina. Lips locked, her body pressed against mine. When I cup her ass and drag her dress up under her coat, I expect to feel her typical cotton underwear. Tonight, I'm met with something different. Thin, satiny, fragile. I snap the strap against her skin and ask, "What is this, Kit?"

"I'm calling them my plucky panties."

"You are plucky," I say, smiling against her lips. "Do I get to see them?"

"As soon as you get me home after the best first date I could have asked for."

By the time I pull into her driveway, she's visibly antsy, rubbing her thighs together for most of the ride. Once inside her house, she fumbles with the latch on Nightmare's kennel and sighs in frustration.

"Kit," I say with more authority than I've ever used with her before. "Find a comfortable place to sit that pretty ass down. I'll take care of Nightmare, then, I'll take care of you."

She nods, and I pick up Nightmare, taking him outside to wander in a few circles. Eventually, he finds the perfect spot.

Kit has the sexual drive of anyone realizing for the first time that sex can, and should, be exciting and fun. She's still shy about vocalizing what she wants. Or taking charge of it. That will come with time, I think. The distance she's traveled in such a short time is already impressive. Yet, I want her to be empowered enough to tell me to drive faster, to get her home and fuck her brains out.

With how sexual she is once she's comfortable in the moment, I have no doubt she's going to be an increasingly adventurous partner. I'm here for it. I'm here for *her*.

Nightmare's paws scratch on my leg, trying to get my attention now that he's done with his business.

"You want a cookie, don't you, pal? Me too," I say, then lead him back inside. Kit keeps a treat jar by the door and I toss one to him. He grabs it and runs to the corner to eat it. Kit isn't in the living room or the kitchen. Walking down the hall, I see the bathroom door is open. It, too, is empty. I'm about to call out for her when I get to her bedroom.

She's sitting on her bed, having removed her jacket, boots…everything other than the small bit of lingerie covering her pussy. The music that nearly always plays somewhere in her house is on, but she's turned it down to the lowest volume. Not much more than a vibration in the air that matches the one in my veins as I take her in.

"Hi," she says, timidly.

"I'm feeling overdressed, here," I say, leaning against the doorjamb, content to stand here and stare at her, for a moment. Her flawless skin is on full display—she's petite but curvy. Womanly and strong. Her hair still pulled half up so I can see the flush on her cheeks.

"You could be more naked. I wouldn't complain." I've yet to step foot in her bedroom, her safe space. She looks me straight in the eye, and there is no waver in her voice, no hesitation.

Staying in the doorway, I kick off my shoes, then slowly strip off my clothes. Letting her watch. Loving that she does. Kit doesn't take any of this for granted; she's fully in the moment, as if she's committing every detail to memory.

"Stand up," I tell her when I'm more naked than she is. "Show me."

Her dark lashes flutter a few times before she complies. I'm fucking mesmerized by her. From her head to her perfectly painted toes that dig into the carpet. The more territory my gaze covers, the more relaxed she becomes. The tension in her shoulders falls away, and her fingers relax at her side.

"Tyson."

"Spin," I say. She turns, her hands moving to the thin strings of her new lingerie. "No. That's my job."

She lets out a huff and it's all I can do not to laugh out loud.

"Tyson," she says again, but this time, with some frustration.

"In all your studying of pornography," I say, stepping to stand close enough that she can feel my heat on her back. "Did you ever come across videos with needy, bratty women?"

"None that I watched."

"You might find you like it. The same way you liked when I nipped your fingers, earlier. The way you like that I'm telling you what to do, now, even though it's frustrating you." Placing my hands where hers tried to be,

I run my fingers along the waistband. The frail fabric would be so easily torn off her, but I don't want to ruin her new prize. Something tells me they weren't purchased for me, but for her. "Place your hands on the bed, Kit. And let me hear you."

"Hear me what?" she asks, leaning forward to brace herself while I squat behind her, dragging the delicate bit of lace down her body with me. When my face meets her core, she curses. "Fuck. Okay. Oh, God."

I spread her ass and lick from her pussy, slowly up, paying close attention to how her body reacts. The sounds she makes, the muscles she moves. I don't want to make her uncomfortable. Quite the opposite, I want to make her squirm with pleasure. I want her to experience everything our bodies are capable of.

All I notice is a small gasp when my tongue hits there. Well, that, and her pushing back into it. Kit has a naughty side. One I'm excited to explore. I grip her right ass cheek with slightly more force, pushing it out and up, repeating the path with my tongue. Dipping into her cunt as far as I can with my tongue, much more shallowly in her ass.

"I said, let me hear you," I tell her again, then gently bite the meat of her butt.

"Why do I like it when you bite me?" she asks with a whine.

"Because," I say, dipping my finger into her pussy, getting it as wet as she is. "A little dull pain makes the pleasure brighter." I press my finger against her asshole, rubbing small circles until she relaxes and I can push in the tiniest bit. It's only a hint, an idea for her to think about. Something to ask for some day, maybe.

"I need—Oh, fuck. I need something," she stammers, her hips beginning to rock.

"You need something to fuck?" She hums at my question. "You want my tongue or my cock, Kit?"

18

KIT

He asks again when I don't answer. It's not that I'm afraid to say the word—it's that I can't decide. There's so much to learn, to know, to try, to perfect.

I want the slide of his dick inside me, but I also love the way his mouth works me over. And whatever he's been doing to my ass is so beyond anything I could imagine. Statistically, it's not a high percentage of women who enjoy anal sex. Of those, most prefer anal surfacing, or shallowing, as opposed to penetration.

I wonder what demographic I'd fit into.

"Kit." He bites high on my thigh between kisses. "Fine, I'll decide—my cock it is. Do you have a condom?"

"No, but you said you were tested last week. Did you get the results?"

"Yes, clean. Are you okay with this?"

"Yes, please," I say on a sigh, and he chuckles. Seconds later, he has one of my legs lifted on the bed and he slams inside from behind. "Yes, that's what I want."

The sensation of him raw is so different than it was the first time. Intimate in a new way, as if we couldn't be closer or more connected.

Tyson traces my spine with his fingers—a light touch, almost a tickle, but not. A stark difference from the smart sting of his bite, yet it accomplishes something similar. He leans over me, licking and nibbling my shoulder.

"The way I feel when I'm inside you," he whispers. I'm unable to tell if he's talking to me or himself. Either way, I like hearing it. "It's almost as good as when you smile at me."

"Tyson," I cry out, turning my face to his as best I can. He doesn't know. He can't know that he's just said the sweetest thing I've ever been told. I don't want him to know; I'll keep my silly romanticism to myself. "Kiss me."

"Anything you want," he says, then seals his lips to mine. "Everything you want."

He pulls out long enough to flip me around to my back, then, he's pushing back in. My knees ride up over his hips and he stares down at me as he pistons in and out. Harder, faster. With a palm under my neck, he lifts my face to his and kisses me again, again, again.

"Tyson," I repeat, my nails digging into the skin of his pecs.

"Fuck, yes, Kit. I'm not going to last much longer. I need to fill you up."

"Oh, God. Please."

"You need to come with me, love. We do this together."

I slide a hand between us, administering what I need on my clit, all while my fingers skim his cock moving in and out. It's enough—the feel of slick skin—more than enough to shove me over the edge.

"Come in me."

"Fucking hell, Kit." His body tenses around mine. After a handful more pumps, he's doing what I asked. The warmth pouring from him to me is shocking ecstasy. I moan, and it spills more. "Holy shit, the things you do to me."

"I think you did it to me," I say when I catch my breath and he's collapsed atop me.

"No. It's you. You make it feel new again. I have no stamina with you," he says, and I preen.

"You're going to give me a complex if you keep saying such sweet things."

"Good—you deserve to know how fucking perfect you are. Stay here."

He pulls out, and I instantly decide I don't like that very much, at all. He sees my grimace and apologizes as he rushes to my bathroom. A few minutes later, he returns with a wet washcloth and meticulously cleans me up.

"Thank you," I say, pulling the bedding down and climbing into my covers. "Will you stay?"

"Of course. Let me kennel Nightmare."

"Oh, shit. Yeah," I say, feeling badly that I've completely forgotten about the one thing in life that wholly relies on me.

"I got it," he reassures.

"I'm a bad fur mommy," I say when he comes back and crawls into bed with me.

"No, you aren't. You were distracted, is all." He brushes my hair off my face and presses a kiss to my nose.

"It's been an eventful night." I snuggle closer to him. He hums when he pulls me closer still, his heart beating against my cheek. I listen as it calms and mine begins to synchronize with his. It doesn't take that long. Strange how our bodies become so easily in tune with each other, even if our brains might fight it. I don't want to fight it—fight the idea of him. Or us. But there's more for him to know. More I need to share of myself.

"Tyson?"

"Yeah?"

"My father knew," I say, feeling like a boulder is stuck in my throat. "He saw and didn't stop it."

"God damn it, love," he curses, squeezing me tighter. "I'm so fucking sorry."

"He said I was like her—my mother. That I was just asking for men's attention. But I never did." My face is buried in his chest, and I keep it there.

I don't want to see the look on his face. Nor do I want him to see that I quit crying about this years ago.

"I know, I know you didn't," he says. "You should have had someone on your side, Kit."

"I dreamed of it," I tell him. "But I have that now."

"You do. You have a lot of people on your side. A lot of people who love you," he says, pressing a kiss to my hair. "You are safe here."

He squeezes me tighter, and I know the truth of his words as I lie in his arms.

"Good morning," Tyson says when he notices me watching him.

I woke up hours ago. Wanting to let him sleep, I snuck out of bed and went straight to my computer. With my headphones on, I started a replay of *Skyrim*. Probably my twentieth playthrough, or close to it. I didn't even notice he'd gotten up until about fifteen minutes ago.

He's doing his usual morning yoga routine, only this time, it's in my living room with Nightmare stretching and rolling around next to him.

"Has he perfected his downward facing dog, yet?"

"Surprisingly, no. But he's getting there," he says with a laugh. "Aren't you, buddy?" Nightmare yips and spins in response. Tyson ends with a warrior pose. Dressed in nothing but boxer briefs, every muscle is a feast for my eyes. The bruises spattered here and there are an enhancement rather than a deterrent to his athletic beauty. I don't think I'll ever tire of simply watching him. Even the way he walks toward me is with an air of graceful power.

"Hi," I say when he's in front of me and pulling me in for a kiss.

"Hey." His lips are cool; his tongue still has a hint of his morning coffee. "I wanted to apologize."

"For what?"

"Last night, I suggested you talk to your father. Knowing what I know now, I wish you'd stay no contact."

"You didn't know," I say. "I thought about what you said, though."

"Which part?"

"Learning about my heritage," I say. I lay in bed for a good half hour, mulling over his suggestion, analyzing the truth of why I've never explored that part of me. I'm surrounded by Native culture here in the Pacific Northwest, and I've never let myself appreciate any of it. It's easier to ignore it, to lie and say it doesn't mean anything to me. That's not honest, though. "I haven't done it before out of fear that he's right. That I am like her. Like someone who could leave her family without a word."

"Kit, no. You would never," he says.

"I know, but a lifetime of intrusive thoughts are hard to ignore."

"Especially if they're reinforced by a parental figure," he says, not leaving out his obvious disdain for my father.

"Right. So, thank you for being a voice of reason for me."

"You're welcome," he says, pressing another kiss to my lips. A girl could feel spoiled with such free affection. "I had something else I meant to talk to you about last night."

"Good something or bad something?"

"Good. Or I hope you think it's good," he says, his brow wrinkling. "The Blades have their foundation gala in a couple of weeks. I was hoping you'd go with me."

Dates don't get invited to the gala. Wives and girlfriends do. Tyson and I haven't put labels on what's happening between us; we've had no conversation about it. Which is something I've appreciated. He lets me go at my own pace, whether that's as slow as a sloth or speed-running through it.

With my limited experience, I can't say how many men would have shown the amount of care and patience Tyson has. I suspect it isn't a high percentage—especially of men who look like him, are successful pro athletes, and have a line of women waiting and willing.

Which reminds me of something I've been meaning to ask him about.

"Can I ask you something, first?"

"Anything."

"Why the sex worker?"

He releases a deep sigh. Worry wrinkles around his eyes.

"I was in my head after Isla and Cillian got back together. Had my own daily pity party and everything. I was reckless and stupid, picking up random women at every opportunity to try and fill some void," he says. "I constantly felt like I was walking around with a chip on my shoulder and something to prove. My competitive nature was getting the best of me in the worst way. When she approached me that night, all I saw were her freckles. Not the price tag, the potential ramifications, or my career."

"So, you're not that great at compartmentalizing," I say, remembering what he said last night on the boat. I'm not sure how it makes me feel, that he hired her because of an attribute that reminded him of Isla. My gut twists some, but my head knows that's stupid. He has a past—we all do. His just involved other people in ways mine hasn't. That's not his fault. If only my jealous side could catch up to my logical side.

"I am," he says with conviction. "For a few months, I was messy, then I got my shit together. I'm not the man I was then." His mouth opens, as if there's more he wants to say, but he stops himself.

"Tell me the rest."

"Don't let this scare you," he says with that grin I've come to look forward to. "But I'm not even the same man I was when I came to Seattle. And I have you to credit for that."

"Me? Why? All I've done is be a spying neighbor and a test of your willpower," I say, and he bursts with laughter.

"No, Kit," he says, lifting me by my underarms so I can wrap my legs around his waist and my arms around his neck. He walks us to the kitchen, perching me on the edge of the counter. "You've been oxygen to my lungs. You are the most refreshing thing to ever stumble into my life. You make me think from a different perspective and contemplate things I've never considered. You've made me a better man in mere weeks."

"I'm the air you breathe?" I ask, wrinkling my nose.

"Yes, you fucking brat. Do you want some breakfast?"

"Yes, please."

"Can I ask you something, now?" He takes eggs from the refrigerator, first, then digs around, inventorying vegetables.

"It's only fair."

"How close are you to your grandmother? You don't talk about her much, either."

"We're complicated," I say.

"How so?" He grabs ham, cheese, an onion, and a red pepper, and begins chopping.

"I love her, but I don't have a lot of respect for her. I mean, she's done the best she knows how. But has never had the courage to try for better," I tell him. She's not a strong woman and, by default, centers men in her life—when it should have been me who was most important to her as a child. She never complained about watching me while my dad worked, but she also never stood up to him when he was cruel to me. "I know she loves me, too. But neither of us makes much effort. I haven't been home since moving here, so I haven't seen her in a decade."

"This is your home. Not Maine," he says, reaching over to massage my hand that is clenched into a fist. I hadn't even noticed I'd done it, but he had. Tyson is always so calm, a balm for me every time my edges start to fray. I'm jittery and tense so often, and he's like a warm lavender bath soothing it all away.

I'm not sure how he notices everything that he does about me, while I also wonder how I can offer anything of equal value in return. What do I bring to his life that compares to how he supports me?

Do I *refresh* him enough to be an equal in his world? Can I give him what I think he eventually wants in life? Marriage? A family?

I don't know.

"Sticking feathers up your butt doesn't make you a chicken," Tyler Durden once said. Just like dating a man doesn't make me wifey material.

Once again, I'm left clinging to whatever I can get while all this lasts.

"Yes, I'll go to the gala with you."

"Yeah?"

"Yeah." I nod several times, until he stills me with fingers on my chin and a kiss to my lips.

"You know that makes us…more, in the eyes of the rest of the team."

"Are you okay with that?"

"Fuck yeah, I am. As long as you are, too."

"I am," I say, sounding more confident than I should. I'm good around the team, having spent plenty of time with them in casual settings over the years. That's not worrying—being labeled a wag is. That's not really my scene, and I have little interest in invites to all their bachelorette parties or baby showers with women I barely know. While I like to dress up now and then, primping daily sounds about as fun as walking over hot coals barefoot.

The ladies are nice enough, but they're also reminiscent of the girls who relentlessly shunned me and called me a weirdo nerd my whole life. I'm not sure I'll ever be truly comfortable in that environment, and I don't know how that would impact Tyson over the long run.

"Hugo is going to be so sad."

"The poor guy. I should probably break up with you and date him."

"Try and see what happens, Ashcroft."

19

TYSON

I skate behind the net, crashing into Svetsky, our sticks battling for control of the puck. The regular season is coming to a close. If we win this game, we clinch our playoff position. We're tied in overtime; whoever scores first, wins. I want that win. We all do, of course, but Colorado isn't a contender in post-season play. Their win would only mean we have to fight that much harder to secure our place.

Fuck that.

I jostle the puck loose, passing it off to Wallin, who keeps control down the ice. Then, it's my turn to take a break on the bench. This was a long shift—I could use the breather. Cillian hops the boards, beelining it to where Wallin and Letty pass the puck back and forth, waiting for a clear path to goal.

Colorado's defenseman tries to get in his way, but Wylder anticipates it, maneuvering around him. He finds a clear line, and Wallin passes to him. The timing is perfect; their goalie's line of sight blocked as Cill shoots… and scores!

The bench erupts, along with the spattering of Seattle fans in the stands. If this were a home game, it would be so loud we wouldn't be able to hear ourselves over the crowd. Whatever, though—securing a playoff spot is fucking amazing no matter where we are.

It's been years since I've been in a real run for the cup. The last time, we were taken out in the first round. The time before that was the same. The Blades have won it once. I hope, more than anything, they get it again this season and I'm here with them through it all.

It's been my biggest dream for as long as I can remember. Every hockey player dreams of that, of course. It's hard to remember when it's within reach, though. It's impossible to believe anyone could want it as badly as me. And it's easier to lie to yourself that you deserve it more, have worked harder than everyone else. The competitive drive digs in deep, takes a firm hold, becomes your sole focus.

The chase is all I know. Seems I'm always chasing something—the NHL, the cup, a woman.

"Great job getting that puck away from Svetsky," Cillian says once we're in the locker room and the excited chatter has calmed down.

"Thanks, and nice shot. Heading to playoffs feels better than I remember."

"It's been a spell since you've had a post-season."

"Too fucking long," I agree. "Not much I want in life. The cup is one of the few."

"I remember that feeling well," he says. "Even after you get it—after you get everything else you want—you find something new to want. A second cup, a third…that, I don't think, ever changes."

"It's not enough?" I ask. I understand always chasing the championship—that's the biggest part of our job, after all. But when you have the rest—a wife, a kid, a family to love, success, wealth—is it still not enough?

"It's more than enough. I have everything important," he says. "Competition never leaves, though. That sticks. I always want another year on the cup, better stats, or to break someone else's record."

"I guess I can understand that."

"You'll see soon enough. We'll get there, I have a feeling," Letty chimes in. "And my feelings never fail."

"I'd say that sounds creepy as fuck, man," Cillian says. "Except you've said that shit before and it's always been true."

"My ma was a witch. I get it from her," he says with a toothless grin.

"Jesus, you're scary."

"Good," he says to me, adding a maniacal laugh as he heads toward the shower.

"For the life of me, I'll never understand how he finds women to sleep with him, let alone talk to him," Hugo says. "Speaking of women, I hear you're bringing Kit Kat to the gala."

"She's agreed to be seen with me, yeah."

"Of course she has, fucking Pretty Boy," he says. "You better watch out, though. Odette's suiting me—I'm going to be dashing as hell. So, we'll see if she agrees to leave with me."

"You can try, fucker. But don't forget, I like to fight."

"Yeah, yeah," he says, smiling. "For real, though, I'm happy for you."

"Me too," Cillian adds. "Kit's good people."

"She's amazing, man. Probably the bravest person I've ever known. And so fucking smart."

"She's like a walking encyclopedia," he agrees. "It blows my mind how much she knows about the most random things."

"Yeah, her mind is always working. A couple of times, I've woken up in the middle of the night to find her wide awake and researching some crazy thing. The other night it was black holes; the time before that, she was near tears reading about the ivory black market."

"She told me she doesn't sleep much," he says.

"She doesn't. A few hours here and there, mostly. She's slept through a few times, now, though."

"How are you dealing with that?" Zander asks, taking his seat on the bench across from us. Concern shows—his mouth a slight frown.

"It's fine," I say. "Once I know she's good, I fall right back to sleep. You know how it is—you learn to sleep when you can with a schedule like ours."

"I don't just mean the sleeping situation," he says. "Kit struggles with change and spontaneity. You seem the opposite."

"I mean, yeah. I'm very much a go-with-the-flow type who will happily dive into whatever comes up. I know that's not her, though. She's a homebody who'd rather pop on a video game than go out for a night on the town with a crowd. And I don't mind that at all," I say. I've never believed that couples need to live in each other's pockets. It's healthy to have not only your own interests but shared ones, too. "I don't expect her to come work out with me or go play golf. Hanging out with her is relaxing, forces me to take time to just…I don't know…be."

"And if you got traded again?" Zander asks.

"Fuck, man. I just got here—I don't even want to think about that."

"I hear you, but that would be very difficult for her."

"To be fair, that would be hard for Isla or Willa, too," Cillian says. "All of our women have roots here."

"True," Zander agrees. "Willa's strong enough to handle it, but she'd hate being away from her family."

"Fuck, I think I'd rather retire, at this point. That would be easier than asking Isla and Sadie to move away," Cillian says.

Shock is my first reaction. I've never heard a player say anything like that. Everyone normally says some version of *we'd figure it out*, because we all know it's part of the gig. We could be traded at any time, without notice, and for those who have a wife or girlfriend, the weight of a move falls on them. They're the ones who have to pack up, sell the old place, find a new one, re-establish any career they may have in a new location—not to mention finding new friends or whatever—while we would just be thrown into the only work we've ever known.

My shock fades to understanding of just how much Cillian Wylder loves his family. I haven't doubted his commitment to them for a long while now, but him saying he'd give up his career for them cements that, for sure.

It's one more thing to be jealous of the guy for.

***

My entire body freezes in the doorway when Kit opens to my knocking. Dragging my eyes over her from head to toe, I start the climb back up even slower.

"I knew this dress was the wrong choice," she says, her voice shaking with anxiety that's already set in. "It's not right, too much. I fell in love with it and convinced myself it was going to be okay. But it's obviously not."

"What?" I ask, trying to focus on the dress itself, rather than her as a whole. It's all shimmery black, calf-length, and long-sleeved. It hugs her form and has boxy shoulders and hips that accentuate her already perfectly curved figure. Hardly any of her skin shows, other than under the sheer fabric covering her chest, but it's sexier than anything I've ever seen her in.

"I'll change. Willa said everyone is wearing pink and black. She brought me some options to borrow. But you said you'd pay me back if I wanted to shop for myself," she rambles, her bare toes digging into the carpet, a nervous gesture I've noticed almost as often as her fist clenching. "I'm not going to fit in. They'll all be in tiny, pink, sparkling dresses."

"Kit."

"I'm sorry I'm freaking out. I thought I had myself under control, and then, I got a text from a coworker that asked if I'd ever thought birds weren't real. Like, instead, they're little robots, and that's why they sit on power lines—so they can recharge. Then, all I could think about was how far artificial intelligence has come and how bad our education system is, and I spiraled."

"Kit," I repeat, all while I try to wrap my head around robot birds.

"I'll go change. I'll be quick, so we won't be late. You look handsome, by the way. I should have led with that."

"Kit," I say again, moving to her and grabbing her trembling hands in mine. "If you change that dress, I will put your bare ass over my knee until it's red. Then, force the dress back on you."

"What?" She blinks up at me. My goal was to get her out of her head—or at least steer it in a different direction. The redness on her cheeks tells me it worked.

"You heard me," I say in a softer tone. "The dress is amazing. You're gorgeous, and who gives a fuck if you fit in with what the other wags are wearing?"

"Be so for real with me, Tyson," she says, her voice a little steadier. "If we show up there and all the other women are dressed in little pink party dresses, and I'm like a goth power boss bitch next to them, you're not going to feel some kind of way about it?"

"Oh, I'll feel some kind of way," I say, dropping my head to the crook of her neck and peppering it with a few kisses. "I'll feel proud that you walked into the room on my arm and that I'm the man you'll be going home with."

"Are you sure?" she asks breathlessly. "It was an expensive dress."

"Worth every fucking penny."

"You don't know how much I spent," she says, stilling my head between her hands and forcing me to look at her.

"How much?"

"Six hundred," she says, scrunching her nose up the way she does whenever she's feeling cringey. "The shoes were on clearance, but still cost almost three-fifty."

"For less than a grand, I get to stare at you looking like this all night? That's a steal," I tell her, trying to hide my amusement.

"You're crazy," she accuses.

"My current contract is a four-year deal for twenty-one million. You could have spent more."

"I'm already terrified I'm going to spill on it or rip it." She's looking at me like I've lost my mind.

"I had ties that I've thrown out that cost more than the shoes you bought. I promise, if anything happens to the dress, it's going to be fine."

"You throw your ties away?" she asks, aghast.

"I meant, donated," I say, laughing. "I'm not a heathen."

"Good, I was rethinking everything I know about you," she says, then takes a couple calming breaths. "Thank you for talking me down."

"Anytime, love. Go get your shoes; I'll take Nightmare for a quick walk."

"Okay," she says, and starts walking toward the bedroom but pauses to look back at me. "Can we try that whole spanking thing sometime? Maybe not until I'm red, but…"

"I knew you had a bratty side," I say with a grin and the beginnings of a hard-on.

20

KIT

Tyson's words play repeatedly in my head during the drive to the event venue. If someone had asked me months ago if I ever thought about a man spanking my ass, I'd have laughed in their face. The way he said it, though, with that sexy, authoritative growl, it went straight to my pussy and pulled me out of my chaotic thoughts.

For the first ten minutes of the drive, I kept taking surreptitious looks at him. I've seen him in suits—since they wear them before every game. Tonight, though, he's wearing a more formal version. Smooth black over crisp white, his broad shoulders and thick thighs only looking larger under the fabric.

After he catches me staring the fourth time, he tells me to quit hiding it.

"I hope you always look at me like this," he says.

"Sometimes I watch you while you sleep," I say. He laughs, but I'm not teasing. I really have watched him a few times.

"Okay, Cullen."

"I'm kind of sparkly like a Cullen tonight," I say. "Also, how do you know *Twilight*?"

"I'm more than a meathead jock; I'll have you know."

"I do know that," I say. "I still wouldn't peg you for a Twihard."

"You want to peg me, Kit?" he asks, feigning shock.

"Oh my God." I hide my face in my hands.

"Lottie loves all things vampires," he finally says after he's done laughing.

"Me too—maybe that's why I like it when you bite me," I say. "It's sweet that you embrace the things she loves."

"She's always been my best friend. It's easy to do what she wants when I just want to be around her," he says. "When she got into reading, I did, too. We'd lounge in complete silence right next to each other and just read. But it was still valuable time, you know?"

"I can understand that," I say. Only because that's how I've always felt with Willa.

"So much of our childhood centered around my life and hockey. Often, I felt guilty about that. She deserved more but was always happy to make sacrifices for me."

I imagine that's what you do for the people you love. It would be easy to fall into my childhood sadness for not having that. Fighting isn't as easy, but I try to push it away. Pulling my phone out, I send my grandmother a text. Tyson and I took a selfie before we left my house, and I attach that for her.

ME:

This is the guy I was telling you about.

The last time I spoke with her, Tyson and I had only begun talking about dating. She was excited for me, though—happy and hopeful. She'll enjoy seeing me all dolled up, too, since that isn't something I ever had the opportunity to do as a kid.

She won't see my text until tomorrow, as I'm sure she's long asleep, by now. After Tyson and I talked about my mother on our date, I've thought about my family dynamics a lot. Every day I grow closer to wanting to find my mom. I'm keeping my expectations low and in check. If she wanted to know me, she knew where I was for so long, after all. Yet, I can't deny that I'm missing something in my life. Roots, maybe. A sense of grounding. History, for sure.

Who knows how much family I have in the world. What if it's not too late to get some of what I always wanted? Or some of what Willa has, or Tyson has. I shouldn't continue to let my fear stop me from finding out if something good can come of it. That's easier to say when I know I have Tyson standing beside me.

"You ready?" he asks. I look out the window to see we're parked. I hadn't even noticed we'd arrived.

"Yeah, sorry. Zoned out there, for a minute."

"You want to talk about it?"

"Not necessary," I say, not wanting to bring down the mood for tonight—well, any more than I already did with my micro-freakout earlier. I'm so embarrassing.

"If you say so," he says. "Let me go show you off, then."

Tyson holds my hand as we walk inside. The event is being held inside a warehouse basement that's been renovated to look like an old wine cellar. Tonight it's dressed up with soft pink linens and twinkling white lights. Every year, the team's charity foundation picks a charity for the gala to raise money for. There will be a silent auction, with proceeds going to a local domestic violence shelter.

The first people we run into are Coach and his wife, who has begun insisting that we all call her Mama Cole. Zander and Damian both have complicated family situations; the Coles have taken them in the same way they have me.

"You look beautiful," she whispers while giving me a big hug. "I'm so thrilled you're here."

"Thank you."

"Enjoy yourself," Coach tells me after he, too, gives me a hug.

"I will," I promise.

"Take care of my girl, here," he tells Tyson.

"Always, Coach."

The next group of people are the rookies who were recently called up and I've yet to meet.

"Killer, Sammy, this is Kit. She's the mastermind statistician for the team, and my girlfriend," he introduces me. My stomach flips and flutters at the moniker that we've never discussed.

"Hey, Kit. Nice to meet you," Killer says. His government name is Victor Kirill. His nickname is an obvious one and I know it's been a joke with the guys that attract all the league murderers with 'Victor Kill' and 'Cill Wylder'.

"What he said," Sam Vogel says, pushing his buddy out of the way to hold his hand out to me. I give him mine, thinking he'll shake it, but instead, he lifts it to his mouth and presses a quick kiss. His shaggy hair falls over his baby face as he does.

"She's out of your league, fuckwit," Tyson says, wrapping an arm around my shoulders.

"Dude, I'd say she's out of yours," he shoots back.

"I'm smart enough to know that."

"Nice to meet you guys, too," I say as Tyson leads me away.

"Wash that hand," he mutters, making me grin at his jealousy.

"Miss Kit," I hear from my right. "Zhivago looks damn good on you, darling," Odette says when I turn to her.

"Thank you! I was worried I wouldn't fit in, but I love the dress so much."

"Standing out is superior to fitting in, every time, my dear," she says, winking before she walks back to where Gavin Vaughn is waiting for her.

"I told you," Tyson says.

"You did. I should learn to listen to you more."

"Easy now, you're by far the smarter one in this relationship." He leans down, I think he's going to kiss me, but instead, he smells my hair.

"Did you just smell me?"

"Maybe."

"Now, who's a Cullen?" I ask, and he just grins.

"Do you want a drink?"

"A white wine, please."

"I see Willa." He nods to the next room. This time, he does kiss the top of my head. "Head in there, I'll grab drinks and find you."

I don't move right away, deciding to take a minute to admire my date. His suit is tailored to perfection, and his ass looks juicier than ever. For a gal that had little to no interest in sex a couple of months ago, I sure do have a healthy libido, these days. Shaking my head, I move through the archway that separates the bar area from the ballroom.

I pass by a small group of women and hear the catty comments from them as they discuss what other women in the room are wearing. It's exactly what I expected tonight, even if this conversation isn't directed at me. Or—yet, anyway. Women in this world tend to gather in cliques and get as competitive as the men. Only, they're competing for attention rather than a cup.

It's one of the things that makes me most nervous about a relationship with Tyson, because I don't want any part of that pettiness in my life. Nor do I want to feel like there is a woman around every corner trying to steal my man—especially when I already feel like I'm not on equal ground with him. It's an anxious girl's worst nightmare.

I hold my chin high as I pass, though, remembering Odette's words. She's a fashion icon—if she says I look good, I'm going to believe it. Besides, fuck those bitches.

"We're all a little mad around here," Willa is saying as I arrive at the group that includes her, her fellas, Isla, and Cillian.

"At me?" I ask.

"What? No!" she protests, and I smile so she knows I'm joking. "Fuck, look at you. You sexy beast."

"Damn, Kit," Damian says. "Did Tyson drop dead when he saw you? Is that why he's not with you?"

"Yeah, but I didn't want to pass up the free food, so I came anyway," I deadpan.

"Atta girl," Cillian says. "I heard they're feeding us some fancy wagyu dish."

"I don't know what wagyu is—other than it's delicious," Zander says.

"It's Japanese cow, raised in a comfortable environment with traceable lineage. It also has more good fat and amino acids than other beefs. But you have to cook it quick and hot," I say.

"How?" Cillian says in awe. "How the fuck do you know everything?"

"She doesn't sleep," Tyson says from behind me.

"True," I admit. "But I don't think my limited knowledge of wagyu is all that impressive."

"I guarantee none of us knew all that," Zander says, and everyone nods their agreement.

"You all need to read more," I say, rolling my eyes.

"Why, when we can just ask you?" Isla teases.

"I'm going to go see what I'm buying tonight," Damian says. He was born wealthy—not like how the Coles are wealthy, or even like Cillian and Tyson are. Damian is old Southern money. You wouldn't know it by hanging out with him, though, and when he gets the chance, he enjoys spoiling Willa and Zander.

"I'll go with you," Tyson says before looking to me. "You want to look?"

"No, I'll wait here," I say. My meager checking account wouldn't get me anywhere in a room full of professional athletes and local celebrities. I know from past purchases by both Damian and Cillian, that the silent auction items are always extravagant, luxurious, and expensive as hell.

"Okay, be back soon," he says, kissing my forehead.

Conversation continues around me, mostly about nothing of importance. I keep stealing looks at Tyson as he makes his way down the line of items. He writes on a couple of pages, so I know he's bidding on things. My curiosity almost pulls me toward him, but I resist. It's not my business anyhow. And the view of him from here is better than if I was up close.

"You're cooked," Willa says, nudging my shoulder with hers.

"Fully fucking baked," I mutter, looking away from Tyson. In all my admiration of the man, I hadn't noticed that our little group grew even smaller. It's only us three ladies, now.

"Does he know how toasty you are for him?" Willa asks me.

"I haven't said. Neither has he—though, he did introduce me earlier as his girlfriend."

"A title is meaningful," Isla says. "Tyson wouldn't have used that word if he wasn't committed."

"I agree," Willa says.

"And for what it's worth," Isla adds, "he's a very loyal guy."

I look back over to him to see that a woman—Renee from the Blades' social media team—approaches him. As they talk, she keeps touching his arm.

"So, you are saying the urge I feel to go rip Renee's hair out right now is unnecessary?"

"Oh, no. I'm not saying that at all. Some women can't be trusted," she says, speaking from an abundance of experience. "But I believe Tyson can be."

I hope she's right. She once thought that about Cillian, though, and that didn't work out so well. Maybe we can never truly trust anyone. Human nature isn't the most reliable thing in the world.

And how can we ever be sure if we know someone or not? People can be excellent liars and deceivers.

"Jealousy is weird," I say. "It's uncomfy, but also sort of exhilarating."

"It's like an adrenaline rush," Isla says. "It makes you want to fight. Also makes for great sex."

"That's the truth," Willa confirms.

"Does it ever go away?"

"Yes and no," Isla says. "I'll never like the attention Cill gets from women. The knowledge that he has other options will always tickle the back of my brain. But the stronger we get as a couple, the easier it is to ignore those thoughts and be secure in our marriage."

"You're saying that, in time, I'll still want to stick her hand in a waffle iron, but I won't be picturing them in bed together while I do it?"

"Something like that, yeah," she says with a small laugh.

"I'm kind of digging this side of you, Kit," Willa says. "It's like your gamer girl attitude has bled out of cyberspace and entered the real world."

"Well, if she tries to show him any more of her tits, I'm going to have to change my gamer tag to Murder She Wrote, or some shit," I grumble.

21

TYSON

Fucking hell, this woman couldn't be more obvious with her intentions if she was wearing a blinking sign flashing the words *WILL FUCK FOR AN NHL HUSBAND*. She's a pretty woman, but her forwardness would turn most men off. This is a charity event, not speed dating.

This is always how it is for the single men on the team. Once women know you're in a committed relationship, it simmers down, some. Usually. Not completely, but mostly.

"I've never skated before, which is so funny since I work for an NHL team. You know?" she says, once again reaching out to touch my arm. The number of times women have fished for skating lessons from me could fill Lake Ontario. It's been a common theme since I was twelve years old. Renee is trite, obvious, and desperate.

"Well, I hear they give free lessons at the Iceplex once a month," I say, scanning around for someone to help me make a polite exit. Kit and I make eye contact. Like every time I see her, I feel instantly lighter.

I watch her say something to Willa, then start to walk toward me.

"That's so awesome, but I think I'd learn better privately," she says, practically purring the last word. Thankfully, Kit's close enough that I can ignore Renee without the silence becoming overly awkward. She works for the team—I don't need animosity from her—but fuck, take a hint.

"Hey, lover," Kit says, sliding between me and Renee. Her arm wraps around my waist as she presses herself to me.

"Hey, baby." I kiss her—nothing vulgar, but possibly more passionate than the event calls for. I'm only thanking her for interrupting this nonsense woman. "You taste good."

"Thank you," she says brightly. "Did you find something to bid on?"

"I did," I tell her, looking over her shoulder to see that Renee has walked away. "She's gone—thank you."

"Thank fuck," Kit whispers. "She was making me crazy."

"Crazy enough that you walked up on me like a sexy succubus—which was hot as hell."

"Glad I pulled it off, then. It's very much out of my comfort zone. And I didn't try and trip her as she left. I should get brownie points for that," she says, frowning. "What was she even on about?"

"She was spouting the usual bullshit."

"Well, that's her first mistake. I could have told her all she needed was a wayward puppy."

I pull her closer, my hand dropping lower from her waist to the top of her ass. Her face—especially when she scrunches her nose—is my favorite part of her, but her ass is high on the list, as well. "Thank fuck for wayward puppies."

"And spur-of-the-moment hockey trades?"

"That, too." I rub my nose against hers. "Thank you for coming to this with me."

"All my friends are here," she says, shrugging and grinning slyly.

"You're angling for that spanking, aren't you?" I whisper. She drops her head to my chest and nods. "I love how brave you are."

"I don't feel brave. I feel like a scared rabbit most of the time."

Lottie and Kit share that personality trait. Self-awareness is hard. Kit is more in tune with herself than she gives herself credit for. I'm not sure I've known anyone who is as honest about everything as she is—including how she's feeling at any given time. Which is brave as hell.

"Admitting that is brave, Kit," I say, just before the MC asks for us to take our seats for dinner.

We end up at a table with Zander, Cillian, Damian, Isla, and Willa along with Brom and Wallin, who are both here solo tonight. Letty is solo, too, but he's attached to Gavin and Odette, who sit at a neighboring table.

Dinner is served while we watch a presentation by the director of the domestic abuse shelter. She speaks on the statistics of abuse toward women and children. I notice when Kit grows vacant. I think it's something she does when she needs to remove herself from the moment—or she's remembering a painful moment of her childhood. I rub the small of her back, hoping it gives her some sort of comfort.

There isn't much else I can do. If I could, I'd take it away—change her past to nothing but happy memories. Every kid deserves that.

The presentation turns heavier as some of the women the shelter has helped share their stories. One woman, a mother of four, needed the shelter before her oldest child was six years old. For years, she wanted to leave, but over and over again, he promised he would change. Then, he'd remind her that she didn't have a job, no money, no local family to help her out. She felt trapped. The decision to leave only came after he raised a hand to one of her children. That's when she found the shelter.

Having the women speak proves an effective strategy, because as soon as dinner is over, all of us guys move back to the silent auction items and bid them up higher.

We're not powerful enough to change the world, but we can help the most vulnerable in our own city, surely. Kit is still quiet. She's adding to the conversation, but isn't fully invested, and I can't help but wonder if she's thinking the same things I am.

What about all the children in the world that don't have a parent to get them out of a terrifying situation? What if the only parent you have is the one you need to escape from? We don't have shelters for children running away from abuse. There's little option for them, other than to survive eighteen years.

Jesus, what a downer.

As if they sense the shift in mood, music starts to play and trays of champagne get passed around for the last few minutes of bidding. Willa pulls Kit to the dance floor with Hugo and Letty. I watch Kit become lighter, her smile brightening.

"She's good at that," Damian says next to me, following my line of sight. "Pulling her out of her head."

"Was my worry that obvious?"

"Yes, but that only makes me like you more," he says. "Not everyone would even notice, Kit's good at hiding it."

"She can be," I agree. But I see it. I see her. All the strengths she doesn't believe she has, all the vulnerability she wishes she didn't have. They're all part of her, they're all what makes her so special. Sweet, kind, sassy, and strong.

She raises her arms above her head, spinning in a circle and jumping to the beat. I know, without a doubt, I've fallen in love with her.

When I least expected to find much of anything good, I found great. I found amazing. I found someone I want to take care of and support. Someone who sees me as a man, rather than a paycheck. A woman I could spend a lifetime with and never have a dull or complacent day. I don't think those are possible with Kit's natural curiosity.

One of the items I bid an outrageous amount of money on tonight is a trip to Palm Springs. We can check Joshua Tree off her list, first, then work on the others. When I saw the auction item, it seemed like fate, though she'd laugh at that. A week with her, without work, midnight phone calls, or traveling to games across the country, sounds like a dream.

After being traded to this team, the most I'd hoped for was a chance at playoff hockey. Now, I'm getting that with a solid shot at the cup. And it's coming in second on my list of priorities. Playoffs haven't crossed my mind all night, until just now. In every past season, it would have been my focus.

I'm not sure what to think about that or how to feel. Until now, I always thought I was the one in control of my life. All the decisions were mine. Now, it's as if I'm watching my puzzle pieces move by an invisible hand.

My head spins as quickly as Kit does on the dance floor. I'm almost dizzy with it all, can't tell up from down, left from right. Is this head over heels? Or fear that I've moved too quickly into a life-changing relationship? We haven't talked about the future. There's a long list of what-ifs that we may not be on the same page with. What if we don't align on the important things? Are we both willing to make the necessary sacrifices and compromises?

If we aren't, is it too late to live without her?

"Hey, Cill just announced Isla's pregnant," Zander says, coming to stand next to Damian.

"That's what Willa's been dying to tell us all week," Damian says with a wide smile.

"Probably. She was with Isla when she found out, but was told not to say anything until they told Coach."

I glance around the room, looking for Coach. Isla and Cillian are with him and his wife. Isla's mom puts a hand to her daughter's stomach, and my own twists with some feeling I can't quite label.

22

KIT

Tyson changed after dinner. After Isla and Cillian announced their pregnancy, he grew quieter as everyone else celebrated. It's hard not to overthink the reason for that.

Overall, the night was great. Despite briefly descending down the memory lane of my childhood, I had fun. Us ladies danced together; eventually, the guys joined in. Tyson doesn't have much more rhythm than Cillian, but it didn't matter. I liked swaying in his arms, even though he was growing a bit distant.

After a couple of songs, Hugo got bored and goaded me and Letty into a dance-off. It started with samba and quickly escalated to dances like The Running Man and The Tootsie Roll—which is impossible to do in this dress. By the time the event ended, my face hurt from laughing. Hugo's a good dancer; I guess that shouldn't be a surprise, considering how he moves in the net. Letty is absolute shit at it, though, and his version of The Electric Slide was the most hilarious thing I've ever seen.

"Where did you learn to dance?" Tyson asks me on the drive home.

"Self-taught," I say. "My grandmother loves any show that has dancing. We watched it all, and I mimicked what I could from an early age." It's one of the happy things from my childhood. She encouraged me to dance with abandon. It was the only time I let go of everything.

I would have loved to have taken lessons and learned different styles. Some things you can't catch on to by imitation—like tap dancing, which I was obsessed with when I was seven. So much so that I glued pennies to my shoes and jumped around the kitchen like a maniac. My dad was irate.

"If you can't respect the things I buy for you, then I'll just stop buying you things," he'd yelled. Everything he bought me was secondhand, which I never minded. But he stopped doing even that. I squeezed my feet into shoes that were too small, for well over a year, until my grandmother noticed the holes wearing through the toe. From then on, she took me to the thrift stores at least once a year to get the basics I needed. It was never much, but at least my feet didn't hurt anymore.

"You had a good time tonight?"

"I did. Thank you for taking me," I say, and again, he grows quiet. "Did you win what you wanted from the auction?"

I know he won something, but he hasn't said what it was.

"I did."

Okay, then. Good talk.

I rack my brain for any misstep I may have made tonight. All I can come up with is that I was too morose when the women from the shelter were speaking. But how could I not be? They spoke from the heart about their struggles with domestic abuse. Only one of the three women had children, but I instantly related to those faceless babies.

So, yeah, it affected me. Had he hoped for me to be a plastic woman with a painted-on smile? That doesn't seem like him.

"Did I do something wrong?" I finally ask.

"No, Isla. You didn't do anything wrong, of course not," he says, and all the air leaves my lungs.

That's not my name, I inwardly scream. My chest tightens, right along with every muscle in my body. It's hard to breathe or see as the blood rushes through my head. He's talking, but I don't hear it—I can't over the thumping of my heart. The beat, beat, beat that steadily increases.

I've never felt more foolish. I knew his feelings for Isla, and I ignored my instinct, in favor of believing him. But I knew. Real love doesn't just come and go. A night with his ex-girlfriend proved that.

I'm just the stupid girl whose name he couldn't remember. Who doesn't have hockey intuition or a face full of cute-as-hell freckles. The one that fell for his sweet charm and patience.

Oh my fuck, I had sex with a man who is still in love with one of my best friends.

"I'm so stupid," I say. I hear his protest, but don't listen. "Just take me home."

"Will you talk to me?"

"I can't," I rasp out. Even if I wanted to—which I don't—I can't do it right now. All I can do is not break down here in the car, with him to witness it. I don't want to work through this with him. I feel so alone, yet I can't wait to get away from him.

"Okay, okay, I'll get you home." He tries to take my hand, but I move farther away, tucking them under my thighs.

"Kit."

"No."

"All right," he says, and then, nothing more for the few minutes it takes to get to my house.

I can't get out of the car fast enough. These damn shoes and this fabulous fucking dress make it hard to move quickly—which is okay, because even though I want to run away, I need to keep my head high. Falling apart can wait until I'm safely ensconced within the walls of my home, with my puppy, who would never dare to fuck me over emotionally or otherwise.

He calls after me again as I walk up to my front door.

"Go home, Tyson."

My hands shake as I type in my code. It takes me three tries, and I'm nearly to the point of tears from frustration. The first one doesn't fall until I'm on the other side, my back to the door as I slide down it and let my anxiety attack take hold.

My sobs come with every gasping breath. I kick my shoes off and struggle to unzip my dress. It's too confining when it feels like I have a boulder sitting on my chest. Nightmare whines from his crate. I need to let him outside, but I can't do that in my underwear, and getting to my bedroom seems like a monumental task with my whole body shuddering with… what? Anger? Grief? Sorrow?

A mixture of it all and more, probably.

Focusing on my breathing, I inhale and exhale, counting to five with each one, until I start to settle the fuck down.

When I'm able, I run to my room to throw on some sweats and a hoodie.

"Come on, buddy," I say, unlatching Nightmare's crate. "I'm sorry that took me so long."

Once out in the yard, I try not to look across the street, not wanting the reminder of who's there and what he called me. Nightmare's halfway through his nightly shit when I finally give in and peek.

Tyson stands in the same spot where he does his morning yoga. He's removed his jacket and unbuttoned his shirt, and when he sees me looking, he places a hand over his heart. As if I hold a place there.

But it's not me he keeps space for, is it?

Tears stream down my cheeks. I don't hide them from him, even if I'm not sure he can see them from here. It's dark, but I don't feel the cold. It can't penetrate this sorrow—the feeling of never being good enough or worthy. It would be unfair to blame all of that on Tyson, but I won't make excuses for him, either. Being predisposed to feelings of abandonment or neglect doesn't give him a pass on treating me like I'm a second-string player in his life.

The kicker is that, when we connect—which is most of the time—it's the highest high. Some of the best moments of my life happened with him, all in such a short span.

But I'm not sure where we go from here.

"Let's go, Nightmare," I call softly, looking away from Tyson.

My phone chimes a moment after we're back inside.

TYSON:

I'm so sorry, Kit. I hope you'll let me explain. On your timeline, of course.

How do you explain calling the woman you're currently dating by your ex's name? The short answer: you can't. The long answer isn't something I'm interested in right now.

Even though he sleeps in his crate, I bring Nightmare to bed with me. Like the best friend he is, he curls up with his nose in the crook of my neck and watches over me as I fretfully sleep.

I wake up with a headache and a cell phone that won't stop ringing. I ignore it the first two times, burying my head under the comforter. Nightmare whimpers the third time it rings.

"I feel the same, buddy," I murmur. It must be Tyson—who else would call this urgently, this early? The sun's barely up. "Ugh, fine."

When I grab my phone off my nightstand, my blood runs cold at the name on the screen. It's not Tyson. It's not anyone I've spoken to in a decade.

My father never calls. I don't call him, either. Which means, this must be an emergency.

Grandma.

"Hello?"

"It's about time you answered," he says, making me instantly retreat into myself. It's what always happens, and one of the many reasons I don't talk to him.

"It's four in the morning, here. I was asleep."

"My mom died last night."

"What?" I sit up, as if that will help me process the words.

"She didn't want a funeral," he says, ignoring my shock. "She'll be interred with my dad. If you want to be there for that, you need to come home."

His voice is cold, without emotion. Which, I guess, is better than anger or cruelty. He could at least pretend to be sad, but he's never been good at hiding how he feels.

"I'll get there as soon as I can."

"Her house is yours, now. You can stay there. Text me when you get here; I'll drop off the key."

"Oh. I didn't know she did that," I say. When he doesn't respond, I add, "I'll let you know when I land."

"All right," he says, then ends the call.

I stare down at my phone, wondering what I've done to deserve the last twelve hours of my life. Then, I start making a mental list of everything I need to do—except, I can't focus on any of it because the only family I had just died.

With watery eyes, I call the only person I can count on, right now.

"What's wrong?" Willa asks immediately. She knows I wouldn't call this early unless it was urgent.

"My dad just called to tell me my grandma died," I say, surprised I'm not in tears. None of this feels real—maybe I'm still asleep.

"Shit, Kit. I'm so sorry. What do you need? Is Tyson with you?"

"No. We had…not a fight, but something happened."

"What?"

I almost tell her. I will tell her. But right now, what Tyson did isn't as important as going to Maine. That's what I need help with, first—because I don't know if I can go back there alone. I'm not sure I'd mentally survive it.

"I need to go to Maine. He's going to inter her with my grandfather, and if I wait too long, he'll do it without me there."

"Okay, I'll have Damian get us on a flight today. Will that work?"

"Thank you," I say on a soft sob, loving that she doesn't hesitate.

"Of course, babe. I'm not letting you do any of this alone, okay?"

"Okay. I'll let work know I need time off. I guess she left me her house. I don't know what condition it's in, but we can stay there."

"Did you know she was doing that?"

"No," I answer. "I had no idea. Do you think Isla would keep Nightmare for me?"

"I'm sure she would, and Sadie would love that. I'll call her and work out dropping him off on the way to the airport. You just pack what you need, okay?"

"I can do that. Thank you again, Willa."

"We've got you," she reassures. "Do you need anything else, right now?"

"No. I'll shower and pack so I'm ready."

"If you think of anything else, text me. We'll be there soon. I love you."

"Love you, too," I say, ending the call.

By now, Nightmare is scratching at the door. Wrapping myself in a blanket, I take him to the yard, sit on the damp grass, and try to organize my thoughts while he takes care of business.

Even though we didn't talk often, I can't believe she's gone. Or that I'll never hear her voice again. It's complicated—this tangle of emotions running through me. I'm sad, yet guilty for not being sadder. What does it say about me that I'm not breaking down, bawling my eyes out?

Or that I'm more afraid of going back to Maine and facing my father than I am about living a life without my grandmother.

I've spent years protecting myself, keeping my peace. Once, not long after I moved here, I tried to explain that to her. She was sad I wasn't coming home for the holidays. But Maine isn't safe for me. Going back is terrifying.

More than anything, I wish Tyson and I were in a place where I could have him with me. If last night hadn't happened, he'd have been my first call—because he was my safe space.

And now, he's just one more thing I'm scared to face.

23

TYSON

My call went straight to voicemail. Even though I told her last night that I'd stick to her timeline, I was worried. So, I called Kit. Well, tried to, anyway. She obviously isn't ready to talk to me. Not that I blame her.

I fucked up.

It's not what she thinks, though, and I'm not giving up. Not fucking ever. Blowing up her phone won't do any good. I need a better plan, and she, understandably, needs space from my dumb ass.

Last night, after I dropped her home, she looked so small in her yard, waiting for Nightmare. It was my fault. I did that to her. I propped up her fragile confidence at the beginning of the night, only to shatter it completely, hours later. Because I got caught up in my own head instead of telling her all the things I was thinking.

She may never forgive me. Not when she trusts so few people. Not when we were so new, still. Kit's the type to cut her losses and move on. Who could blame her?

"Fuck," I mutter, dumping my wallet and keys into my cubby.

"I feel you," Cillian says from his spot next to mine. "If Isla had to leave for a death in the family, I'd be agonizing over it, too."

"What?" I ask. "Who had a death in the family?"

"You didn't hear?" he asks.

"Hear what?"

"Kit's grandmother died," he says, except, now, he sounds like maybe he wasn't supposed to say anything. "Why don't you know that?"

"Willa said Tyson and Kit got into a fight last night," Zander says as he walks up to us. "She didn't call him."

"You fought? About what?"

"It wasn't a fight," I say, shaking my head. "Back up, her grandma died?"

"Yeah, man. Last night, I guess. Her dad called early this morning," Zander says.

"She talked to her fucking father?"

"I guess," Zan says. "It all happened quickly. She called Willa, and Damian got them on a flight first thing this morning."

"To Maine?" Anger and worry swim in my gut. I don't want her anywhere near her father, but especially not without me by her side to make sure he doesn't hurt her. Again. I promised her he couldn't do that. I promised myself I'd never let it happen.

"Yes," Zander says.

"No," I say. "Fuck, no. She can't go there alone." I sit on the bench, drop my head in my hands. What do I do? We have practice today, and a game tomorrow. How do I fulfill my responsibilities here, and to her?

"She's not alone. Willa and Damian went, too."

"Damian is with them?" I ask, and he nods. "Where's Nightmare?"

"My house," Cillian says. "Sadie is puppy sitting."

"I bet she loves that," Zander says, and Cillian rambles about how Sadie was so excited to have him at their house that she almost peed her pants because she didn't want to take a break from playing to go to the bathroom.

This isn't right.

"Isla had to carry Nightmare to the bathroom with her, just so she'd go," Cillian says, laughing. "We can't quit holding out on the kid, she wants a puppy so badly."

"This isn't right," I say aloud, this time. "I can't be here."

My heart beats wildly, a painful banging inside my chest, as if it's trying to escape me and run to her. It wants to be with Kit. Not here. *Not here.*

"Damian and Willa will keep an eye on her," Zander says.

"That's not good enough," I argue. "Do you know what happened to her in Maine?"

"Not entirely. But Willa does."

As much as I trust Willa to help Kit, it's not enough. Again, I picture her like she was last night. Alone, shaking and upset. Even on her strongest day, this would be a difficult trip for her.

"It's not right," I repeat. "I need to be there."

"Does she want you there?" Zander asks.

Would she? I can't answer with certainty, not after last night. But I think she would. Kit is emotional, but not in that way. She isn't petty or immature. She'd set aside my infraction and take my support. There's plenty of time to hate me after she buries her grandmother and comes back home.

"I won't know until I show up."

"What about the game tomorrow?" Cillian asks, sounding…approving.

"You guys can win one without me," I say, and he nods, smiling.

"We'll hold it down, you go help your woman," he says, patting me on the shoulder. "I'd do the same in your shoes."

I can't help but wonder if he'd have a different reaction if he knew the reason Kit isn't talking to me. That's not as important, right now, as getting to her, though. Like everything else, there's time to deal with that later.

"Do you know what flight they're on?" I ask Zander.

"They're already in the air," he says. "I'll forward you what I know, but it isn't much."

"Get in touch with Willa when you get to Bangor," Coach says. I hadn't noticed him lurking behind us. "I'll handle things with management, here, to keep you out of as much trouble as I can with them."

"Thank you, Coach."

"I'm relying on you and Damian to take care of my girls."

"We will, sir."

It takes me all day to get to Bangor. It was already late when I landed and got a rental car. Then, there was another ninety-minute drive up to the small-town Kit grew up in. Willa gave me the address of Kit's grandmother's house. They plan on staying there, but she let me know of a motel nearby. Zander had let her know I was on my way, when they landed. She told Kit, who, I got the impression, was indifferent to the information.

Skipping the motel, I head straight to Kit. There won't be any sleep until I see her; I'm far too amped up with concern. Maybe it's stupid to be this worried. I'm not trying to treat her like she's too fragile to handle this. I know she's not, and I know she'll get through this like she does everything. With shaky confidence and an abundance of courage.

If she wavers, I want to be her crutch. That's all. If by the time she's ready to fly home, she still wants space from me, I'll take that shit like a man and give it to her. I'll hate every fucking minute of it, but that's the bed I made.

My phone chimes as I pull up to the postage stamp of a house that Kit's grandmother lived in.

LOTTIE:

Are you there yet?

I'd called both Lot and my mother while I waited at the airport to board, this morning. Neither is happy with how I screwed shit up. Lottie ran me through the wringer, using every swear word in her arsenal at least twice, before she let me explain what was rattling through my brain when I used the wrong name with Kit.

After that, she settled down and told me she was proud of me for putting my career aside for a woman. Something she didn't think I'd have done for Isla, when we were dating.

My mom tried to be more understanding, but I think she wanted to use some foul language with me, too.

ME:

Just pulled up.

LOTTIE:

Glad you made it safe. Don't fuck up anymore, dickhead.

ME:

I won't. Promise.

The house isn't much bigger than Kit's in Seattle. This house has seen better days. The pale yellow paint is dingy and peeling, several of the shutters are hanging on for dear life, and I'd be shocked if the roof isn't leaking. I'm scared the front door will cave in if I knock too hard, so I rap on it lightly.

"Hi, Tyson," Damian greets when he opens the door.

"Hey, thanks for getting her here."

"Of course, family first," he says, moving aside to let me in.

Following the sound of voices, I walk down the short hall. There's a bathroom at the end, a bedroom on either side. Kit and Willa stand just inside the door of the one on the left.

"That's where I slept if I stayed over," Kit says, pointing to a futon mattress lying on the floor in the corner. "I wonder why she never got rid of it."

"Maybe she wanted to keep a place for you, just in case," I say, and she spins around to face me. She stares at me, her eyes haunted. I don't say anything more, not with words, anyway. If I can convey them silently, that's what I'm attempting to do. There's something intimate in the silent eye contact. Something transcendent. If I vocalized that, she'd laugh at me and ask if I want to go look up my horoscope. So, I keep my sappy lips shut, for now. She bounces on her toes, and I just know she's curling them inside her shoes. "Hey, Kit."

I hold my arms out at my sides, and she steps into me, letting me wrap them around her.

"Hi."

"I'm sorry about your grandmother," I say.

"You shouldn't have come, Tyson," she says, the words muffled in my shirt. My heart cracks, but I knew this wouldn't be easy.

"I'll leave if you want, go check into the motel. But I'm not leaving Maine until you do."

"You have a game tomorrow."

"I made a promise," I say, cupping her face. "When you're back at home safely, I'll go back to work."

"I haven't forgiven you," she whispers.

"You don't need to forgive me for me to keep my promises to you," I say. "You don't owe me that, or anything else. Okay?"

"Okay," she agrees after a moment.

"Did you see your father?"

"He dropped the key under the mat before we got here," she says, shaking her head.

Thank fuck for small miracles.

"How are you holding up?"

"I don't know, really. It's weird being here," she says. "It's weird you're here, too. I appreciate it, Tyson. I do. I just don't…"

"I get it, Kit," I say. I wish things were different, but the last thing I want is to make any of this harder for her. "I'll go to the motel. I'm only here as a friend who cares about you. A lot. I needed to see you. I know I fucked up, and we can talk about that back in Seattle, whenever you're ready. But I meant what I said. I'm here until you aren't."

"I'll…I'll call if I need you," she stammers.

"Thank you," I say, and drop a kiss to the crown of her head. "Try and get some sleep."

"I will." She looks over her shoulder at the makeshift bed. I can't guess what's playing through her mind, I can only hope it's not all horrible. "Thank you, Tyson. For…well, thank you."

"Anything you need, love."

Reluctantly, I walk out of the room, leaving my heart behind. My whole world used to be hockey. Now, it's that woman, her hair in messy braids, her feet in worn out Converse, with tears in her eyes and her chin held high.

I love her. Irrevocably.

I only hope I have the chance to tell her, someday.

"We'll keep an eye on her," Willa tells me, patting my shoulder as she walks with me out the door.

"Never doubted that for a second." I try to smile at her. "Did she tell you?"

"What you did? Yes."

"It was bad, but it's not what she thinks. I'm not in love with Isla. I never was," I say. "This isn't to get you on my side or anything. I'm in love with Kit. I have been for weeks, now."

She looks at me with a mix of sympathy and something else. Probably pity, since I fucked my chances so miraculously.

"Actually, I knew that as soon as I heard you were flying here."

"It felt important that I tell someone," I say, not understanding my reasoning enough to vocalize it. I only know that I had to tell somebody. "I told her I'm not leaving Maine until she does. Whether she wants to include me in anything here is up to her. I'll be here, though. In case."

"That's sweet of you, Tyson," she says as a truck pulls down the driveway. "I wonder who that is. Her father?"

A man drives the truck, a cap on his head making it hard to tell his age. Unease tickles the back of my neck. There's no man in this state that Kit would want to see.

"Go inside, Willa," I say. "If Kit wants to talk to whoever it is, she can let me know. Okay?"

"Okay," she agrees, and rushes into the house while I wait for the man to exit the vehicle.

He hesitates when he gets closer to me, as if he underestimated my size—or maybe the scowl on my face. First impressions matter, and I want his first one to be clear: he must get through me to get to her. Friend or foe, I'm his first obstacle.

"Uh, hey," he says.

"Who are you?" I cross my arms over my chest, my stance wide as I block the path to the house.

"I'm a friend of the family."

"Whose friend? Be specific."

"Of Carl's. Kit's dad. We go way back," he says, and my veins chill. Did this motherfucker think he could show up here and take advantage of her vulnerability? Again.

"What's your name, man?"

"Derik."

Fuck my life, I'm going to jail tonight.

"Derik what?" I ask. The front door of the house opens behind me; a quick glance tells me it's Damian who has stepped out—not Kit.

"Johnston."

"Hey, Damian?"

"Yes," he replies slowly, his single word dripping with pleasure at what he knows is about to happen. He comes across as polite, mature, classy. But Damian March has a darker side, I'm sure of it.

"I'm going to need a witness."

"It's self-defense, my friend. I saw him swing first," Damian says.

"What the fuck?" Derik says, taking a step back. Not far enough, because I easily grab his shirt with my left hand as I jab with my right. The crack I hear when my fist meets his nose is the most satisfying thing I've ever heard. The instant gush of blood makes my heart pump faster.

"What the hell? I'll call the cops."

"You think a night in jail scares me more than the pleasure I'll get from putting a rapist in the hospital?" I tighten my grip. He tries to push me away, but I have height, reach, and strength on him. Another swing makes contact with his eye.

"Rape?" he protests. "I didn't rape anyone!"

He swings his arms wildly. The only one that finds purchase on my face feels more like he hit me with a pillow than a hand. It may still leave a mark, but it's nothing compared to what I'm used to from a little brawl on the ice.

"Did she say yes, you motherfucker? Coercion isn't consent," I say, and I don't stop swinging. Nor do I stop yelling in his face, which is becoming slick with blood, now. "Did she fucking say yes? Answer me, asshole! Did she say yes?"

"N...no," he finally stammers.

"What was that?" I ask, landing another blow to his side while I hold his weight up against the side of his truck. He's already weak—this didn't last nearly as long as I'd like.

"No," he repeats.

I shove him, and he falls to the ground, covering his face with his hands.

"I'm going to find out if you've done this to other women," Damian says, stepping up beside me. He rolls Derik over with a shove of his foot. "In fact,

I'm going to find out everything about you. Every horrible thing you've ever done, you piece of shit. If it's as bad as I think it is, I'm going to share it all with my friend, here, and then we're going to ruin your fucking life."

"Fuck you, I have a family," he mumbles.

"Yeah? Do they know you're a rapist?" I ask.

"No, I didn't—"

"Be very careful with what you say to me, right now," I warn, squatting down to get close to his face. "You're able to drive out of here, but that can change quickly."

"I didn't mean to. I didn't mean to hurt her."

"But you did. And what the fuck did you come here for, tonight?"

"I…I have a daughter, now," he cries.

"So, you came here to what? Relieve your guilt?" Damian asks. Derik nods.

"Selfish prick." I spit on the ground next to him. "You came here for you, without thinking that it could hurt her more. Get the fuck out of here. Don't ever come near her again, or I'll fucking kill you. This was your warning."

He scrambles to his feet and fumbles with the door to his truck.

"Seek some fucking therapy, asshole," Damian says, giving Derik a final shove into his truck. Neither of us moves until his truck has turned out of the driveway.

24

KIT

I watch the scene from behind the living room curtain. The house is old, the windows have never been replaced, so I hear most of everything they say through the single-pane glass that separates me from them.

When Willa came in to tell me someone was here, I expected it to be my father. It being Derik was infinitely worse. For the first time since Willa told me Tyson was coming to Maine, I felt no apprehension about it. I'm glad he's here. Also, I'm afraid of what could happen to him because of this—not what Derik can do physically. It was perfectly clear Tyson dominated in the altercation. But the legal ramifications that may come later...I'd hate for him to get in trouble for standing up for me.

Damn, it was hot. He's always so caring with me that I forget he has this side of him—as if the Tyson Murphy on the ice and the Tyson Murphy in my life are two different characters.

His dominance in the situation was a great distraction from the traumatic flashbacks my stupid brain was conjuring. I can never forget. Not all the words he said.

"You'll like it, I promise."

That was a lie.

The feeling of his hand on my chest, forcing me to still while he unfastened my pants, will never leave me. Ever. Nor will that first sharp pain, or the tears that silently spilled from the corners of my eyes. Or the screams that were only loud in my own head because I was too stunned, confused, and terrified to vocalize them.

Those are things I'll live with my entire life.

I hope his nose breaking under Tyson's fist lives with him forever. If it does, it's not enough. We're not even. The scales can never be balanced. But it helps—that small amount of justice. It helps.

Willa stands behind me, her arms wrapped around my waist, her chin resting on my shoulder while she watches the scene with me.

"Tyson's okay," she says when Derik's car drives off. "Are you?"

"I think so," I say, trying to take stock of myself. My pulse is racing, my toes curled, I'm trembling, but not uncontrollably. "I'm not alone anymore."

"Never again, bestie," she says, leaning her head against mine.

My eyes don't waver from Tyson as he walks back toward the house. He stops just short of the porch. Damian comes back in, but nobody follows. When I look back to the window, I see Tyson walking toward his car.

"Tyson," I call, running outside to him.

"Are you okay?" he asks, turning to face me.

"Are you leaving?" I ask, nodding. There's a red spot low on his cheek; I touch it with tenderness. "Are you okay?"

"I'm fine," he says, grinning. "If anything, I'm disappointed he didn't put up more of a fight so I could have gone at him longer. And yes, I'm leaving. I'll go to the motel, and you'll call me if you need me." He gives me a pointed look, and again, I nod.

"Can I—" I start, then stop to compose myself. Looking down at my sock-covered feet, I laugh. "I don't have shoes on. But can I hug you?"

"Of course." He wraps me in a big bear hug, lifting me off my feet and walking us back toward the house. When we reach the porch, he sets me back on my feet. "It's been a long day. Go get some rest."

"Okay," I say, staring up at him. My emotions war with each other inside my chest. "Goodnight, Tyson."

"Goodnight." He presses his lips to my forehead. I don't move back into the house until he's gone and I'm certain he's not coming back.

"He left," I say when I'm back in the house, the door locked tightly behind me.

"He didn't want to trauma bond," Damian says.

"What do you mean?"

"A part of you wanted him to stay, right?" I nod, and he continues. "Was that because you want him here, or because you want the safety he provides?"

"Can it be both?" I ask, because I don't really know the answer.

"Absolutely. But he doesn't want you to forgive what he did last night because of what he did tonight. He'd protect you, even if you never speak to him again."

"And wanting that protection from him shouldn't be a factor in whether you two work things out. Or not," Willa adds.

"He's being a gentleman. Again," I say.

"Yeah, babe," Willa says. "He knows you're fragile from everything going on. He doesn't want to take advantage."

"That's good. I'm not sure I like it, right now, but it's good," I say, pouting a little—which only underscores what they're saying. I'm not ready to have the conversation with him about calling me by another woman's name, but what he did for me tonight was what I've dreamed of a man doing for me for as long as I can remember.

I hate to think of myself as a damsel in distress, but everyone needs a support system. I never felt I had one, until tonight, when three people showed up for me in huge ways—no questions asked.

"Emotions are hard," Willa says.

That's the damn truth. Today has completely wrung me out. It's probably a good thing I have friends here to help me keep my shit straight.

The following day, we get to work cleaning out the house. Luckily, my grandma was tidy and didn't like clutter. We move from room to room, sorting piles for donation, trash, and a small stack of things I want to keep.

There's a meager teaspoon collection that I know was her mother's, a coffee mug that I made her in a pottery class I took in the tenth grade, and a small box of her family pictures. There are more from her childhood than there are from mine, reinforcing my thoughts on her adult life. She didn't lead a happy one.

It makes me sad for her. For women like her, who get trapped in unfulfilling or abusive relationships. It makes me sadder for the children trapped in those situations. It's the cycle of thought I repeatedly end up with. Like always, I remind myself that I got out of the situation. I found a way to live on my terms, by my rules. I'm no longer anyone's victim. And as much as I wish I could have changed my grandmother's situation, she made her own choices.

My phone chimes with a text, bringing me out of my depressing thoughts. It's a message from my father, telling me that the funeral home will have her ashes ready to inter inside the same mausoleum as my grandfather, two days from now. These were arrangements she made prior to her death. To me, it feels wrong for her to be resting eternally with her abuser, but that's not my call. He also says that the attorney who prepared her will has paperwork for me to sign and will be coming by the house.

The house that I don't know what to do with. Damian offered to find a property management company to upkeep it, if I decide not to sell it. I'm not sure what benefit there is to keeping it, though. I have no interest in being a landlord, nor do I have any reason to come back here in the future.

Selling it is logical, but that doesn't feel quite right, either. It conjures an icky swirl in my stomach, like I'm profiting from her death.

"You don't need to make a decision, now," Damian says when I express that. "Whenever you decide, whatever it is you decide, we'll be here to help take care of it."

This is my family—Willa, Damian, Zander, the Coles, the Wylders. They are the type of family everyone deserves. The type that shows up, not only when you need it most, but always. Maybe I should have been more of that for my grandmother, but she should have been more of that for me, too.

Now, it's too late for either of us to make those amends.

If anything, it gives me more perspective on my situation with Tyson. I don't know if I'll ever be secure as anything more than a friend to him. There are still discussions that have to be had. What I do know is that I won't shy away from those conversations. I'll give the opportunity for amends to be made—even if, after it's all said and done, Tyson isn't my man, after all.

Because another thing I'm sure of, is that I won't compromise by being second choice. I won't settle for what I can get, instead of what I deserve, only to die lonely anyway. I won't live a life of what-ifs, like my grandmother did.

I do hope we'll always be something to each other, though. He's given me so much in such little time. It wouldn't be right to share so much with someone, only to end up never speaking.

"We should order pizza, tonight," I suggest, as we finish up in my grandmother's bedroom. The only thing staying is the nightstand, lamp, and bed that Willa and Damian are sleeping on. The rest is being donated. "And I'll ask Tyson to come over. I feel bad that he came all the way here and he's been hanging out in the dingy motel all day."

"Pizza does sound good," Willa says.

"The car is full," Damian says, poking his head into the room. He's been making runs all morning to the Goodwill. "Need anything while I'm out?"

"Pizza," Willa and I say in unison.

"Got it."

"Enough for Tyson, too," I add.

"No problem. Be back soon. Call if you think of anything else."

"Thank you, Damian."

"No worries, Kit."

I text Tyson to ask if he'll come over.

TYSON:

I'd love to, thanks for the invite.

Next, I shower, and try to make myself presentable after a day of cleaning. As soon as I turn the hair dryer off, I hear a knock on the front door. Damian is already back and hollers that he'll answer it. Shortly after, Willa knocks on the door to tell me the attorney is here.

She's a woman in her late fifties, if I had to guess. Introducing herself as Susan, she tells me she met my grandmother years ago, when they both joined a cribbage group that met one night a week at the community center.

"It's too bad they didn't catch the cancer earlier," she says.

"Cancer?" I ask.

"Yes, dear. She didn't want to tell you she was diagnosed with late-stage colon cancer early this year. I figured your father would have told you since she passed."

"He didn't. We're not close," I say, not asking why my grandmother didn't tell me. It's not surprising, since we didn't tell each other a lot of things. Mostly, we kept every conversation to good news only.

"Of course," she says, as if she knew and forgot. "So, I have some paperwork you'll need to sign. Essentially, she quitclaimed the house to you. There wasn't much money left over, as she used everything she had to ensure there wouldn't be expenses left unpaid for you to take care of from inheriting her estate. She did add your name to her bank account, though—that information is in here." She hands me a manila envelope.

"Thank you, I appreciate you coming here to do this." I sign each page where little red flags are placed.

"Sure. Anna was a friend. She loved you, Kit. It wasn't easy for her to show, but she did."

"I know, I loved her, too."

"She knew that," she says, rubbing her hand down my arm. "There's a letter from her in there, as well."

"Oh. Okay." I peek in the envelope to find a smaller one inside, my name written on it.

"That's it for paperwork. My card is in there—if you need anything from me, you just let me know."

"Thank you, Susan," I say, and walk her back to the door. Opening the envelope back up, I take out the letter, and within minutes, everything I knew about my life changes.

25

TYSON

The scene I walk into at Kit's grandmother's house is not the one I was expecting. She's ghostly white and struggling to gain control of herself, in a full-on panic attack, a crumpled piece of paper in her hand.

"Hey, hey, what's going on?" I move to sit on the floor in front of her. Willa is next to her, an arm wrapped around her friend. She looks horrified, and I just know, whatever has happened is worse than I can imagine. "Kit, breathe with me."

Cupping her face, I softly blow out air, hoping that she'll exhale with me. I rub my thumbs along her temples and keep whispering to her. It's long minutes, but she starts to regulate. A few moments later, she pushes the paper into my chest.

"She's dead," she gasps.

"Your grandmother? Yeah, sweetheart, I know."

"Read it," she says, shaking her head wildly until I take the paper and look at it.

Kitpu,

There is a long list of things I should have told you. It's almost as long as the list of reasons I never did. Let me start with some of the easy ones.

I love you. You've been the greatest joy in my life, the brightest light. I regret that I didn't tell you that every day. And that I was terrible at showing it. My weak excuse is that I didn't know how.

I'm sorry I couldn't save you. It was my job. The most important job I ever had, and I failed. You should have been protected, you deserved that. I'm so proud of you for protecting yourself, for leaving this place, and never looking back. You were always stronger than anyone gave you credit for.

I'm sorry I didn't tell you the truth. I'm sorry I didn't tell you the truth in life, instead I took the easy way out and wrote you this letter. Hopefully, you won't hate me for it, but I'd understand if you do.

Promise you'll never feel any guilt for how you feel about me or the complicated relationship we've had, Kit. You've learned to put your own happiness and peace first, and I could never ask for anything more than that. You are a woman of value, of worth, who is deserving of every good thing you want out of life. And you are those things because of the choices you made. You are you because of you, not because of him. Do you understand?

I hope so.

Now comes the hard part. The secret I've kept from you because your father said I had to. He threatened to take you away if I ever told you, and I stupidly believed him. I also didn't want to be the broker of more pain for you, which I can admit was selfish of me.

With this letter, you'll find the name and phone number of a detective in Billings, Montana. Jack Silva is retired now, but he'll answer any questions you have.

Nimii didn't leave you, my sweet girl. Not intentionally.

She went to Montana for the funeral of a childhood friend. While there, she planned to find work and a place to live. A place for you both to escape your father who had shown his true colors by then.

She went missing, later found murdered.

I'm so sorry you never got to meet her or learn what a sweet woman she was. She loved you more than anything in this world.

When your father found out her plan was to come back and pack you up, he hated her for it. Instead of blaming himself, he blamed her and then you.

He erased her from his life because it was easier for him. Maybe he thought it would be easier for you, too. I can't say.

Her name was Nimii Marian Ray-Ashcroft. I don't believe she had much family by the time she met your father. Hannah Markle is the name of the friend whose funeral she went to Montana for. She has a brother who handled the arrangements for your mother's burial in Montana. Your father didn't bring her back here.

I hope it's enough of a trail for you to find any answers you'll need. It's all I have.

This will be hard information for you to process. I'm thankful you have a support system now to help you. Nimii would love that for you, too. Though I didn't get to know her as much as I wish, I'm certain she would be as proud of the woman you are as I am. Please live with that knowledge strong in your heart, Kitpu. You have always been wanted and loved.

Don't follow in my footsteps. Stay on your path. Live for yourself, live without regrets and fear. Shower your love on others and take the love they give you with the same exuberance.

It's the most important thing in life.

I've loved you always,

Grandma Anna

Holy fuck.

No wonder she's such a mess.

"I'm so sorry, Kit," I say.

Sorry isn't a big enough sentiment, but what do you say in a situation like this? How is she supposed to handle finding out her mother has been dead for over twenty years from a death bed letter?

Jesus, the shit she's been through in her life would bring anyone to their fucking knees.

"Why is he so horrible?" she asks, speaking about her father. She's calmed down since handing me the letter. Silent tears fall from her eyes; other than that, her anxiety has subsided. Or rather, morphed into despair. She still looks like the saddest woman I've ever seen. I'd do anything to change that. What, though? There's nothing that can take this away from her.

"I don't know," Willa says.

"What do you want to do?" I ask, rubbing my hands along her thighs to comfort myself as much as her. The heaviness is a cinderblock on my chest. The shock of it all is difficult to process, for me, and I'm much more removed from it than her.

Finding out you've been lied to your whole life by your entire family is a soul-crushing level of bullshit. Her father has a lot to answer for, and she still hasn't seen him. Not only will she be facing him for the first time in a decade, but it will be with the knowledge that he didn't tell her that her mother is dead.

"My thoughts are all over the place," she confesses. "Right now, I want to eat pizza. I want to watch something stupid and mindless until my brain defrags and I can think coherently."

"We can do that," Willa says. "Stupid and mindless. You leaning toward something in particular?"

"*Schitt's Creek*?" Damian suggests, but she shakes her head.

"*Love Island*?" I ask.

"No, I can't take all that screaming and cheering tonight."

"*Midsommar*," Willa chimes in.

"Fuck. Yes, that's it." If this conversation was happening at any other time, I'd be laughing my ass off. Because what the actual fuck? *Midsommar* is anything but mindless. Though, Kit doesn't relax the way most people do. Easy television is true crime documentaries and the goriest horror movies. If a pagan cult flick that violently murders people is how she sorts through her brain, who am I to tell her differently.

We all sit on the floor around the television, pizza boxes spread out in front of us while the movie plays. There isn't much conversation, and all three of us watch Kit for any sign that her anxiety is taking hold again. Other than how she normally retreats into herself when she's contemplating something, she seems okay.

I can't imagine how I'd react in the same situation. Truth be told, I've never had real trauma. The worst I've been through is a breakup, which is trivial to anything Kit's been through. But I imagine I'd rage. At life for being cruel and unfair. At a father for keeping such detrimental information.

Yeah, I'm sure I'd rage.

I want to rage for her, bury everyone that's ever caused her offense. This sweet, unexpecting woman who only wants to exist in the world as who she is. A brilliant mind, a heart full of love, and a little bit of chaos to keep things interesting.

My heart hurts when I look at her. It hurts for her, and it hurts that she's not mine. She should be mine. I believe we're meant to be. Kit is my person. All the messy thoughts I had the night of the gala are gone. I'm clean. It's clear to me.

This woman is my future. She's all that matters.

"What?" she whispers.

"What?"

"You're staring at me."

"You're staring at me," I say.

"Oh my God," she says with an eye roll. A soft smile tries to play on her lips. It's enough to let me know that she's going to be okay. Whatever she learns from her father, about her mother, she's going to be okay.

Whether we will be, or not, remains up in the air. But she's going to be okay. And that's all I can ask for right now. The rest…I'll fight for.

Until the day I fucking die, I'll fight for Kit Ashcroft.

26
KIT

Today, I see my father for the first time since I left for college.

Today, I see my father for the first time since learning he lied to me about my mother.

Today is going to be a hard day.

But at least I'll be doing it with friends, and not as the same weak little girl he's used to pushing around. Tyson is with me, too. He sat by me all night, after reading my grandmother's letter. I caught him staring at me more than once. At first, I thought he might be waiting for the powder keg to explode. Like I was going to start breaking everything in the house or something. Then, I realized he was probably expecting another anxiety attack.

What I appreciated most last night was that the three of them didn't handle me with kid gloves or try to force me to talk about it. Tyson even flirted some, like he did at the beginning.

The initial hit from that letter was hard. Devastating, really. In the back of my mind, finding her was always an option. Not a desire, but an option. There was a chance at…something. That's gone, now.

I was up most of the night researching. I searched for my mother's name and found few hits—a couple of news articles that mentioned she was missing, an archive from her high school that had her name attached to a varsity volleyball team that went to the state championship her senior year in Massachusetts. I didn't even know that was where she was from. Other than that, all I could find was basic vital statistics for her.

What I did find was a big, deep hole of information on missing and murdered Indigenous women. The Crow reservation, where she initially went missing from, is riddled with similar stories. Very few are ever entered into the U.S. Justice System database, and far fewer are ever solved. The numbers are terrifying—and grow too quickly because of a flawed system that lets perpetrators take advantage of jurisdictional red tape.

My mother is nothing more than a statistic, now. All but forgotten by anyone.

That breaks my heart. More than not ever getting to know her, because that's just a selfish want I'll never be able to fulfill. She should be remembered by someone, though. If nothing else, I could have been that for her—a person who knew she existed and mattered. He stole that from both of us.

Which brings on a slew of questions. Did he ever love her? How could he dismiss her in death so callously, if he did? Not that my father's version of love has ever made sense to me. Is he why I'm so distrusting in love?

What even is love?

It's not an emotion I understand. It's not the only one, but it's the biggest one that makes little sense to me. If I'd experienced it more in my life, perhaps I wouldn't be so gun-shy of it. My lived experience has jaded me, I fear.

I don't want to be fearful of anything—especially not something that brings other people so much joy. For the first time, I want to experience being in love. With Tyson, I thought I was heading there. But I'm not sure if that's because of the sex. Was it just a stimulation high? Is my brain addled from our physical connection? I've seen people do stupid things because of lust.

But lust is foreign to me, too. Not that I'm not ridiculously attracted to Tyson—just looking at him sometimes makes me blush with the things I want him to do to me. Except, I think that's desire and curiosity, not so much lust.

Are desire and lust the same thing? I'm not sure.

What a stupid thing to be thinking about while I'm walking through the doors of a funeral home to bury my grandmother. There's time to figure those thoughts out. There's time to figure everything else out, later—and there is a lot of everything else.

It all falls to the wayside when I see my father waiting for me by the mausoleum wall that will be my grandmother's final resting place. The marble block behind him has already been removed, one urn already sitting inside, just waiting for the other.

There is no *till death do us part*. Not for Anna Ashcroft. She never found her escape. For the first time since her death, tears well. She deserved better—if for no other reason than that she created the smallest of safe spaces for me as a child.

It wasn't large. It was a small hope. Never underestimate how hope blooms.

"Kit," he says as I approach. "I expected this would be only family." His eyes bounce around my three companions, lingering on Tyson the longest.

"This is my family."

"I meant mine," he says, tight-lipped.

"You have no family," I blurt. The girl he used to know wouldn't have been able to say such a thing without retribution. I'm not that girl anymore. Even with my heart racing, it feels right to speak my mind. To stand up to him. "It died with her."

His eyes narrow dangerously on me. I've caused offense—he always hated that.

"Who are your friends?" He says the word like it's an insult. Though, he's probably never experienced true friendship, so maybe it is to him. Can narcissists have friends? I can't imagine.

"This is Willa, Damian, and Tyson."

"Tyson Murphy?" he asks, surprising me. I remember him casually watching hockey, but I wouldn't expect him to know all the players.

"Yes," Tyson says with a dismissive nod as he steps closer to my side. My father's gaze bounces between us, trying to interpret the situation. His mouth opens to say something, but Tyson beats him to it. "We'll put Anna to rest, now. You can make your assumptions and ask your questions after."

The funeral director, who has awkwardly been standing to the side, clears his throat. He says some words—nothing I can focus on—but it sounds like he knew her. Not surprising, in a small town, and I can be thankful that someone has nice words for her. I scan the wall, full of names. Some I recognize. Some have fresh flowers in their vases, most are empty.

This isn't what I want for myself in death—to be placed in a concrete wall, or a concrete box and lowered into the cold earth. I don't want even my ashes to be confined. Spread me in a flowerbed where I can become something else. Something fresh, colorful, and alive. A renewal instead of an ending.

I'm not religious or spiritual. I do believe in a circle of life, though, and I like to think that I was part of something before—an atom, an organism that morphed or mutated time and time again. And will continue to do so. Like a continuous cycle of fertilization.

Maybe I'll be used for growing carrots in my next cycle. I'll be someone's beta-carotene.

My father stands like a statue throughout it all. His shoulders heightened, the vein in his neck bulging. If I had to guess, I'd say he's not thinking about his mother. No—he's fuming over what Tyson and I both said to him. His ego could never take such slighting.

That's okay. My, albeit much smaller, ego can't take his lies. And I'm long past putting up with his verbal abuse.

When the funeral director—whose name I didn't catch—finishes speaking and places my grandmother's urn in the space, I place the small bunch of flowers we stopped to buy on our way into the vase on the wall. Coneflowers tied with string—simple flowers for a simple service. She would have hated an extravagant display; that wasn't her style.

My father follows us out to the parking lot. I feel him looming behind us—the same dark cloud he's always been. I wonder if he's proud of that? Does he get a kick out of ruining people's day?

I bet he does.

"You gonna leave, never to be heard from again?" He asks the question as we get to Tyson's rental car.

He's not wrong; that is exactly what I did. I left and went no contact with him. There wasn't a point in it; there was nothing left to say. Until now.

"I'll say what I have to say, here, then yes, I'll leave and go back to pretending you don't exist."

"Ungrateful," he spits. "You always were."

"Ungrateful for what? You didn't give me anything to be grateful for."

"I put a roof over your head. Food on your plate."

"You did the bare minimum to take care of a child," I bite back, incredulous that he thinks his own flesh and blood needed nothing more than shelter and an occasional peanut butter sandwich. "*Your* child. Not some random kid you found on your lawn. The daughter of the woman you loved enough to marry. Me! The child of your dead wife."

He flinches, looking away from me, surprised that I know. Quickly, he schools his features back to his signature scowl. Willa and Damian stand by my side, Tyson at my back. Towering over me, his silent anger radiating around me.

"She told you," he states.

"It should have come from you, years ago. I deserved to know the truth, to know her."

"Don't blame me for that," he snaps. "You don't know her because she left. I told her not to go, I told her not to leave us."

"She didn't choose to leave me," I say.

It doesn't come out as strong as I'd like, the weight of what I'm saying truly hitting me for the first time. Willa's hand grasps mine. Tyson's lands on the small of my back. I love that they want to give me support, but this is a fight that I think I've needed for a very long time, now.

"You don't know that for sure, do you, Kit? She didn't take you with her. She was there to look for a different life. While you were here. With me. She could have taken you."

The words cut deeper than anything he's ever said to me or anything he's ever done. Or not done. It's one of the things I've asked myself the most since reading my grandmother's letter. Why leave me behind?

"What have I ever done to make you hate me?"

"I hated the situation—you're just a casualty of it," he says, almost looking remorseful for a half second. "Of the circumstances I was pushed into. I look at you and I see her—a constant reminder of the woman who left us. I didn't know what to do with you, and you never cared. You were indifferent to everything."

"I wasn't indifferent to anything. I felt it all; I just didn't know how to show you. No matter what I did, you'd scold me for it. You knew your friend raped me and blamed me for it. How could you do that to your own flesh and blood?"

"That is not what happened," he says, and Tyson steps up next to me.

"I need you to be careful and intentional with whatever words come out of your mouth, next," he tells my father. "If you think for a second that you will argue with her about her lived experience, you'll be having that argument with me. Understand?"

"Yeah? You going to punch me like you did him? I heard about that."

"He got off easy," Tyson says. "It's not a mistake I'll be making again."

"That's exactly what happened," I say when the stare-down between the two men proves to be unwavering on either side. "I didn't want any part of what happened. When you walked in at the end, you told me I was just like her—chasing men."

He has enough shame to look at the ground, his feet shuffling. He looks nervous—something I never dreamed of seeing.

"At the time, I didn't realize what had happened. By the time I did, you were long gone."

"Just like my mother." He flinches at my words. It's a small victory, and enough for me to find the peace I need to say the next words. "I'm leaving, again. I won't ever be back. You'll never see me, and we'll never speak again."

"Kit," he says, taking a step forward.

"No," Tyson says, blocking his path. "If she wants to come to you, she will. It will never be the other way around."

"Goodbye, Dad." I say it with my whole heart. This needs to be over with—I've said all I need, and he can never say anything that could make it better or right. Even an apology, which I likely wouldn't believe, doesn't do me any good. It doesn't bring my mother back or make my childhood happy. There is no *forgive and forget* for us. Forgetting isn't an option. Moving on is.

He must sense it, too; he nods at me once, then walks away.

There's no love lost, here. Him being my father was never enough for me to love him, in the same way that being his daughter wasn't enough for him to love me. *Blood runs deeper than water* is a lie.

The only person I share it with drives away without so much as a glance back in my direction. A finality settles over me like a warm blanket. This was long overdue. Maybe I'll dwell on the conversation—wish I'd said more, fought harder. Maybe he'll do the same, though I wouldn't expect it of him. I said the most important thing.

Goodbye.

"I'm ready to go home, now."

27

TYSON

When she said she was ready to go home, she meant Seattle. Kit was determined we find a flight as soon as possible. Especially me.

"You can't miss another game," she said. "I won't allow it."

Within hours, we'd closed up Anna's house, dropped a key to Susan for emergencies, and boarded a flight. I don't know how Damian pulled it off, but he got us all on the same last-minute flight. As soon as the plane took off, Kit passed out. She slept the entire flight. A testament to how emotionally draining this trip was for her.

The only time she ever sleeps this well is after a major life moment. Or an especially chaotic day. She had said her mind is always all over the place, and I think that's why she keeps her life simple. She doesn't keep a busy schedule—a good day for her is living her best homebody life.

I overheard her speaking to Willa, earlier. She said she hated dragging the rest of us into her vortex, these past days. But none of us wanted to be anywhere else. And honestly, her storm isn't the tornado she thinks it is. Her childhood trauma, her mother's tragedy, those are huge. Everything else, though, only feels overwhelming to her. She's not the burden she's been taught to believe she is.

I'd weather a million of her hurricanes.

Because on the other side is her, looking at me like I've hung the moon. When, really, it's her who has. I don't know if she'll be able to forgive me. I'll live with whatever she decides, as long as it isn't cutting me out of her life completely. Loving her is the easiest thing I've ever done. Losing her would be the hardest.

My future, whatever it looks like, includes her in it.

Her father is a piece of shit for not seeing how great she is. What he said, about her being indifferent, was bullshit. Had he cared enough, he'd have tried to learn why she doesn't process and react the same way as most. Instead, he put the responsibility on her, a child. A child who didn't understand that what she was doing was different from everyone else.

I understand how challenging it can be to live with a neurodivergent person. When you love someone, though, that challenge isn't difficult. It becomes part of life, of who you are. It becomes precious and beautiful. Different isn't bad. I happen to think it's better.

Fuck him for not seeing that. Fuck him for dismissing her. Fuck him for not begging her forgiveness.

Also, bravo to Kit for having the strength to tell him goodbye.

Kit will always be my priority, but she's right about one thing. I can't miss another game. The regular season ends with the next game, which is only twelve hours away.

Flying from one side of the country to the next, and still being ready to suit up, is part of the gig. I'm not worried about that. With our playoff spot secured, I'm not worried about that, either.

I can taste the cup, though. Fuck, I want it.

Zander picks us up at the airport. I help load luggage, while Damian gets Kit and Willa settled in the backseat. They're both practically dead on their feet after a long few days.

"Fair warning," Zander says after shutting the hatch. "Cillian wants a word with you."

"A word, or right hook to my jaw?" I ask, assuming my fuck up with Kit has finally found its way to him.

"Could go either way," he answers.

"I'll take whatever he decides. Hopefully, we can squash it and not fuck up the team dynamics."

"You both damn well better. I want the cup."

"You and me both, man."

Me calling Kit his wife's name was always something I knew Wylder would find out. There was no way around it, just like there's no way around him being pissed off about it. I get it—I deserve some level of retribution. Avoiding it only makes things worse.

So, when I get to the arena, he's my first stop.

"You want your shot before or after I attempt an explanation?" I ask, dropping my game duffel into my cubby.

"Explain, first. That way, I know how many hits to take." He looks up from the bench, a scowl on his normally smiling face. "You're not leaving the locker room without new bruises, though."

I take a seat next to him, releasing a heavy sigh. This conversation should be happening with Kit, first. She's not ready, yet—her plate is full of more important situations. It's understandable, but still, I wish it was her sitting next to me to hear this.

"As a kid, did you have a picture in your head of what your life would look like?"

"Yeah, to an extent," he says. "I daydreamed of The Show, like we all did. As I got older, I imagined a wife, lots of kids, family."

"Me too. Exactly that," I say. "It shifted as my real life changed. I mean, as a shithead kid, I imagined a new woman in every city for my first few years as a pro."

"Most of us did. I thought the same until I met Isla," he says, a brow raised pointedly.

"Again, me too."

"Murphy, you are dangerously fucking close to being taken to the floor," he says, jaw tight. "I've spent days dreaming about beating the shit out of you for calling Kit my wife's name."

"I know, I know," I say, raising my hands in peace. "I'm not in love with your wife, Cillian. I thought I was, once. Now, I know better."

"Because you love Kit?"

"More than fucking life itself," I say, dropping my head into my hands, rubbing them through my hair that's getting too long. "I'd give everything up for her—no regrets."

"That doesn't explain how you ended up calling her my wife's name." He sounds calmer, but the threat is still evident.

"The night of the gala, when I heard you were going to have another kid, it all shifted for me again. I don't know if Kit will ever want kids. She's said she's never even entertained the idea. With the path her life has taken, it's understandable," I say. "I came to Seattle wanting what you have. Now, I want something else, but I didn't fully realize that until I heard about the pregnancy. My head was full of this realization—sorting through it all, trying to be certain. I couldn't make declarations to Kit without being sure, you know?"

"So, what? You were so in your head that you didn't know who you were talking to?"

"No, of course I knew who I was with. But yes, I was so in my head that my mouth moved faster than my dumbass brain. I was thinking about how clear it was that I hadn't ever been in love with Isla. I care about her, of course, I do. It's not the same, though. And I was thinking that I don't want what you have. Not Isla, not a floating house full of kids, not a hockey empire family. Just Kit—and whatever that looks like."

"I'm not sure I buy that," he says.

"Really, dude? I was confused about a fork in the road I didn't expect to be at. You, of all people, know what that's like," I say. Because he had his own crossroads when he got to the NHL, and he fucked his path up, too. It cost him years with the love of his life, and his daughter.

"You're getting an extra fist to the jaw for that," he says, eyes narrowed. "But you have a fucking point, asshole. When I ended up in Boston, my dream didn't change. I still wanted Isla, and a family with her. My circumstances got in the way, and I couldn't see it as clearly. I'll regret my bullshit for the rest of my life."

"We're human, dude. We fuck up sometimes. I wish I hadn't—I never want to hurt her, and I did," I say, looking up to the ceiling and sighing again.

"Is she still upset? Or did you work it out in Maine?"

"We haven't discussed it yet, at all. Not with everything else that happened. Maine was heavy," I tell him. "You can't even guess how heavy. It might be a while before she gives me another chance."

"What are you going to do in the meantime?"

"The same thing I've been doing. I'll be supportive of her, I'll work my ass off for the team, and I'll wait until she's ready."

He stares at me, contemplating something I can't guess, exactly. A few moments pass before he speaks again, quieter this time.

"The boys expect a fight. I think they're amped about it. Let's make it good—get the blood flowing for everybody before we hit the ice."

"Get your shots in," I say, suppressing a smirk as I stand up. "Make them good, Wylder. You've been waiting for this for a long fucking time."

"You bet your pretty face I have," he says before he takes his first swing. Moving into it, I take the hit on my jaw. Shoving him off, I brace for his next. It lands on my side.

The guys crowd in, all talking some level of shit. Letty whoops the loudest, but it's Hugo's comments that have me laughing. He thinks Wylder bloodying me up will finally give him a chance at "his Kit Kat."

"In your fucking dreams, Blom," I say. "You next, man? I'd love to see your little goalie arms try to bruise a real hockey player."

"Ooh, them's some fighting words if I ever heard them," Letty says.

"Goalie arms? My arms aren't small," he protests, holding them out in front of him and inspecting them.

"Does your mommy tell you you're a big boy?" Letty asks him.

"Yeah," Hugo answers before he catches himself. "Fuck off!"

The ribbing and shoving lasts until nearly every member of the team has insulted everyone else. It serves its purpose—Cillian got to relieve his aggression toward me, and the boys got out a bit of pre-playoff pent-up energy.

As a team player, I don't mind being the brunt of it all. When we take the ice, it's with renewed morale, which shows in our play. We're faster, in sync, our passes landing more than not, and our shots on goal beat out our opponents almost by double digits.

Cillian and I won't ever be anything more than friendly, but it's nice to know he can put aside his annoyance with me for the sake of the team.

Per usual, the other team gets chippy in the third period. Everybody acts froggy when they're down by three goals. I get it, but I'm tired of getting checked into the fucking boards every time my stick connects with the puck.

Mullins, their defenseman, who I've known since camp as a teenager, blows into me from behind within seconds of Wallin passing me the puck. It's a shitty hit and he knows it. When I spin to face him, he's ready for the fight.

Blame pent-up frustration from this past handful of days, or the shit between Wylder and me, earlier, or maybe just my love of how physical this game is. Whatever the reason, I fly at Mullins—fists first. Despite being prepared for it, I surprise him with my enthusiasm. My first hit takes him to his back. I go with him, because my coaches always told me to follow through.

Of course, we both end up in the box, and I get a few minutes for my blood rush to subside. The fucker got one good hit, which happened to be on top of where Cillian punched me earlier. It smarts, now, it's going to be a bitch of a bruise, later.

It doesn't matter, though. We win the game and the fans are all hyped as we head into the playoffs.

"As much as I'd love for you two to bury your bullshit, I'm going to advise against it until after we win that cup," Coach Cole says to Cillian and me. He wears a wide grin as he walks to his usual place in the locker room for his post-game speech.

There's a text from Lottie waiting for me after I've showered and changed.

LOTTIE:

OMG, great game, bro! I wish I'd
been there. CALL ME!

"What's up, sister?" I ask, calling her on my drive home from the arena.

"Dude, you got beat up tonight."

"You should see the other guy," I say.

"I love it when you fight," she says almost wistfully. Lottie is a pacifist in her own life, but damn, that girl loves a good sporting rumble. "That's not why I called, though. Or you called…whatever. How's Kit?"

"As well as can be expected, I guess. She's got a lot to work through." I don't hold secrets from my family. They know all about my fuck up the night of the gala, and I filled them in on some of the details from my trip to Maine. Kit's full story isn't mine to tell, but they know enough.

"I've been thinking about her a lot. Every time I do, I start to cry. She really doesn't have any family, and I can't imagine what that's like," she says, even now, getting a little choked up. "Would it be okay if I texted her?"

"Of course it would, Lot."

"Okay. I just…I just want her to know she's not alone. You know?"

"I know, sweetheart. I'm sure she'd appreciate that," I tell her, holding back my own emotion. How lucky am I to have such a loving and supporting family, and what have I ever done to deserve them? When someone like Kit gets so little, it makes me painfully aware of how unfair life can be.

"Even if you can't fix things with her, I'm going to be her friend. Okay?"

"Yes, and I fucking love you for it."

"I love you, too, Tyson," she says before she goes on a rant about how I need to ice my face. "In fact, you should probably ice bath. Did you do that at the arena tonight?"

"Yes, Coach."

"That's good. You need to be ready for the next game. Dad says we'll try to get to as many games as we can. Mom's already clearing the calendar of any other commitments. Whatever that means, it's not like we're the Kardashians or something."

This then leads to a whole conversation about the latest celebrity gossip. Something about a book to movie controversy and lawsuit. I don't know what the hell she's talking about. It never matters, though; I just like listening to her.

Kit calls her ADHD her squirrel brain. Lottie is the same, jumping from one topic to another faster than I can sometimes keep up with. I've never minded it. It keeps my life interesting, and who wants a boring life?

28

KIT

I see when Tyson gets home. Of course, I do. Since I'm sitting at my front window, waiting for him to get home. I've become that girl.

Willa called after the game. She told me he and Cillian had a "scuffle" because of the night of the gala. There's no reason for me to feel badly about that, yet, I do. Or maybe badly isn't the right word, I feel *sorry* for Tyson.

I also feel turned on, because I watched the game, and his fight with Mullins in the third period was hot as fuck.

Again, I've become that girl.

For the last half hour, I've sat here at my window, staring at the dark house across the street and trying to sort through every feeling I'm having about the man that lives there. When I asked Willa what she thought I should do about Tyson, she told me to trust myself.

"For as long as I've known you, you've made the best decisions for yourself. Why would that change now?" she'd said.

Except, I haven't always trusted my head. Especially now, because my grandmother's last words linger and repeat on a steady loop.

Don't follow in my footsteps.

Would I be settling for Tyson? If I'm his second choice, if he is settling for me, does that mean I'd be settling for him, too? I don't want to settle. I don't want a life where I love my partner more than they could ever love me.

What I want is the epic love the likes of…I don't know, Jane Eyre. Where she and Rochester find their way back to one another. Not because it was convenient or easy, but because they were meant to be.

Not that I want Tyson to go blind while figuring it out or anything. Maybe his team captain kicking his ass is the equivalent of his Thornfield Hall fire.

Or maybe I'm just silly and looking for reasons to be near him.

I like being with him. I like myself when I'm with him, which is a profound thing for me to think after a lifetime of being uncomfortable with my place in the world.

My phone chimes with a notification, and I'm surprised to see it's a text from Lottie.

LOTTIE:

I was very sorry to hear about your grandmother, Kit. I wanted to tell you that days ago except I know that when my grandpa died, anyone that said anything nice to me made me cry my eyes out and I didn't want to do that to you. Tyson told me he's a fuck up. I already knew that, but I was sorry to hear about his bonehead move. Whatever happens, I hope we can still be friends. I like you more than I like most people. That must mean something.

A small laugh escapes, mixed up with gratitude for her reaching out to me.

ME:

> Thank you, Lottie. I appreciate you reaching
> out. And of course we're friends! I like
> you more than most people, too.

Nightmare stirs from his position in my lap, rushing to the door. It's time for his pre-bedtime potty.

When we step outside, Tyson spots us. Nightmare notices his friend, his tail wagging wildly as Tyson approaches.

"Hey, buddy," he says, bending to pet Nightmare's head.

"If you pick him up now, you risk getting peed on."

"Noted," he says with a laugh. "Do your business, bud."

My dog runs off to his favorite corner of the yard, staring us down as he relieves himself. As if he's afraid he's going to miss some monumental moment while he takes a poo.

Dogs are weird.

"Do you have time to talk?" I ask. I don't want to put this off. For both our sakes, it's important that we have this talk. He's heading into the play-offs, with the best shot he's ever had at the Stanley Cup. He doesn't need a distraction like me. I've been such an emotional vampire as it is. And the longer we put it off, the more I'm going to dwell on it.

"Always," he says without hesitation.

After Nightmare is finished, we both follow him back into the house. He immediately runs to his kennel and starts the routine of twirling in a circle about twenty-three times before he deems his bedding to be just perfect.

"I need you to try and explain," I say, sitting cross-legged in the middle of the room and staring up at the bruise blooming on the left side of his jaw. From Mullins or Wylder, I wonder. And how does it make him look even sexier?

Tyson mirrors my position, sitting less than a foot away. Close, but no contact. His eyes scan over my face. What for? Do I look different, now that I know I'm truly without blood ties? No, of course not. That's a dumb thought. Something like that can't possibly change my physical appearance. It only takes shape inside the deep voids waiting to be filled by the despair we let loose on ourselves.

I refuse to let it take hold.

Shoo, you dumb bitch.

"What's funny?"

"I don't know, what?" I ask him.

"You tell me," he says, grinning widely. "You're the one smiling."

"You are," I accuse, pointing a finger at him.

"Only because you did it first."

"Your smile is bigger; you're probably using all forty-three muscles."

"I'm not sure what that means," he says, "but I like it when you smile. It's my favorite thing."

"I doubt that," I say, my head tilting with skepticism.

"I know you do," he says, suddenly looking far sadder. "I wish you didn't. That you could pop into my head for even the smallest moment, so that you could have the same certainty that I do."

How much easier life could be if that was such a thing. Or, how much more horrifying and complicated. There are plenty of minds I'd never want to have intimate knowledge of. Like—I can't imagine how horrible it would be in the head of a serial killer, or the CEO of a mega-billion corporation, or some vapid asshat, for that matter. Tyson's, I would, though.

"Certainty of what?"

"Of you. You're so honest about who you think you are. But I'm not sure you see how incredible you truly are," he says, holding my gaze. "And of us. I know without any doubt that you're my future, and I'm yours."

"How? How can you say that, let alone know it?"

"It's simple for me. When I conjure an image of the future you—whether it be a wedding day, a fiftieth birthday, an eightieth—it's me by your side. If I try to replace myself with some faceless man, my chest literally hurts," he says, placing a hand in the center of his chest and rubbing it. "Right here.

When I see my own future, it's with you by my side, holding my hand as Lottie tells me she's going to marry some dumb schmuck that I don't think is good enough for her. When I win the Stanley, it's you I imagine looking for in the crowd of people. You wearing the obligatory wag playoff jacket with my name on the back."

My eyes dart to the box on my couch. The one Isla dropped off when she brought Nightmare home, earlier.

"Less than a few months ago, you didn't know my name. Less than a week ago, you called me by another woman's name. It's hard for me to believe you, now," I say—though, fuck, I want to believe him.

"I've never lied to you, Kit. I never will," he says, reaching out to tuck a wayward strand of my hair behind my ear. "I didn't mistake you for her. I wasn't wishing she was with me. instead of you. Haven't you ever been so deep into your own thoughts that your mouth says something you didn't mean for it to?"

"Regularly," I say sardonically.

"That's what that was. It was me, confused by how my life plans were shifting so rapidly, and how utterly okay I was with it all. You know how surprised you are by how comfortable you are with me? It confuses you. That's the headspace I was in. I always have a plan, a goal that I'm working toward. You disrupt all of it, and I fucking love it. It terrified me, for a minute."

"Only a minute?"

"Okay, an hour or two," he says with a soft smile. "Only long enough for me to realize that what's far more frightening is a future without the love of my life in it."

I must give him a funny look because he laughs.

"I'm talking about you, Kitpu. You are the love of my life."

"You're not even thirty, yet; you have a lot of life left."

"And I want every day I have to be with you. If that's what you want, too."

That's the big question, here. What do I want? What can I trust? Or what am I willing to risk if I'm wrong about Tyson? I guess that's several questions.

Love is risky. It must be, because we place so much reliance on another human being to accept it and care for it the same way we do theirs. When I look back on the time we've shared, he's done a lot to show me that he can be careful with me.

Is it worth throwing away over one misstep? Can I live with mere friendship with Tyson Murphy? Or no Tyson in my life, at all?

Sure, I can. The truth is, I don't want to. Like him, it physically hurts me. I try to imagine the things he said—him marrying a woman who is tall, blonde, elegant, and graceful. It makes my stomach turn. I see her holding a red-faced, bald baby, Tyson's arm wrapped around her. Him teaching a little boy who looks nothing like me to skate for the first time.

It all pains me.

Then, I think of Lottie and what she said earlier.

"I like you more than I like most people. That must mean something."

"I hope it means you're giving me a second chance," he says, though it sounds like a question.

"I didn't mean to say that out loud."

"Well, fuck," he says, completely dejected and looking sadder than I thought he could.

"Even if I didn't mean to say it, it's true," I say, crawling into his lap. His arms immediately wrap me up, and it's what I've been missing for so many days, now. "I don't know how to trust what you say. So, I'm going to trust myself—which is also hard for me."

"What are you saying, love?" he asks after I grow quiet.

"You make me want things I never considered before," I finally say. "A possible future I never saw as an option. When I imagine those things, I see you doing them with some woman with far less baggage than me. I don't like what I picture."

"Your baggage isn't yours to carry alone," he whispers over the top of my head as I snuggle into his chest. He smells good, the same as he does after every game. "Let me share the load."

"No, Tyson." I shake my head before looking up at him. "It's time for me to unpack. I've been thinking about it all day. After playoffs and when work slows down, I'm going to Montana."

"Yeah?"

"Yeah," I confirm with a nod. "I want to visit her grave site and see if there's anyone left that knew her. I also thought about what you said about my heritage. You're right, it's time I learn about that, too. I wasn't ready before because I was afraid to know more about her."

"Now, you want to know everything."

"All of it," I say. "I'm done living in fear of things, Tyson. So, I don't need you to carry any weight for me, but I do need you to keep showing up for me. I can't do this with you if I don't feel like a priority."

"You are *the* priority. I'm in love with you, Kit. I'll be in love with you until the day they slide my cold bones into the incinerator," he says. It's a creepy declaration that makes me smile. "I'll still be in love with you in whatever form we take after this life. You are it for me."

"It?"

"It," he confirms. "The one. My endgame. Did you know bald eagles mate for life?"

"I'm the one named after an eagle," I say.

"Whatever you are, I'm the same."

He doesn't pressure me to say anything similar back to him, and, like always, I'm thankful for how he lets me be me. I think I'm in love with Tyson Murphy. But I'd rather let that thought stew before I blurt it out. If it's uncomfortable for me to think, it's going to be awkward to say. And that's not what I want when I tell him for the first time.

It should be said with surety and confidence. Like when he says it to me, I know he believes what he's saying. The words need to breach my age-old armor, but I know he believes them.

"I was given something today," I say, untangling from him and walking to the box sitting on my couch. I tried it earlier, so I know it fits perfectly. Of course, it does; it was made by the infamous Odette Quinn, who wouldn't dare let anyone she dressed outside without looking fabulous. "Wait here."

I take the box into my bedroom, stripping off all my clothes until I'm completely bare. I return to Tyson wearing only my new jacket—a short trench style, cut from the deepest teal-blue fabric, his last name and number emblazoned in red down the sleeve, the team's logo proudly displayed on the back. It's simple and classy, yet still flashy.

"Fuck," he cusses when I tiptoe back into the living room. "You are the hottest damn thing I've ever seen."

"It's not your name on my back, but close enough."

"Where'd your other clothes go?" he asks, a brow raised as he comes to stand in front of me.

"I won't need them for this next part."

"What's this next part?"

"Where you fuck me," I say boldly, meeting his eyes—determined to be the strong woman he sees me as. It's time for me to be the woman who asks for what she wants and demands what she needs. "Up to ten percent of women struggle with sexual urges bordering on addiction. I might become another statistic."

"Oh no, we wouldn't want that," he teases, before he hauls me over his shoulder and takes me to my bed.

For the first time, he doesn't hold anything back. While he still pays close attention to my physical cues, there's no verbal check-in. Tyson is trusting me to tell him if it's too much.

He starts by devouring me with his mouth, his talented tongue bringing me to the first of several orgasms within minutes. All my senses—so ragged from this past week—are on high alert. The jacket stays on when he flips me over and takes me from behind.

"My colors look as good on you as my cum does," he says, and I die a little at how hot his dirty talk makes me. The Kit Ashcroft of a few months back would never have dreamed of a life that included this. Could never imagine how good it would feel to have his hips pump against my ass as he drives into me.

I wonder what other dreams my anxiety and fear have gotten in the way of.

He changes our position again, and as he throws my leg over his shoulder—his fabulous cock pistoning in and out—I realize how much trust is a game of give and take. So is love.

I never want to stop playing this game with Tyson.

KIT

They won the Stanley Cup. After a few moments of the team celebrating on the ice, Tyson, Cillian, and Zander skated together toward the red line. All three scanned the crowd where the family section was.

I'm sure we weren't visible in the sea of celebratory fans, but the trio blew kisses up to us, regardless. Lottie jumped up and down next to me, arms thrown in the air, tears pouring out of her eyes as she cheered as loud as she could.

The two of us became quite close during the playoffs. She's even talking about moving down here to be closer to us.

It's the proudest I've ever been of another person. It's a pretty special thing to watch someone you care about fulfilling a life's dream. That night, back at home, Tyson told me he needed a few days to get through necessary press and celebrations, but that he wanted to leave for Montana as soon as he'd fulfilled his obligations.

I argued that there was time. He ignored that.

"No. We put it on hold for my career. It's time to go find out who your mom really was," he'd said. I didn't argue after that. It was time. And it felt right having him, and Nightmare, with me on the drive to Montana.

I'd already reached out to Jack Silva, the detective who'd worked on my mother's case. We'd set up a time to meet. I was surprised when we got to the designated park to find Jack wasn't alone.

Hannah Markle's brother, Daniel, was there, too. As we listened to Jack describe what he knew, I caught Daniel staring at me several times.

"Sorry," he apologized sadly, after the third time. "You look so much like her."

It turns out, there was never much evidence to go off. There was footage from hotel security cameras of her leaving the lobby and walking across the parking lot toward a diner. A waitress there had remembered her, said she'd eaten alone and left without any incident. That was the last she was seen. The hotel was on the reservation, right near the border. Her body was found five days later, off reservation by nearly eighty miles.

Jack had been a junior detective, at the time. He has Crow family members and is sympathetic to their struggles with missing people. However, the higher-ups in his department, at the time, had little interest in working with tribal police to pursue her case. There's no way to know where she was murdered, what jurisdiction it fell in. Jack's department didn't care enough to figure it out. My mother was just one of many. Tribal police had even less to go on, since her body was found outside of their reach.

"It happened like that a lot, back then," he'd said. "It hasn't gotten much better. Part of the reason I left the force."

He suspects that night—the night before she was supposed to fly home to me—someone had grabbed her on her walk back to the hotel. They brutalized her, murdered her, and dumped her body.

Just like that.

All too common, all too easy. A night for them, a lifetime for me. They gained whatever it is one gets from such an act; I lost my world. Maybe whoever did it was eventually caught for some other crime and is sitting in prison, now. I doubt that, though. It's far more likely they've gotten away with it—and countless other offenses.

Jack apologized profusely for never finding justice for Nimii.

"You did your best, I'm sure," I'd tried to reassure him. "It's not you who failed her."

That made Daniel cry. Before we left the park, he asked me if we'd have lunch the following day and he'd show me where my mother's plot was.

That's where we're at, now—at the diner she last ate at, only a few blocks away from the cemetery. It's a run-down place, clean and busy, but with signs of wear. A lot of life has been lived in these four walls; you can feel it when you walk in. The staff all look like they've spent their careers here. I wonder, for a minute, if any of them were here to serve my mom that night.

I don't ask. I don't want to make it any more real than it already is. This was my choice, it's where I wanted to be—this last place where she was alive. Free to be herself.

Daniel arrives and comes to sit across from me in our booth.

"Hi," he says, almost timidly, as if he doesn't know how to handle this situation any better than I do.

"Hi, Daniel," Tyson says. "Thank you for this."

"Of course," he says. "I want to help any way I can. I...I tried before. When it happened, I tried appealing to your dad. Nimii had so few people in her life, I wanted to be a part of yours. For her."

"She didn't have family?" I ask.

"You really don't know?" His shock is evident.

"He didn't talk about her. I learned early on that my questions would be met with anger, so I stopped asking," I say, almost ashamed that I couldn't stand up to my father as a child and demand answers. "All I know, I've only learned since my grandmother passed."

"Hell, I'm so sorry, Kit."

We're interrupted by the server, all of us ordering whatever we see first on the menu. I'm not sure any of us has much appetite.

"We grew up outside of Salem, Massachusetts," Daniel says. "She was raised by her grandparents—her mother had perished in a car accident when she was young. I'm sorry I don't have any information about her dad, but I got the impression he was never in the picture. Unfortunately, both her grandparents died within a couple of years of each other, when Nimii was in college."

"She went to college?"

"She did. Damn, she was smart. She had a scholarship to the University of Maine for mathematics."

Tyson asks questions, keeping the conversation moving while I take everything in, latching on to the small details that connect me to her. By the end of it, I feel more a part of her than I ever could my father.

"I have pictures."

Daniel opens a manila envelope and pulls out photo after photo. I study each one for long minutes.

"You're right, I do look like her," I say, looking at one of her in a volleyball uniform, her arm wrapped around another girl.

"That's Hannah, my sister. Hannah moved here with her husband. When she got sick, I came to help, intending to go back to Salem after she died. But then, everything with your mom happened," he says, his voice growing sadder. "I stayed. The two women I'd loved the most spent their final moments here, and I couldn't leave."

"You loved her?" I ask, popping my head up. His eyes shine, and mine begin to water, too.

"I did. I had for years. It was unrequited, but I'd have done anything for Nimii. She was a special woman with a special spirit. I'm sorry you never got to know that."

"It matters that she was loved," I say. "Thank you for sharing that with me."

When I've methodically viewed every picture, Daniel packages them back up and hands the envelope to me. A gift, he calls it.

The most precious one I've ever received, I think, as we walk to the cemetery. He doesn't stay for that. Once he's shown us the way, he leaves to give me time.

Another gift from him—because I sob while sitting on the earth above where she's interred. Tyson sits behind me, arms tightly holding me together as I try to fall apart.

"It's stupid, she's not here," I say. "I know that, but I've never felt closer to her."

"It's not stupid, love. It's natural. It's human," he says. "Let yourself feel it."

TYSON

We've been home from Montana for over a month. Kit and Daniel have established a friendship, they talk regularly. Any time she thinks of a question about Nimii, she asks him. He loves to talk about her, and I think it's been healing for them both.

Something else that has been healing is Kit's therapy. She found someone to talk to as soon as we got home, and she's learning new techniques to deal with her biggest anxious moments.

She's also been learning about her heritage. The team works closely with the local Muckleshoot tribe, and she's connected with a few of their members, who are helping her dip her toes in. Plus, Daniel has invited us back to Montana to attend the annual Crow Fair. It will be Kit's first Powwow experience, and she's giddy with excitement. She wants to connect with folks from Mi'kmaq at some point, too. For now, she's soaking up everything she has easy access to.

Every day, she grows stronger, braver.

Every day, I fall more in love with her.

We don't spend nights apart. That will change when the season starts back up, of course. I'll hate being away from her, so for now, I soak up every minute we spend together. Cal's house has become nothing more than a place I store my shit. I've practically moved into Kit's little bungalow.

I'd offer to buy us a bigger space; except we like it here—at Kit's shoebox home. She said we should construct an outbuilding in the backyard. A yoga studio and gym. A space that's mine, free of her sensory clutter.

The truth is, I like her clutter. But she wants me to have everything I need, here, and it's one more thing to love about her.

"Plushie," Lottie yells into her microphone.

"Fuck yeah," Kit replies, excitedly. The three of us are in party chat while we play *Palia*. It's a cozy game that is not at all my speed, but it's Lot's current obsession. If we want to spend time with her, this is how we do it. If it means I run around a fantasy landscape mining ore and hunting magical creatures, that's what I'll do.

What the fuck does it matter, as long as I'm hanging out with my two favorite people.

"Okay, I'm exhausted, now," Lottie says, the high from her prize wearing off as quickly as it hit. "I'm logging off."

"Get some sleep, love you, Lot."

"Love you guys, too. Talk tomorrow."

Kit tosses her controller and headset aside and crawls into my lap, her hands wrapping around my neck.

"I want to tell you something," she says, her eyes nervously bouncing between mine.

"What is it?" I cup her cheek, trying to ease whatever she's feeling.

"Earlier…when Lottie talked about her imaginary future kids," she says, referring to Lottie daydreaming about someday playing farming simulation video games with her children. "Something popped into my head."

"Okay," I say when she pauses, as if she's nervous to go on.

"I thought about us, you and me, playing with a child of our own," she says, nibbling at her lower lip. "I see things like that more and more. I'm not saying it's what I want, because I'm still not sure. But I see it, sometimes."

"You know I'm okay either way," I say. I'd love to have a family with her. But I don't need that more than I need her.

"I know," she says. "I need you to know, though. It's too hard to keep to myself and I don't want to. I don't want to keep anything from you."

"I don't want you to, either."

"Okay, so then, I need to tell you this other thing, too."

"What?"

"That I love you," she says confidently. "Every day, you show me how much you love me, and it makes me fall more in love with you."

Unbidden, a tear of joy drops from the corner of my eye.

"That's the best news I've ever heard, Kitpu."

"There was a survey once that found only sixty-seven percent of Americans have ever felt true love. I always thought I'd be forever part of the thirty-three percent that didn't."

"And then, Nightmare escaped his harness?"

"Thank fuck for that little escape artist."

"Thank fuck." I kiss her.

Life can be a whirlwind. I'm glad we're weathering it together.

AFTERWORD

Thank you all for making it this far. I appreciate each and every one of you.

Missing and Murdered Indigenous Women is a movement I don't believe gets nearly enough attention. Nimii's story, while fictional, is all too real for so many. I encourage you to find a MMIW chapter to support in any way you can. Even if it's simply sharing their social media posts to help raise awareness. Everything helps. #NoMoreStolenSisters

FROM NATIVE HOPE:

Native American women make up a significant portion of the missing and murdered cases. Not only is the murder rate ten times higher than the national average for women living on reservations but murder is the third leading cause of death for Native women.

This is startling as Native people only make up 2% of the US overall population. Urban Indian Health Institute reports the youngest MMIW victim was a baby less than one year old and the oldest victim was an 83-year-old.

According to the Centers for Disease Control and Prevention (CDC) National Intimate Partner and Sexual Violence Survey, non-Hispanic American Indian and Alaska Native (AI/AN) females experienced the second highest rate of homicide in 2020. Additionally, in 2020 homicide was in the top 10 leading causes of death for AI/AN females aged 1-45. More than 2 in 5 non-Hispanic AI/AN women (43.7%) were raped in their lifetime.

If you, or someone you know, has experienced sexual assault and needs help 24/7, connect with a trained support specialist:

Call 800.656.HOPE

Text HOPE to 64673

MORE FROM ALISON RHYMES

Subscribe to Alison's Newsletter for Early News and Bonus Scenes

RAINFALL

I met the love of my life at ten years old.

At sixteen, I gave him my heart.

Three years later he was drafted to the NHL and moved across the country.

Five years after, he's back. And he's meeting his daughter for the first time.

I still hate him.

Even if my heart says that's a lie.

At ten years old, she changed my life.

At sixteen, I told her I loved her.

Three years after, I left and broke her heart.

Five years later, I'm coming back home to the surprise of my life.

I hate her for it.

Even though my brain says this is all my fault.

FLURRY

Willa

I've been in love with him for years, despite knowing he could never be mine.

Now his charming new boyfriend is determined to include me in all their plans.

Zander

I've been infatuated with him for years, despite us being in different states.

Now we're living in the same city with the only woman who's come close to holding my heart.

Damian

I've been intrigued by her for years, despite us never knowing each other.

Now I just need to convince the two people I care most about that three is better than two.

Flurry is an MMF Hockey Romance

TEMPEST

You can fall in love in a matter of days.

It can take years to recover from the loss of it. I know that all too well. When I fell for Gavin Vaughn, I never expected to watch him marry someone else. The experience changed me, shaped the woman I became.

Now he's divorced and wanting to reconnect after twenty years. As if that same shattered heart doesn't still beat inside me.

He's as charming as he ever was, better looking, too. And a star player for the NHL team in the city I just relocated to.

I'm not that same girl who loved him and watched him leave. I'm a woman who built her own empire from scraps. I'm also the woman who will be mentoring his daughter to do the same.

I'm the woman who can still be brought to her knees by the only man she ever cared about. But it's going to take more than sly smiles and bouquets of flowers to convince me he's worth my time. Or my heart.

BROKEN PLAY

They have ties that bind.

June grew up in the shadow of her brother and his best friend, Drew McKenna. She stood back while Drew dated his way through high school and college, watching and waiting. Waiting for him to realize he loved her as much as she loved him.

When he did, it was the happiest she'd ever been. Until she found him with another woman only five years after their marriage.

Leaving her husband was a simple decision, but there was no easy way to cut him out of her family.

When June receives a fresh start to her career, she also finds what could be a new lease on love. Reality hits Drew with a vengeance.

He wants her back.

She wants to make him suffer.

BRUTAL PLAY

Mistress.

Whore.

Lorelai has been called every name in the book. Except for the ones she's always dreamed of.

My love.

Mine.

Noah Anders is the only man to have ever owned her heart. But it's her soul he wants.

Theirs is a battle of wills, tempers, ego, friendship, and loyalty.

He wants retribution.

She just wants to survive.

BITTER PLAY

Reed Turner has loved his sister's best friend, Leighton, for damn near a decade. He's given her space to grow in her career and her life. Now he's ready to claim the woman he's always believed was his. It's too bad another man in her life keeps getting in the way.

Leighton Ward has never been in love. Now, just as so many things are changing in her life, she finds two men vying for her heart. Both hold strong ties to her future and making the wrong decision comes with heavy consequences.

He knows what he wants.

She's as confused as ever.

DECONSTRUCTING DELILAH

A modern-day retelling of Samson and Delilah…

As the son of a preacher, Pope Blackwell believed he learned the difference between good and evil early in life. After all, it was beaten into him regularly. Now as an adult, he's traded in his life of abuse for one where he holds all the power.

When a young woman strolls into his life full of more bravery than she should possess, he becomes consumed by her fire.

Delilah believed escaping her family's abusive ways would be the hardest challenge of her life. Then she met Pope Blackwell.

One sinner and one saint. A world of differences between them.

Faith. Experience. Age.

His obsession only grows as she challenges him until he's ready to topple any pillar that stands in her way, and she'll fight every demon to be by his side.